SHARP TURNS

SHARP TURNS

BOBBE TATREAU

SHARP TURNS

iUniverse books may be ordered through booksellers or by contacting:

iUniverse
1663 Liberty Drive
Bloomington, IN 47403
www.iuniverse.com
1-800-Authors (1-800-288-4677)

Because of the dynamic nature of the Internet, any web addresses or links contained in this book may have changed since publication and may no longer be valid. The views expressed in this work are solely those of the author and do not necessarily reflect the views of the publisher, and the publisher hereby disclaims any responsibility for them.

Any people depicted in stock imagery provided by Thinkstock are models, and such images are being used for illustrative purposes only.
Certain stock imagery © Thinkstock.

ISBN: 978-1-5320-2031-5 (sc)
ISBN: 978-1-5320-2032-2 (e)

Library of Congress Control Number: 2017905005

Print information available on the last page.

iUniverse rev. date: 04/10/2017

CHAPTER 1

When Charlie returned from Heathrow, the Bankside Hotel's lobby was crammed with rows of luggage ready to be delivered to the rooms of a busload of frazzled Canadian tourists wearing bright green name tags and clutching bottles of water. Not having taken her room key with her—a real key, instead of the plastic cards used in the more expensive hotels—Charlie would now have to wait in line. She'd just delivered the fifteen Summer Session drama students and her Theater Arts colleague, Tessa, to the airport for their flight to San Francisco and was in need of a hot shower and an uninterrupted evening in the room she and Tessa had been sharing. Tomorrow would be her play day. She'd added two extra nights to her trip so she could wander London on her own, do some shopping. Browsing the ceiling high shelves at Waterstone's was so much more satisfying than scrolling through Amazon.

When she finally got her turn at the desk, the gray-haired concierge, who always looked like he was having a bad day, handed her the room key and a folded sheet of the hotel stationary. "A message for you, Dr. Ames. The man on the phone said to call him as soon as possible. It's urgent."

In no mood for anything *urgent*, she smiled her thanks and headed for the ancient elevator. The call surely couldn't be from the university; they would text her cell number, as would Sam. She'd texted Dean Fitzpatrick's office from Heathrow as soon as Tessa and the students successfully cleared security. The end of her official responsibility. Once inside her room, stuffy from being closed up all day, she tossed her oversized purse onto the bed and opened the sash window. To keep expenses down, the university, in its infinite wisdom, had booked a non air-conditioned hotel, assuming London never got warm in July. Someone seriously missed the mark on that decision.

Shoes off, sitting on the bed, she opened the note: *Call Earle Donovan, Attorney at Law, Vienna, Virginia*. A phone number and the US international code were scrawled underneath.

She had no idea why a Virginia lawyer was looking for her on a Monday afternoon in July. Actually, it was still morning in Virginia.

And how had he obtained the name of her hotel? Neither the university nor Sam would give out that information, and her father probably wouldn't even remember that she was in London. He was too busy planting houses on all the available vacant land in Southern California.

She entered all the numbers into the hotel's landline and waited.

"Donovan and Pierce. May I help you?" The female voice was young.

"This is Charlotte Ames. Mr. Donovan left a message for me."

"Oh yes. One moment."

"Dr. Ames?" An older male voice, raspy.

"Yes."

"Am I right that you're currently in London?"

"Yes. I've been teaching a summer class for Humboldt State. The class ended yesterday." Probably more than he wanted to know. "Can you tell me what you need from me?"

"Of course. Is Melissa Enright your cousin?"

Missy.

Charlie rarely let herself think about Missy and her husband, Rick. "Yes."

"I'm sorry to have to tell you," he cleared his throat, "both Melissa and Richard died a week ago. The small plane he was piloting crashed in Florida."

For a long moment, Charlie felt as though someone were standing on her throat. News like that shouldn't be delivered by phone. When she finally had enough air, "Elizabeth too?"

"No, she was at a summer camp in Maine."

"Where is she now?"

"With Richard's sister. The one who lives in D.C."

Ah yes, Rowena, the lobbyist. Missy had never liked her much.

"I'm calling because I'm the executor of their estate. It took a while to track you down. The only address we had was Sacramento. You're named as Elizabeth's guardian."

Elizabeth's guardian!

Charlie resisted the words. They expected her to take care of Elizabeth? Surely there was some mistake. Missy would not have done this to her.

Protest rose in her throat. "No one ever consulted me. Is that legal?"

"I don't know any of the reasons for the Enrights' choice or why they didn't tell you. Their trust and wills were written by my partner, who retired last year. I'm acting in his stead."

"But I can't." *Really, really can't.*

No response.

She tried again. "I can't care for Elizabeth." Taking care of herself was hard enough sometimes. And fortunately, Sam took care of himself.

More silence.

Then, "If you refuse, she'll have to be placed with Child Protective Services," his voice became disapproving, "and ultimately she will end up in Foster Care. At sixteen, she isn't a good candidate for adoption. You do know she was adopted by the Enrights as an infant."

"But—surely there's someone else." Charlie was trying to remember where Missy's parents were. "What about grandparents?"

"Melissa's father is in poor health, and her mother is taking care of him at their home here in Vienna. She can't handle anything else. Richard's parents are deceased." He cleared his throat. "This situation is too complex to discuss long distance. Can you come to my office as soon as possible?"

Go to Virginia? In her head, she screamed, *No!*

"Dr. Ames?"

Her hands were shaking. She'd spent most of her adult life avoiding complications. Avoiding Virginia and her family. Reluctantly, "I guess so." This catastrophe would probably not go away on its own. She gave

3

him her email address and cell number, "I need to change my flight," then broke the connection so she could process what had just happened. A few moments ago, she was looking forward to enjoying London without fifteen college students in tow. Now a teenage girl had been dumped in her lap.

She wasn't fond of the unexpected. Surprises rarely turned out well.

The earliest available flight from London to Dulles International was at 2:10 p.m. the next day. She changed her ticket, then left a message on Sam's cell phone. *Something's come up. I'm stopping in D.C. before coming home.* She wished he'd answered, but he was scheduled to be at Castle Rock this week, counting nesting birds for the Humboldt Wildlife Refuge. Reception was problematic up there.

She slept badly, her dreams a creepy collage of past and present. Missy as a teenager, blonde, petite, a popular cheerleader in the same high school that Charlie would attend five years later. Missy on her wedding day. Bubbly and beautiful.

Rick was Missy's high school sweetheart, the son of a wealthy horse breeder. They married as soon as Rick graduated from college. Five years younger and five inches taller than Missy, Charlie was one of the bridesmaids. The clumsy cousin who dropped her bouquet during the ceremony, hoping no one in the audience noticed. But of course Missy's mother had. Aunt Grace was good at finding fault with Charlie.

Three hours was barely enough time to navigate Heathrow's Terminal 5, especially since she had to stand in line to pick up her new boarding pass. At least British Air would serve a meal on board, but she barely had time to buy a bottle of water at W H Smith before dashing to the departure gate. Instead of running through the airport, she should have been shopping for a sweater for Sam, then having lunch at a tearoom, leafing through the books she'd bought. She was feeling badly used.

Typically, she could sleep on long flights, but the specter of being forced to be the guardian of a teenager kept her awake and anxious. She did not want to take care of a girl she had only seen once before. Charlie's teaching devoured most of her time and thought: she taught two, sometimes three classes as well as writing for academic journals to satisfy academia's publish or perish demands. In two years, she'd be eligible for tenure. Her career was her first priority. She did not want to be Elizabeth's guardian. Had never wanted to be responsible for anyone but herself.

Sam understood that. Loved her anyway.

They did and didn't live together. Though he'd moved into her house a year ago, he'd kept his apartment in downtown Eureka, three sparsely furnished rooms over an antique shop. Charlie's 1930's Craftsman house in Arcata had more space, three bedrooms and two bathrooms but, whenever one or both of them needed personal space, Sam would retreat to his apartment for a few nights. Separately together suited them. Adding a grieving teenager to their lives would unbalance everything.

Reentering the US was almost as complex as entering the UK, and less efficient. Lines snaking everywhere. As soon as she'd jumped through all the bureaucratic hoops, she caught the train from Dulles to D.C.'s Union Station, snagged a cab, and checked into the hotel she'd found online last night. It was 3:30, too late to go to the law office to plead her case. Instead, she made an appointment for 9:30 the next morning. She could look forward to another sleepless night, rehearsing all the reasons she couldn't and shouldn't fulfill Missy's request.

And Sam still wasn't answering his phone.

The next morning, listening to Earle Donovan read Missy and Rick's wills, Charlie felt her stomach twist into a knot; the legal language was intimidating, sounding as though she had no choice but to become Elizabeth Ann Enright's guardian until her eighteenth birthday. As Donovan turned another page, Charlie broke in, "Is there an alternative? Can I opt out? There's really no way I'm prepared to take this on." She wished she knew how to cry on demand, but tears probably wouldn't move him. He'd undoubtedly seen plenty of tears from distraught clients. She wasn't usually given to crying anyway.

He laid the wills on his desk, obviously annoyed by her continued reluctance. Spacing out his words, "Dr. Ames, your cousin has entrusted her only child to you. She must have had a good reason. Doesn't that mean anything to you?"

It means that I'm expected to turn my life upside down. Years of concentrating on her career hadn't left time for family. Her mother had died several years ago, and her father remarried two years later. It had been a year since she'd seen him. Undoubtedly, some of her colleagues at the university saw her as driven, but she preferred the words focused and ambitious.

"Dr. Ames, you do know that, if you refuse, Elizabeth will go into the Foster Care System." He sounded like a character out of Dickens—sending children to the workhouse.

"You said that before."

"Do you have any idea how difficult Foster Care is for a child? Particularly a child like Elizabeth, who has had a loving, stable home. She attends a private school, has traveled extensively with her parents. Going into a foster family could be traumatizing, no matter how loving the foster home is. Her parents have, of course, left their entire estate to their daughter; most of it in trust until she is eighteen, much of it earmarked for her education and eventual wedding. There is also a generous monthly stipend for her support."

"Money isn't the issue." *Not entirely true.* "I don't have the time or ability to take care of her. I live in Northwestern California. Compared to Virginia, it's like living in a wilderness. We're a full day's drive from San Francisco. What about a boarding school?"

"There would be money for that, but an institution might be lonelier than Foster Care. And there are the holidays to consider. She should not be punished because her parents died."

Hard to argue that.

He reached across the desk and handed Charlie a brown clasp envelope. Inside were two sealed, letter-sized envelopes. One addressed to Charlie, one to Elizabeth. Charlie opened hers. Read through it once, then read it again.

The knot cinched tighter, thanks to the heavy dose of guilt stirred by Missy's words.

For the briefest of moments, Charlie was tempted to walk out of

Donovan's office, fly back to California, and pretend this conversation had never happened. But if she ran, would the legal system track her down and deposit Elizabeth and her belongings on Charlie's doorstep anyway?

The intercom on his desk buzzed. He picked up the receiver, "Yes?" He paused. "Good. Please send them in."

A moment later, his secretary held the door open so the two visitors could enter. Charlie recognized the blonde wearing tailored gray slacks and a matching jacket as Rowena. Missy had once called her *Rowena the terrible* because she had a sharp tongue and always had to be right. Qualities that probably made her a good lobbyist.

Behind her was a slender teenager.

Elizabeth.

Where Rowena was austere, the girl was softly pretty, with shoulder-length, richly dark hair. Elizabeth was wearing the tight-fitting leggings young girls favored these days, a t-shirt hoodie, and flip flops, a flowered purse, perhaps a Vera Bradley, slung over her shoulder. Her eyes were red-rimmed, a bit swollen. The ravages of the last week smudging her features. Faced with the reality of this girl, Charlie was doubly sure she should run. And not look back. For much of her life, she'd perfected not looking back. Not getting close to anyone. Except Sam.

Donovan stood up, "Thank you, Irene." The door closed.

"Dr. Ames, I think you've met Rowena Enright." Charlie nodded in Rowena's direction, "and this is Elizabeth."

Charlie turned to meet the gaze of Missy's daughter. Though Elizabeth's wide-set eyes were in danger of overflowing, they were surprisingly steady, carefully taking the measure of this stranger.

Uncomfortable under Elizabeth's scrutiny, all Charlie could manage was "Hello."

No reply.

Donovan turned to Rowena, "Perhaps we should step outside, leave Dr. Ames and Elizabeth alone."

Charlie considered going with them.

The door closed.

After a few moments, "I'm sorry about your parents." Not a platitude.

Charlie *was* sorry. Melissa had been a big part of her childhood. And really sorry because now she was supposed to assume Missy's role.

Elizabeth looked away, staring out the window.

"That's what everyone says because they're uncomfortable with the subject." Elizabeth did not pull her punches. "I'm the only one who is truly sorry." Her voice was deeper than Charlie expected.

"Do you know why we're here?"

The dark eyes returned to Charlie's face. "Because you're supposed to be my guardian but you don't want to do it. He probably thinks you'll change your mind once you see me. Like some sort of stupid magic." Her tone was angry. Trouble was, Charlie felt like she had a right to be angry too. "I wish my dad didn't know how to fly a plane or that they'd taken me with them so I'd be dead too." Matter of fact. "Now, no one wants me. So for the second time, I'm on the open market. My birth mother didn't want me either."

Though Elizabeth's fierce expression didn't change, soft tears were dripping over her cheeks onto the front of her hoodie. She didn't try to wipe them away.

A few moments later, Charlie realized there were tears on her own cheeks.

CHAPTER 2

Not until Charlie was telling Sam about the hours in Donovan's office did she admit to herself it was Elizabeth's silent weeping, not compassion or even Missy's letter, that made her capitulate and accept the guardianship. She felt a grudging respect for Elizabeth's composure even as her world was falling apart. Donovan's comment that *she shouldn't be punished because her parents died* probably figured into the acceptance somewhere. Flying back to California, Charlie played and replayed the scene in the office, read and reread Missy's letter, wondering what she could have done differently and how she was going to explain what had happened to Sam.

When the McKinleyville taxi dropped her off in front of her bright yellow house, Sam was in the kitchen, unpacking the groceries he'd shopped for after listening to her rather cryptic voicemail message: *My flight lands at 5:20. No need to pick me up. I'll take a taxi.* He heard exhaustion in her voice and something else he couldn't identify.

Without a word, she walked straight into the safety of his arms and held on for dear life. He was so solid, always on her side. Often reading her better than she could read herself. She'd needed him with her in Virginia. Maybe he could have helped her say no.

Into her hair, "Hey, you okay?" Clearly she wasn't.

Against his chest, a muffled "Not really."

He waited until she finally pulled away, "Bad flight?"

She shook her head.

"What then?"

Charlie always loved looking at his face, more rugged than

handsome, amused gray eyes, salt and pepper hair in need of cutting. She loved him as much as she let herself love anyone. "Is there wine? It's a long story."

"There's always wine. Give me a minute."

She walked into the living room, slipped off her shoes, and sank onto the couch, letting it soften the edges of her day. A minute wouldn't be long enough to prepare for this conversation about what she'd done, what she'd agreed to. Her life and Sam's were going to change.

He brought two glasses of wine, "We only have white," and sat close to her. She took several sips, then began with the concierge giving her the message from Donovan and ended with Elizabeth's weeping. Then all the legal documents that followed.

Sam listened without comment, watching her eyes fill as she confessed to accepting the guardianship without consulting him. Charlie was seldom bulldozed into doing something she did not want to do. Always good at standing up for herself. Sometimes too good at keeping the world at arm's length. And he'd seldom seen her moved to tears. Whatever had changed her initial refusal must have been powerful. Even more powerful than a young girl's sadness.

But Charlie didn't explain what that was.

The day he met Charlie, nearly two years ago, she was moving into this house. Because it was a sunny day, she was wearing white walking shorts and a faded blue Humboldt State t-shirt, lugging an over-filled box of books from her car to the front porch where she half-dropped, half-set it down. There was another box in the cargo space, so he propped his bike against a tree in the parkway. "Looks like you could use some help."

She straightened. "No thanks, I'm fine." Ignoring her *no thanks*, he picked up the remaining box and carried it to the porch, placing it alongside the first one.

She smiled. "Thank you."

"You're welcome. Those are heavy boxes."

"I always fill them to the brim and then regret it." She had a low, husky voice with intriguing layers.

He held out his hand, "Sam Ledger."

She took it, "Charlotte Ames."

"Are you new to Arcata?"

"Not exactly. I've been renting an apartment for four years. I just purchased this house."

"I'm guessing you're at the university—all those books and the t-shirt."

"English Department. Do you live in Arcata?"

"In Eureka. I'm a marine biologist at the wildlife refuge. I'm test-riding my new bike."

"You rode from Eureka?"

"On the old highway. It's only nine miles and not all that much traffic." He wanted a reason to continue their conversation. She had amber eyes and an inviting smile. "Before I start back, is there something else I can carry for you?"

She shook her head. "I'll empty the books onto the shelves in my office a few at a time."

"Wise plan." He straddled the bike. "Nice to meet you, Charlotte." *Very nice indeed.*

"Everyone calls me Charlie."

Her wine glass was empty long before she finished the Elizabeth story. Sam considered going to the kitchen to retrieve the wine bottle to refill their glasses, but he didn't want to interrupt.

"So when does this all happen?" *When will our lives be re-arranged? Will I still be part of your life?*

"Ten days perhaps. I don't have the exact date. Her furniture will be put on a moving van in a few days."

"Not much time." He was glad she hadn't asked what he thought about her decision because he wasn't sure how he felt right now. He was already a parent, albeit a poor one, according to his ex. And even though Charlie had always been quick to say she had no interest in being a parent, she'd suddenly agreed to parent a girl she didn't know. Something didn't add up.

"Elizabeth needs to be here before school starts on the twenty-third,"

Charlie paused, "I'm so sorry I didn't get a chance to ask you, to reach you, but you weren't picking up," her voice trailed off. Not blaming him, not excusing herself. He admired that and many other qualities in Charlie. She set her glass on the low coffee table. "I need to take a shower."

"Are you hungry?"

"Starved. I didn't have time to buy a snack in San Francisco. Are you cooking?"

"Sure."

She leaned over and kissed him lightly. "I won't be long."

For the next twenty-four hours, Sam and Charlie avoided talking about Elizabeth. Neither was ready to explore the complexities of her arrival, so Charlie told him about her weeks in London and he told her about the semi-annual seabird count on Castle Rock. If they pretended everything was normal, perhaps it would be. Sunday afternoon, Sam drove to Eureka to prepare for a Monday meeting with visiting Federal officials, leaving Charlie to rattle around the house with way too much time to think and worry. And wish this weren't happening. Her imagination was working overtime, concocting worse case scenarios because the Sam, who always wanted to talk through a problem, hadn't weighed in about this change in their lives. She suspected he just might not have her back this time.

Monday morning, tired of her tangled thoughts, she walked the half-mile to campus to deliver the hard copy of her final evaluation of the Summer Session at London's Globe Theatre. Since she didn't want to go back home to face Sam's absence and several loads of laundry, she sorted through the mail stacked on her desk, cleared out her email, and began updating her syllabi for the fall semester courses: one Accelerated Writing Class, one Romantic Poetry class, as well as the Special Topics in Shakespeare class that she and Tessa were team teaching.

Just after 12:30, Tessa appeared in the doorway of Charlie's office in Founder's Hall. "I gave Angela my London materials."

Charlie hit *save.* "I did too and discovered she was the one who helped the lawyer track me down in London."

"What lawyer?"

"It's complicated. Is The Deport open? Do you have time for lunch?"

"Good idea. I could use a hamburger. The English have never quite figured out how to make one properly."

Charlie grabbed her purse and locked the door behind her, hurrying to catch up with Tessa, who was already heading toward University Center. The campus was remarkably quiet, a few students here and there. Charlie always relished the pre-semester emptiness. Once classes started, the walkways would be teeming with student energy, and she would have meetings to attend while her brain obsessively rehearsed upcoming lectures. And stacks of papers to grade.

Charlie found a table by the window, while Tessa ordered two hamburgers with everything and brought glasses of iced tea, their order number clipped into a wire holder. "Only one person ahead of us," she tore open two packets of sugar and dumped the contents into her glass. "Someday I'm going to teach this crew how to make sweet tea."

"This is not Georgia." Charlie handed Tessa the $7 for her share of lunch.

Ignoring the reference to her birthplace, Tessa repeated the question, "What lawyer?"

"Strange story. I ended up in D.C. and didn't get home until Friday. So much for my extra day in London."

"Because?"

Because a cousin I haven't seen in years decided to will me her child.

There was probably nothing to be gained by trying to avoid Tessa's questioning. They'd been friends since Charlie's first Humboldt semester; she had quickly learned that Tessa did not give up until she got answers.

Once again, Charlie began with the hotel concierge and the note.

Halfway through the story, the hamburgers were delivered and the wire holder removed. Tessa immediately bit into hers, but Charlie let hers sit until she finished the story.

"So why did you agree to take Elizabeth?"

"It didn't seem as though I had a choice."

"Bull. There's always some sort of choice. You're not usually a bleeding heart. You don't even know this girl. And transplanting any teenager, even for the best of reasons, is not simple. Especially hard when that teenager has just lost her parents. Isn't there anyone else in the family?"

"One set of grandparents, but the grandmother—my Aunt Grace— is caring for her husband, who's in the last stages of COPD. Not an option. Two aunts. One lives in Amsterdam and is in the Diplomatic Service. The other one, Rowena, has been looking after Elizabeth since the accident. Missy never got along with her."

"How's Sam with this?"

"Quiet." Truthfully, his silence worried Charlie. She was the one who clammed up when differences got in their way. *Talk to me Charlie; let's get past this.* And they always could. But he hadn't called her this morning. When he was staying in Eureka, he usually called to tell her good morning.

"What can I do?"

Charlie picked up her hamburger. "Physically fitting her into the house isn't a problem. I received a message this morning that her things should arrive sometime Friday." She hoped Sam would be back in time to help with the furniture. But furniture and possessions weren't the scary part. Being responsible for a teenage girl was.

"Do you need to repaint? I'm pretty good with a roller."

"I thought I'd wait to see that color she'd like. Once I get her school records, I have to enroll her at the high school. Maybe you could go with us. Since Jimmy went there, you know something about the school."

"That was five years ago, but the office staff is probably the same. I might be able to grease a wheel or two."

"Thanks for listening."

Now, if only Sam would call.

Elizabeth opened her *Facebook* account and stared at her last posting—only three weeks ago. She'd uploaded a picture of herself and her friend Julie in a canoe on the lake at Camp Dodson. Smiling at the counselor who had taken the picture.

Several lifetimes ago.

Now, there were sympathetic messages from friends expressing their shock at what had happened to her parents. Asking how she was. A stupid question. Where she was. At Aunt Rowena's, at the lawyer's office, and eventually she would be in California—of all places. What was going to happen to her? She hadn't been able to answer their questions or, for that matter, talk to anyone about how she was, where she was. She was where other people said she must be. No one asked what she wanted. The woman named Charlie—a cousin she'd only heard about—hadn't been asked what she wanted either and, like Elizabeth, seemed to have no choice in the matter. Only the legal documents mattered—not the people.

The day after the memorial service, Elizabeth would be sent off to California, like a UPS package to someplace called Arcata. One girl with luggage. Her aunt had shown her where Arcata was on a map, but Elizabeth hadn't paid close attention. Where she was didn't matter because her parents would never again be where she was.

It took only a few moments to erase all the photos and information on the site. In place of that *other life,* she uploaded her favorite picture of her parents, added their birth dates and the death date. She was through with social media; she didn't want anyone looking at her life. She didn't want to look at it either. Instead, she bought herself a notebook to use as a diary. So retro. Julie would laugh.

She would miss Julie.

Elizabeth opened the diary—*This is the first day of my strange new life. All my possessions—Aunt Rowena gets upset if I call it my stuff—are on their way to California. My bedroom furniture, as well as everything else in my room. I suppose I'll have to sort out what I want and don't want once I arrive. It all got packed up without my being there because my aunt thought going to our house would be too upsetting for me. My parents dying is upsetting. Boxing up my stuff is nothing. I asked for all our family photographs too, though I have no idea who some of the people are. Mom was always saying she needed to write that information on the back of the photos, but she never got around to it.*

My grandmother brought Mom's jewelry over to Aunt Rowena's and asked if there were other things in the house I wanted. I should have asked for the Christmas decorations, but searching for them felt like too much trouble. So I didn't. Grandma looked awful. I look awful too. I guess that's what happens when people you love die. I wish I could live with her, but she has to take care of Grampa 24/7.

Our house, our big beautiful house and everything in it, will be sold. The Richard Enright family is being erased, just like my Facebook page.

I'm getting my hair cut short tomorrow. Since I have to be different, then I should look different.

Monday evening, Sam finally called Charlie. "Sorry I didn't check in this morning." He'd spent Sunday evening putting together the presentation about his recent visit to Castle Rock, successfully avoiding thinking about Elizabeth's arrival. In his defense, about the time he would normally have called Charlie on Monday, he was setting out coffee and donuts in the conference room at the Administration Center. "Now I have to put together all this information for a new display in the Visitor Center. I'll be back early Friday."

The real truth of the matter was that he didn't know what he wanted to say to her—but whatever he did say should probably not happen on the phone. Too personal. Too important to their relationship. He did not want to lose her. He'd already lost one marriage and daily access to his son. His ex, Diane, had listed his parental failures often enough that he came to believe Greg deserved a better father. As a result, when they divorced and she petitioned to move his six-year old son out of state, he didn't fight back. Didn't demand shared custody, just visitation rights. He regretted letting her win.

Admittedly, he'd managed his family life badly—focusing on his job instead of them. He loved Greg but hadn't understood, soon enough, that Diane expected him to share parenting duties, really share, and was serious that he should change diapers, go to Greg's play groups, volunteer in Greg's kindergarten class. But Sam was always working— away for days at a time. Sometimes in D.C. for a week or two during the yearly budget meetings. One of the plusses in his relationship with

Charlie was that she understood how important his job was to him, because hers was equally important to her.

He'd lost the war with Diane long before he realized there was a war. His punishment was Greg living in Portland. Sam's parenting was now by appointment. The last weekend of every other month, he flew to Portland, rented a hotel room, and spent two days indulging his son.

Would having Elizabeth in their lives wreck this relationship too?

CHAPTER 3

Sam drove into Arcata late Friday morning and parked his aging Land Rover at the curb behind Charlie's much newer Subaru. The garage door was open, ready for the movers. He lifted his bike off the bumper rack, rolled it into the garage for safekeeping, and let himself in the back door. "Charlie, where are you?"

"In the guest room."

She was in the midst of stripping sheets from the double bed. The bright blue comforter was already folded on the upholstered chair, two pillows on top.

"Hi," he pulled her hair to one side and leaned in to kiss the back of her neck.

"Umm, nice to see you too. You're just in time."

"For?"

"The movers called from Eureka ten minutes ago. I'm having them move this furniture into the garage before they bring Elizabeth's things in here." He could sense her nervousness. "Do you mind taking the lamps and pictures to the garage? Maybe put them on the workbench for the time being. I'm betting there will be boxes and wardrobe containers that will temporarily have to go into the garage too." She stuffed the sheets into the laundry hamper in the hall.

A rumbling diesel motor interrupted whatever else she might have said. Looking out the window, she saw the yellow and green Mayflower van parking across the driveway entrance and hurried outside. Sam picked up two framed pictures and followed her. The speech he'd been rehearsing about Elizabeth would have to wait.

Moving the guest room furniture out and Elizabeth's in was amazingly efficient. In less than half an hour, Charlie's furniture was in the garage. Sam stayed behind to cover everything with sheets of plastic while she quickly vacuumed the rug in the bedroom before the movers unloaded Elizabeth's furniture. A three-quarter bed with drawers beneath, a double dresser, a nightstand, a gray leather desk chair that swiveled, an upholstered rocking chair, lamps and, in keeping with the electronically capable generation, an L-shaped desk designed for computer equipment.

Charlie had been expecting feminine furniture, perhaps a canopied four-poster bed, maybe a white dresser or pink chair. Instead, the furniture was pine, with simple lines. Very good quality but nothing especially feminine. At Elizabeth's age, Missy had been a girly-girl with a pink bedroom, a white eyelet dust ruffle on her canopied bed. Clearly, not Elizabeth's style. There was so much Charlie didn't know about this young girl. Had no idea how she would talk to her. What did a sixteen-year-old talk about? Clothes, music, boys? But then Elizabeth might not talk to her at all.

After Charlie signed the moving company's release forms, she sat down on the bedroom floor, her back resting against the closet door, adjusting to the room's new look. Elizabeth's impending arrival was suddenly, tangibly real. Next week, she would land at the McKinleyville airport, and everything in Charlie's well-ordered world would get complicated. Elizabeth was flying to California by herself because Rowena had begged off at the last minute to attend her high school reunion. Who would have guessed Rowena would care about something like that?

After Sam locked the garage, he found Charlie sitting on the bedroom floor. He sat beside her and pulled her into his arms. "Are you okay?" The dark circles beneath her eyes were evidence that she wasn't sleeping well.

"It's really going to happen." She took a deep breath. "I'm scared. I never imagined I would be doing something like this. I'm not prepared." She was short of breath, as though she was having some sort of panic attack. Ever since she'd unwillingly agreed to be Elizabeth's guardian, she'd been a bit numb, keeping this new reality at arm's length. But furniture was real and soon Elizabeth would be real, be in this room putting clothes away or crying because she was in this room putting clothes away. Wanting her parents. Maybe hating Charlie.

Sam kissed the top of Charlie's head, savoring the faint scent of the lemon shampoo she used. "Since it seems too late to undo this situation, let's do something physical instead of thinking it to death." He'd been doing that all week. Not particularly constructive. "Would the sheets for the bed be in some of those boxes or should we go shopping?" One small step. He regretted having stayed in Eureka this week. Charlie wasn't comfortable asking for help; he should have recognized that she needed him.

It took a while for her breathing to smooth out. He was right. Doing would keep her from thinking, from imploding. She wanted to ask whether he minded—about Elizabeth—but she didn't know what she'd do if he did mind, so she didn't ask. Confronting problems head on was never one of her strengths.

Sam and Charlie's relationship began slowly. A week after their first meeting in front of her house, his boss had loaned him to the Merritt Island Wildlife Refuge in Florida, so he didn't see Charlie again until he returned to Eureka three months later. She was in Eureka's Ace Hardware store, holding a handful of paint chips and conferring with one of the clerks when Sam walked in, looking for a bolt to replace the one he'd just stripped the threads on. He saw her before she saw him. Even more attractive than he remembered, her hair pulled loosely back at the nape of her neck with a piece of yellow yarn. She was wearing denims, a blue fleece, and bright yellow Nikes. Not an outfit he'd expect an English Prof would wear.

After purchasing two bolts—in case he stripped another one—he was waiting near the check out aisle when she set three sample paint containers on the counter and gave the clerk her credit card.

"Hi Charlie, remember me? Sam Ledger." Not the most scintillating dialogue, but he'd just spent months sloshing around the East Coast marshes, with only seabirds and other biologists for company.

And there was her intriguing, hesitant smile: "I do. Still riding your bike?"

"Not lately. I've been in Florida on loan to another wildlife refuge."

The clerk returned her credit card. She signed the slip he laid on the counter and picked up the plastic bag with the paint containers. "Do you regularly get loaned out?"

"More than I like. Not enough seabird specialists to go around. One of the guys at Merritt Island broke his leg." Sam didn't want this opportunity to reconnect slip away. "Do you have time for coffee?"

"Actually I do."

He smiled. "I know just the place."

She remembered his smile too.

That winter, they met for coffee whenever their work schedules permitted. The beginning of where they were now. For all sorts of reasons, they had moved cautiously. By spring, they were having dinner at his place or hers at least one night a week, sometimes two. He was a better cook than she was so, even when they were at her place, he cooked.

During Charlie's Spring Break, Sam took some of his unused vacation days, and they drove to San Francisco, rented a hotel room within walking distance of Fisherman's Wharf, and made love for the first time.

Until that week, neither of them had been quite ready to take their relationship to that level. Being friends first and lovers second was new for Charlie. Since Andre's departure, the men she'd let into her life didn't stay long. Mostly her choice, not theirs. Safer that way. During graduate school, she'd learned that falling headlong into love left permanent emotional scars. Once burned, forever shy.

But her relationship with Sam—from its beginning—felt different, deeper. Certainly safe.

Their last morning in the city, they ordered coffee and croissants at a French bakery near their hotel. Most of the business was take away, but there were three small tables near the window looking onto the street. It had been drizzling earlier, but the sun was trying to come out.

Sam pulled a croissant apart and spooned strawberry jam onto his plate. "Perfect days."

Not wanting to return to reality, Charlie sighed, "I wish we had more of them."

"So do I." He gambled. "We could try long weekends at your place." Since it was her house, Sam didn't want to be the one to suggest that he move in, even though he'd been thinking about that possibility for weeks. Charlie looked down at what was left of her latte. Her response was crucial but would mean change. A man living in her house—a commitment she'd never made before. Preferring to run away. Needing to run. But backing off might mean losing this tenderly passionate man, and she was fairly sure she didn't want to walk away this time.

"Or you could just move in." The six words startled her.

A huge leap. Enormous commitment.

After a few minutes, "Are you sure?" His eyes were asking and smiling at the same time.

More minutes. "I think so."

Her *I think so* was why he kept the Eureka apartment—as back up.

On the plane to San Francisco: I don't know if I should be happy about getting away from Aunt Rowena or sad about leaving Virginia. My parents are now buried in a churchyard outside Vienna, and all my friends are moving on with their lives without me. Just as well. They don't know what to say to me so we don't say anything much. I'm different from them now. It's like they're afraid of me or afraid that what happened to me will happen to them. I didn't want to leave, but I'm not part of Virginia anymore.

Waiting in San Francisco: Because I'm sixteen, I didn't have to wear my airline ticket around my neck in a leather case, but one of the flight attendants made sure I got to the right area to catch the plane into McKinleyville. I guess Arcata isn't big enough to have an airport. In an hour, I'll be there. My stomach really hurts. I hate everything about my life.

Sam and Charlie had decided Charlie should meet Elizabeth by herself. "I'll be waiting at the house." He'd made a pot of marinara sauce—what kid didn't like spaghetti—but in case she was a vegetarian, he cooked the meatballs separately. Charlie's nervousness had succeeded in making him nervous too.

By mid-afternoon, the fog had begun drifting onshore. Charlie was at the airport half an hour before the flight was due, anxiously pacing the arrivals hall. She wished Sam were with her—he'd hold her hand, make her sit quietly, talk to her about something else.

At 4:17, the arrivals board blinked and *Landed* appeared after the San Francisco 4593 flight listing. Elizabeth was here. Charlie stood at the window as the small plane parked on the tarmac, and the passengers climbed down the portable stairway that had been rolled to the door.

Elizabeth was the last passenger off, a male flight attendant following her down the stairs, talking to her. She was wearing the same leggings she'd worn in Donovan's office, white sandals that fastened around her ankles, and a gauzy white blouse with a pink camisole underneath; she was almost as tall as Charlie and, since Charlie had seen her in Virginia, she'd cut her hair in a pixie style that made her look rather fragile.

As Elizabeth and the attendant stopped beside the luggage carousel, Charlie joined them. "Hello, Elizabeth." For most people, a hugging moment, but Charlie wasn't given to casual hugging.

Elizabeth stepped back slightly, then a formal "Hello."

Definitely not a hugging moment.

Fortunately, the flight attendant filled in. "Oh good, you're here." He wrote something on the clipboard he was carrying. "Ms. Ames?"

"Yes. Thank you for watching out for her."

"Part of my job." He shook hands with Charlie. "Bye Elizabeth. Good luck," and hurried off.

The carousel cranked to life behind them.

"How many bags do you have?"

"Two." Elizabeth moved around Charlie to stare at the luggage circling toward her.

"What color?"

"Black. Aunt Rowena put bright orange elastic bands around them so they would stand out. There—there's one."

She set her purse down and grabbed for a large suitcase that was too heavy for her to drag off. A man standing close by came to her rescue and, when the second, smaller one appeared, he helped her with that one too. She thanked him, picked up her purse, and took the handle of the larger case. Charlie, pulling the smaller one, headed for the sliding exit door.

"The car is in the front parking lot." Charlie's mouth felt dry but her hands were sweating. She wondered whether Elizabeth was as nervous as she was.

I'm in Arcata. It's done. I'm in a room that has my furniture in it but is very different from my other bedroom. Smaller. Shutters on the windows instead of curtains and only a view of the house next door. Nothing on the walls. Charlie said I could paint the walls another color and hang whatever I want on them, but I don't much care. I have a bathroom to myself—unless there's company.

I met Charlie's boyfriend, Sam something or other. He lives here most of the time. He tried to make conversation during dinner. What did I like to do in my spare time? My favorite subjects in school. Charlie didn't say much. At least she isn't treating me like I'm made of glass. Aunt Rowena kept tiptoeing around, asking if I was okay. I'm not sick. Just alone and pissed. My mother wouldn't approve of that word. But she's not here to correct me so I get to use it.

By the time Sam locked up the house and crawled into bed next to Charlie, it was almost eleven. She was exhausted. Not at all sure anything had gone well, but nothing terrible had happened either. Elizabeth answered Sam's questions during dinner, but you couldn't call it conversation. Bless Sam for trying. Charlie hadn't been able to move beyond giving her a key to the house and explaining about all the boxes in the garage. Telling her they had an appointment at the high school on Friday, asking whether she had her school records with her. Mentioning casually that Tessa would meet them there.

Charlie had never been good at warm and fuzzy, and she was pretty sure Elizabeth didn't want anyone fussing over her. Maybe she should ask if Elizabeth wanted someone professional to talk to about losing her parents. Schools sometimes had counselors. On the other hand, it might be too soon to talk about what she'd lost.

Charlie was pretty sure she could use some counseling of her own.

CHAPTER 4

Elizabeth woke to the smell of coffee, the comforting aroma that meant her dad was up. Her mom always let him make the coffee. *I never get it strong enough for him.* Once Elizabeth had asked how her mother could drink it if it was that strong. *Plenty of milk and sugar, darling.*

And then Elizabeth remembered.

Her dad would never again make strong morning coffee and, although she was in her own bed, the bed wasn't where it should be. Neither was she. As they'd been doing ever since the plane crash, the tears came.

The coffee smell was gone when she woke the second time. Her alarm clock showed 10:35. She almost never slept so late. The unfamiliar house was quiet except for the soft brush of rain against the windows hidden behind the shutters.

She rummaged in her large suitcase—underwear, cut-offs, a long-sleeved t-shirt with D.C. in large yellow letters. Purchased two years ago when they'd been on the Mall for the Fourth of July celebration. No shoes. Charlie and Sam didn't seem like the kind of people who would mind her going barefooted. Aunt Rowena always made her go get shoes.

Charlie was in the third bedroom working on a laptop computer, her back to the door, her earpods connected to an iPod on the desk. She didn't hear Elizabeth until a cupboard door snapped shut.

Carrying the earpods, Charlie stood in the kitchen doorway. "Good morning. How'd you sleep?"

"Okay, I guess. It's late."

"Flying messes with your inner clock. Would you like me to fix you eggs or—"

"I just eat cereal." She already had the box of Cheerios in her hand.

"If there's a kind you like better, we can go shopping today." Charlie reached into another cupboard for a bowl and set it on the counter. She didn't want to help too much—or too little. Tricky balancing. "There's 2% milk in the refrigerator—and orange juice. Bananas are in the bowl." She pointed.

Watching Elizabeth move around the kitchen—slicing half a banana, skipping the orange juice—Charlie was grateful the girl didn't seem to expect to be waited on. None of the *I don't like that* or *Don't you have?* comments Charlie had been afraid of.

But then Missy, despite her girly exterior, had also been a no nonsense sort of person.

"I smelled coffee earlier. Is there any left?" Then, as if reading Charlie's mind, "It's okay. I drink it half and half, like they do in France. My mom lets me."

A bit unnerving that Elizabeth guessed what Charlie was thinking. "There's still some. Sam usually makes it before he goes to work. I'll ask him to fix more tomorrow."

"Where does he work?"

"South of here at the Humboldt Wildlife Refuge. He's a marine biologist."

Elizabeth nodded, then concentrated on her cereal.

Probably as much conversation as Charlie was going to get right now. "I'll be in the office if you need anything." She went back to reading the emails forwarded to her computer from the university. There were a couple of committee meetings next week, the usual command performance at the Freshman Reception, and she and Tessa needed to finalize the details for their combined Shakespeare course. Charlie was lecturing the history/literature portion, and Tessa was directing four performances of *Othello* as part of her advanced acting class, the culmination of their summer work in London. The graduate student in charge of the theater costumes was requesting a meeting before the students reported to classes. The semester was kicking into gear.

She heard Elizabeth go back to her room, then sounds that suggested unpacking. Sam called during his lunch break. "Everything okay?"

"Except that I'm on pins and needles, yes."

"What's she doing?"

"Unpacking her suitcases. In a few minutes, we're going over to campus. I need to pick up handouts that the Print Center is holding for me. Maybe we'll grab a snack at The Depot and then go to the grocery store to find out what she does and doesn't eat. I'll let her choose tonight's menu. What do you think?"

"Sounds good. Your first full day as a guardian."

It already seemed longer than one day.

Friday: It's been mostly wet since I got here. It doesn't rain hard, just drizzles all the time. I thought California was sunny, but I guess that's the southern part. Last night, Sam fixed fried chicken and grits—my choice. He had to look up a recipe for grits. I helped with the dishes and clean up. Good news, Charlie has a dishwasher. So far no one has laid down rules and stuff. I have my own house key.

Charlie and her friend Tessa took me over to the high school today. I've never attended a public school. Never gone to any other school than The Vienna Academy. The high school building is kind of plain, two stories; it looks like an apartment building with outside walkways. Classes start on Monday. The counselor was impressed with my transcript. She wanted to know why I was transferring. I suppose I'm going to have to keep telling people why. It hurts every time. At least I didn't cry.

I wonder what Julie's taking this year. I'm signed up for English 3 CP. I can only do College Placement since I didn't have the summer reading schedule that would let me into Advanced Placement. That's okay. I don't feel like working hard right now. I'm also taking Calculus, French, and European History. I signed up for Madrigal Choir. It sounds like a heavy schedule, but I doubt the competition is anything like the competition in Vienna. This school loans the students their textbooks. Amazing. We had to buy them at the academy. These are rather beat up though.

Bought notebooks and other supplies over at the university's bookstore. Charlie paid for everything. As soon as I get a checking account, the Vienna law office will deposit a monthly allowance for me. I'll have an ATM card to make withdrawals so I don't have to ask for spending money. Charlie will take me to a local bank after classes on Monday. I guess I'm here to stay.

In bed that night, Charlie filled Sam in on what happened at the high school.

"She's been taking difficult classes at that private school. She may think high school here is a breeze or boring."

"Maybe she needs a breeze this year."

"She seemed really interested in the choir. I guess she's done some singing and performing the last few years."

"How are you doing with all this?"

Charlie considered his question, well aware honesty was required. Sam could always sense when she was less than truthful about her feelings. "I'm really out of my element. I suspect this is the easy part. She's still in shock and coping with a totally strange environment. Once she's comfortable, she might not be as easy."

"I'm proud of you." Sam shifted his position and pulled her close. "Let's celebrate surviving the first three days."

Charlie leaned away to turn off the light on the nightstand, a little uneasy that they'd be having sex while Elizabeth was just down the hall.

The weekend filled itself up. Saturday, Sam helped Elizabeth set up her computer and printer with Charlie's wifi and, after considerable swearing and two phone calls to the company, figured out how to hook her small TV set to Direct TV. After dinner, Elizabeth started looking through the wardrobe containers in the garage, pulling out additional clothing.

Sunday dawned bright and dry. A good day to drive to the refuge so Elizabeth could see where Sam worked. He enjoyed showing her around the Visitor Center, probably telling her more about the displays than she wanted to know; then they took one of the nature walks. Elizabeth paid attention, nodded when appropriate, but didn't ask any questions.

To the casual observer, they looked like a typical family on an outing.

Monday, Charlie dropped Elizabeth at the high school, went to her office on the HSU campus, worked on her Shakespeare notes, had lunch with Tessa, and left campus in time to take Elizabeth to the bank.

Tessa had warned her not to ask Elizabeth how school was. "That's guaranteed to produce only one useless word—fine. You have to trick teenagers into talking to you."

"I don't want to give her the third degree, but I need to sound interested. We don't have much to say to each other so far."

"Ask something like *What are your teachers like*—or *are there more supplies you need?* Something that requires a specific answer."

"All of this is so complicated. Conversations are awkward. Both of us standing on ceremony. Sam's handling her better." For which Charlie was grateful. It took some of the pressure off for the moment.

Day 1 at AHS: I learned two things today. One, Charlie was probably more nervous about my first day than I was. Even though it's only a three-block walk, she drove me to school and picked me up at 2:30 so we could go to the bank. Two: Madrigal Choir is the only class I'm going to have to work hard in. Two other students and I have to audition tomorrow. We have to sing Eidelweiss without accompaniment. There are some really good voices in the choir. The English class isn't as hard as what I was taking last year. My oral French is better than that of most of the other students in the French 2 class; the time spent in Provence when my parents had a timeshare helps. Since I had pre-calculus last year, the calculus class won't be a huge problem. Besides, I like math. History is a no brainer.

The hard part is that most of these kids have lived here all their lives. Everyone knows everyone. Lots of inside jokes. There are only five new eleventh grade students. No one has been mean or anything, but I'm almost invisible. If I disappeared tomorrow, would anyone notice—or care? Probably only my grandparents. Maybe Aunt Rowena. I bet Charlie would be relieved.

In case she didn't pass, Elizabeth didn't tell Charlie about the audition.

Choir was the last class of the day. Probably about thirty students, more girls than boys. Elizabeth was wearing the same white blouse over the pink camisole she'd worn the day she arrived. Pink set off her dark hair and dusky skin. Right now it was her favorite outfit. She got to class early and sat in the front row of tables in the chair closest to the door. None of the students spoke to her, most of them arranging themselves in the SATB groupings they'd been in last year, laughing and talking among themselves. If she made it into this choir, she'd probably be either a second soprano or a first alto. The voice teacher she'd had at The Vienna Academy had commented that Elizabeth's voice would be lower by the time she finished high school. She hoped so, because she liked doing sexy, torch songs.

At exactly 1:15, the director, Mr. Hannigan, entered the classroom. He was too heavy for his height but had a welcoming smile. Standing behind the upright piano, he began warm up exercises different from those she was used to. They'd be easier to follow the next time.

When they finished, "Elizabeth," she jumped a bit, "let's start with you."

She took her place in the front of the class, pausing to calm herself and breathe evenly. *Eidelwiess* was a slow piece that required precise control to hold the notes. Her performance lasted only a few minutes. The class applauded politely, and Mr. Hannigan called the next auditioning student to sing the same piece. After the third audition, he handed out the semester's syllabus and spent time reminding the students about the class rules. "Don't forget to bring your black folders for the new music I'll be handing out tomorrow. I'm dismissing you a few minutes early today. Don't disturb the other classes or we'll all be in trouble."

The three who had auditioned stayed behind and, one at a time, were called into Mr. Hannigan's small office adjacent to the classroom. Elizabeth was last.

"Please sit down, Elizabeth." He opened the folder in front of him. "I see this is your first year at Arcata."

"Yes."

She expected he would ask about her parents, why she was living with a cousin she barely knew, but he didn't. Elizabeth relaxed a little.

"You began singing in a chorus when you were twelve?"

"That was as early as they let you take it at my old school." She'd wanted to start sooner. "But it wasn't Madrigal."

He looked up from the pages in front of him. "You have a promising voice. You'll easily fit into the choir. Congratulations."

For the first time in weeks, something had gone right. "Thank you."

"Let's start you in the alto section. If you don't have a black folder for your music, the university bookstore carries them."

"Okay."

He stood up and extended his hand. "See you tomorrow."

Because Charlie was attending a reception at the university, Elizabeth walked to the campus bookstore to buy a black folder. It was the first time she'd been on her own in weeks. Wonderfully liberating. Ever since the crash, someone had been with her—as though she might self-destruct if left alone. Once she located the folder, she browsed through the newsstand and chose two fashion magazines. The store was jammed with university students buying books and supplies for the new semester; the check out lines each had ten or eleven students. Since she needed the folder for tomorrow, she'd have to be patient. She liked being surrounded by these older students. Made her feel grown up.

As she was leaving the store, she heard, "Hi, Elizabeth." Charlie's friend Tessa was buying coffee from the cart at the foot of the bookstore steps. "Shopping for school?"

Elizabeth smiled. "Hi. I needed a folder for my music class. The teacher told me I could buy one here."

"So you made it into Madrigal. Is Bill Hannigan still directing?"

Another smile. "Yes. He seems nice."

"Does Charlie know you passed the audition?"

"She didn't know there was an audition. She's at some reception."

"It's over. I think she's in her office."

"I really need to go back to the house and start on my Calculus, but it's okay if you tell her I got in."

If she went to Charlie's office, they'd go home in the car. Elizabeth was looking forward to walking back to the house, taking time to go into a few of the shops around Humboldt Plaza. She'd seen the plaza each time they drove through town and was curious about the statue in the center. Walking a new place always helped her acclimate—like her first year at camp. She and Julie had walked every inch. During

Elizabeth's first week in Arcata, Charlie had warned her that transients hung out in the Plaza, panhandling, some smoking pot. The warning only served to pique Elizabeth's curiosity.

Charlie didn't cross paths with Tessa until Thursday afternoon when they met with Linda Knightsbridge, the G. A. in charge of costumes for the Theater Arts Department. The three of them spent a couple of hours sorting through the costumes that were in storage, deciding what could be reused in *Othello*. Their wish list and budget would have to be submitted to the chairman of the department in two weeks. Finding money for new costumes would undoubtedly be next to impossible. The budget was always tight.

It was after six o'clock when Tessa and Charlie walked to the parking lot. "I ran into Elizabeth at the bookstore Tuesday afternoon. She said she got into Madrigal. She seemed excited."

"I'm told it's quite an honor to go straight into Madrigal without being in the other choir first."

"Is she settling in?"

"A little. She doesn't want me to drive her to school, even when it's raining."

"Independent."

"I guess so. She spends most of her time in her room, except for meals. I have no idea what she watches on her TV or what she does on the computer. I probably should know those things, but I hate to pry. She asked me to show her how to use the washing machine."

"Does her own laundry. A low maintenance kid. I'm impressed."

"Or she doesn't trust me with her clothes. Just as well since I don't know how to maintain a kid. I did mention that keeping her room clean was her responsibility, and her response was *Do you have a cleaning lady?* When I said no, she asked if she had to wash her own sheets."

Tessa laughed. "She can take care of her own clothes but not her sheets! How funny. What did you say?"

"Just put them in the hamper in the hall. They'll get done."

"Have you noticed her smile?" A question out of left field. "When we were getting her set up at the high school, she never smiled once.

But while I was talking to her on Tuesday, she smiled a couple of times. Her smile reminds me of yours." She paused. "You did say your cousin had adopted her, didn't you?"

"Yes. An adoption agency handled it." Hopefully the answer was firm enough. Charlie wasn't good at extemporaneous lying.

"Maybe I was just imagining the resemblance," Tessa stopped beside her Explorer. "I won't be in until Monday. I need to go to Ferndale tomorrow."

Charlie didn't have to ask why. Tessa's son Jimmy was once again going through drug rehab. She couldn't remember whether this was the second or third time. Tessa's family life had its share of difficulties.

After the Explorer drove away, Charlie sat in her car, ruminating over Tessa's comment about Elizabeth's smile. Though Tessa had only seen Elizabeth twice, leave it to her to notice something like that.

Charlie wondered whether Sam had noticed the same thing.

CHAPTER 5

Sam had.

And it wasn't just Charlie's sweet, quizzical smile. Elizabeth's hands were a younger version of Charlie's, graceful and long-fingered. As a marine biologist, Sam was trained to notice even the smallest anatomical details—the length of a bird's beak, the subtle variations in feathers. If Elizabeth had been Missy's biological child, he'd have dismissed the similarities as family traits. But Elizabeth had been adopted.

In spite of their differences—Elizabeth's dark hair, warmly tanned skin, and dark eyes; Charlie's amber eyes, fair skin, and blonde/brown hair—they could be related. Both were lithe and tall. Charlie was 5'7", Elizabeth maybe an inch shorter but probably still growing. Both moved quickly.

Once the possibility that Elizabeth and Charlie might be biologically related insinuated itself into his thoughts, he couldn't get rid of it. He did the math. Elizabeth was sixteen. Where had Charlie been sixteen years ago? If he remembered correctly, she'd been in the second year of her doctoral program at Yale. She rarely talked about those years. *Not much to tell, just studying and teaching. A few relationships, nothing serious. End of story.* It never seemed she was intentionally being secretive, but one of the first things he'd learned about Charlie was that she had a hard time talking about herself, about what might be bothering her or what her back story was. He often had to coax her to tell him about her day. Ultimately she would—a student had been verbally combative or she had made a mistake in a lecture and was beating herself up over the error. Something that happened in a department meeting.

Sam didn't see her reticence as a problem because, quite simply, he loved her, had loved her from the moment they reconnected that day in the hardware store, though her love for him had come more slowly. He hadn't hurried her. And, in her own time, during those magical days in San Francisco, she'd come to him completely.

He knew all the secrets of her body, but he was pretty sure he didn't know *all* her secrets. He, on the other hand, wasn't given to holding back. She'd probably heard way too much about his failed marriage, about his work at the refuge, his childhood.

While Charlie was teaching in London, he realized it was time to ask her to marry him and shopped for a ring. What were they waiting for?

Then Elizabeth entered the picture.

And now there was her smile.

The first week of a college semester, all things are possible. A brief honeymoon. No student is any better or worse than any other. The academic version of a level playing field. Adrenaline everywhere. Students hunting for classrooms and endless lines in the bookstore. For Charlie, the first meeting of each class felt like a make-or-break audition. Get the introduction to the course wrong and the rest of the semester would be off balance. Getting it right didn't guarantee a good semester, but the odds improved. An intangible chemistry within four walls.

Standing in front of twenty plus Accelerated Composition students, Charlie called roll from the roster she'd downloaded on Friday night. One name didn't come with a student—making room for the first student on the waiting list; then she sent the rest of the waiting list hopefuls on their way. Charlie's class was the only Accelerated section offered this semester. A year of Freshman Comp was the prerequisite for these students so, in theory, all the students should know the basics of essay and report writing and have fairly decent grammar—fingers crossed on that one. The class was a requirement for English majors, recommended for history majors.

She handed out the syllabus, explained the reading list, and focused on the difficulty level of the course. Making it sound too easy would only lead to major grousing when the first papers were returned. Better to start hard and soften later.

In the remaining half hour, she asked them to write a short essay defending the value of a Liberal Arts education, an intentionally dreary topic designed to separate those who could support an argument from those who ran in circles of generalities. At 3:30, one student was still struggling with his essay and reluctantly handed it in when Charlie reminded him that part of the assignment involved finishing in the allotted time.

He began to protest—*But Dr. Ames, I*—wisely stopped, and shuffled out of the classroom.

Charlie glanced at the paper. He'd managed only one short paragraph. Not a good sign. She would have to look at his transcript, see which Freshman Comp instructor he'd had and what his final grade was. She added his paper to the others and laid them in her briefcase.

She didn't get home until after six. Elizabeth was in the kitchen, emptying a storage container of yesterday's beef stew into a saucepan. "I didn't know when you'd be home." She rinsed the container but didn't turn the stove on.

Charlie set her briefcase on a chair. "Sorry. At the beginning of a semester, I get caught up in everything. Sam says I'm a lost cause until the third week. Isn't he home yet?"

"He called. He's staying in Eureka. Something about a stranded seal."

Sigh. No Sam to smooth awkward moments. Charlie felt her neck tighten with the subtle tension that crept in whenever she and Elizabeth were alone and had to talk to each other. She looked into the pan. "Is there enough stew for two?"

"Yes, if we have some bread and eat the rest of the lemon pie."

Charlie was quickly discovering that Elizabeth was more comfortable in the kitchen than she was. Missy had prepared her well. Too bad Missy couldn't have prepared Charlie for looking after Elizabeth. But of course contact between Charlie and Missy's family had not been part of the arrangement.

Donovan's office had forwarded Elizabeth's medical records, reminding Charlie that she needed to put Elizabeth on the university's medical plan. She'd already sent him her checking account number so the monthly stipend could be deposited on the tenth of every month. She'd need to keep track of what she spent. This year's income tax would undoubtedly be more complicated. Elizabeth's allowance would go straight into her new checking account. Charlie had no idea whether Elizabeth would quickly go through the money and then ask Charlie for more. Should she give her more? There were so many ways she could get it wrong. Probably already had.

Two months ago my parents died. When I woke up this morning, I was feeling so lonely. I have a ton of things I want to tell my mother and ask her. I thought about not going to school, staying in my room looking at the photos I brought from Virginia. I keep them in one of the drawers under my bed. Sometimes I look at them when I can't sleep. I already feel like I'm forgetting my parents. I can't hear their voices anymore. I don't want to forget.

Then I remembered we were starting a new piece by John Rutter in Madrigal. I needed to be there. It feels so good to sing. When I'm singing, I can't think about anything else. One of the other altos, a junior named Martha, takes time to talk to me, and sometimes we leave school together, then go in different directions. She has to hurry home to take care of her younger brother. I don't really talk to anyone else much.

Several days later, Elizabeth described the choir uniform requirements to Charlie. "A white, long-sleeved blouse that has a collar that'll look good with a red bow tie like guys wear with a tux. Long black pants, I have those, but I need the tie and a black cummerbund. Black flats."

"How soon do you need everything?"

"We have a performance scheduled in early October. At a nursing home."

"We can get the tie and cummerbund at a tuxedo store. The blouse is easy. You could go online if you know your size."

Elizabeth hesitated. "Is there someplace I could go to try on blouses?

I—ah—don't fit into some of my tops from last year," more hesitation, "and I think I need new bras."

"Of course. There's a mall in Eureka."

"Great. I like to shop." The first time Elizabeth had shared something personal. Missy had loved to shop too. Charlie, on the other hand, shopped only when necessary. Online shopping was her friend. No salesperson following her around, asking if she'd found everything, whether she'd like to see the sweater she was looking at in another color. Charlie had never imagined she'd be helping anyone buy bras. Had no idea how to go about it.

The day she and Charlie went shopping for choir clothes, Elizabeth bought a photo album with plastic pages divided into 4" x 6" sleeves. Instead of shuffling through the stacks of family snapshots held together with rubber bands, she would select the important ones to fill the album. The most recent photos were, of course, on her computer and phone. The album would be a non-digital record of her older relatives as well as her own baby pictures. Being able to look at the photos whenever she began to feel like she was forgetting would be comforting.

Since Charlie usually served dinner at the round oak table in the kitchen, Elizabeth asked if she could lay the photos out on the dining room table while she was making choices.

"No problem."

"Maybe you could tell me who some of the people in the older pictures are."

"If I can't, your grandmother might be able to help. The ones I can't figure out, we'll mail to her." A project to share. Something to talk about.

Sam hadn't paid much attention to Elizabeth's album project. He'd been working late all week and, by the time he got home, Elizabeth was in her room, doing homework. But Sunday afternoon, he paused at the table on his way to the kitchen for more coffee. An 8" x 10" colored picture of Missy and Richard's wedding party—too big to fit into a plastic sleeve—caught his eye. Charlie was standing far left, wearing a frilly peach bridesmaid's dress, smiling. A year or so older than Elizabeth was now. Smiling Elizabeth's smile. The resemblance in the picture couldn't be a coincidence—or his imagination.

Elizabeth was possibly Charlie's biological daughter.

The part of the guardian story she'd omitted.

Something so huge, so personal and important, yet Charlie hadn't confided in him. From the beginning of their relationship, he'd accommodated himself to her reluctance to share certain parts of herself. But this—this was way beyond any other secret she was keeping. He went from shock to annoyance. Why hadn't she told him? He could understand the awkwardness of telling Elizabeth that the cousin who was her guardian was actually her mother. Especially so soon after Missy and Richard's deaths.

He was tempted to confront Charlie right then. She was in her office, working. Elizabeth had gone for a walk. As he poured himself the last of the coffee, he calmed down, backed off. Evaluated why he was upset, finally deciding he was making her secretiveness bigger than it needed to be. Taking out his phone, he scrolled through the pictures he'd shot at the refuge the first weekend Elizabeth was in Arcata. He hadn't taken the time to look at them until now. He'd snapped a couple of pictures of Charlie and Elizabeth on the Shorebird Loop Trail. In the first picture, both had been unsmiling—perhaps uncomfortable standing side-by-side.

Come on ladies—a smile please.

And they'd complied. With his thumb and index finger, he enlarged that shot. And there were the smiles.

He definitely needed counsel.

On his way back to Arcata on Monday afternoon, he called Tessa at her office. "Are you going to be there for another ten minutes?"

"Yes. Something wrong?"

"I need to show you something. I'll be at your office as soon as I find a parking spot in the visitor lot."

Tessa had spent the afternoon in the empty Van Duzen Theater, blocking scenes for *Othello*. The cast had begun read-throughs. They'd start rehearsing in the theater next week.

Sam knocked lightly on her open door. She was pinning the blocking sheets to the cork wall beside her desk. "Hi, Sam. Come in." She moved to her desk and pointed to the single chair on the opposite side. "Use the student chair."

Sam laughed. "The naughty chair?"

"More often than I would like. What's up? I saw Charlie at lunch."

Instead of explaining, he turned this phone on, made sure the photo was still enlarged and handed it across the desk.

She studied it for a moment, then met his eyes. "Yes."

He let out the breath he'd been holding. "It's not my imagination?"

"No. I noticed the similarity a few weeks ago when I met Elizabeth at the bookstore. Their voices are similar too. When I mentioned it to Charlie, she didn't even blink, didn't say yes or no. Have you shown her this? Asked?"

"No."

"Are you going to?"

"Eventually, if she doesn't bring it up first."

"There'll come a time when she's going to have to tell Elizabeth before she gets the information from someone else or figures it out herself."

"Who else would know the truth?"

"Best guess, Missy's parents, Charlie's dad."

"The father?"

Tessa shrugged.

Driving back to Charlie's, Sam couldn't decide whether he felt better or worse. But at least Tessa agreed.

A few weeks into what Charlie was privately calling her *Instant Parenting Phase*, she ordered a book from Amazon titled *Parenting the 21ˢᵗ Century Teenager*. The first fifty pages did not make her feel any easier about her new role. For a dozen years, she'd been teaching students who were only three or four years older than Elizabeth. Sixteen shouldn't be all that different from nineteen or twenty. According to the book however, the students who walked out of her classes after an hour were quite different from the girl who was living under her roof.

The author stressed the importance of establishing trust, but Charlie had no idea how that happened when the child was almost an adult. After all, she and Elizabeth had only been "together" since August. Bra shopping had been the most personal event and ultimately one of the young salesgirls had taken Elizabeth into the dressing room while Charlie waited outside. When Elizabeth emerged and informed Charlie that the new bras were a cup size larger than the ones she'd been wearing, Charlie was selfishly relieved she hadn't had to help with the decision. There were undoubtedly going to be other personal issues. She'd noticed a box of Kotex pads in Elizabeth's bathroom. Would there eventually be a discussion about Tampax? Did Elizabeth have cramps? How much did she know about birth control? Was she a virgin?

I am so in over my head.

CHAPTER 6

Today would have been my father's forty-third birthday. He loved having mom and me make a fuss over him, always wanted carrot cake with lots of cream cheese icing. Mom was going to get him new skis this year. I was saving to get him a good pair of gloves. His hands were always cold, even when he wasn't skiing.

I wish…

It was too hard to write down what she wished.

Charlie's open-handed parenting hit a snag when Missy's mother called Elizabeth and discovered that it was dinnertime in Arcata and Elizabeth was home alone, fixing herself a sandwich.

Seated in Tessa's office, reviewing the cuts they needed to make in *Othello* so it would run only two hours, Charlie felt her cell phone vibrate. She'd shoved it into her skirt pocket when she left her office. Pulling it out, she checked the screen.

Aunt Grace

"Excuse me a minute. It's my aunt in Virginia. Hi, Aunt Grace."

Charlie listened.

"It's not really that late here—only 5:45."

More listening.

"She's doing okay. She's quite self-sufficient."

The voice on the other end got firmer.

"Of course. I understand your concern."

Another minute.

"No, I haven't."

Charlie was trying not to say what she was thinking.

"Well this is today, not the way it was when they were alive." Charlie needed to remember that Grace had lost a daughter and her granddaughter was a continent away. She changed the subject. "How is Uncle Kevin?" She didn't wait for an answer. "Please give him my love. I have someone in my office. I need to go."

Charlie laid the phone on Tessa's desk and sighed.

"Trouble?"

"My aunt, Elizabeth's grandmother, called Elizabeth and discovered I've *abandoned* her at dinnertime, forcing her to fix herself a sandwich. She made it sound like child abuse. I should add that Grace was a stay at home mother, as was Missy."

"Ah, the oversight committee."

"As far as she's concerned, my parenting credentials are suspect."

"Because?"

Charlie shrugged. "Long story."

"I've got time. Does some of the story have to do with your real relationship to Elizabeth?" Tessa knew she was stepping over a line, but her curiosity had waited long enough.

Charlie pretended confusion. "Real?"

"Don't bullshit me, Charlie. You know what I'm talking about."

"I really don't want to talk about this right now." Tessa the interrogator was never easy to dodge.

"At some point you'll have to. You know I can be like a dog with a bone, and I've already had Sam on my doorstep, asking whether I've noticed that Elizabeth has your smile. And your hands."

Charlie leaned back in her chair, as though putting a few extra inches between herself and Tessa would make the questions go away. She let a full five minutes pass without answering, then, defeated by Tessa's tenacity, "What do you want to know?"

"Are you Elizabeth's biological mother?"

Strange word, biological. A cold, clinical mother, only providing genetic material, as opposed to a compassionate, caring mother. Which Charlie hadn't been then, wasn't now, probably never would be. When Donovan's office had called her in London, she knew a trap had been set and, during the afternoon in his office, the full force of the trap had been sprung. She'd spent the previous sixteen years pretending her affair with Andre had been neatly erased the moment Missy and Rick adopted Elizabeth. No harm, no foul.

Charlie was free to finish her doctorate and begin teaching; and Elizabeth had a good home.

Tessa's steady gaze wouldn't let her lie. "Yes."

"Does she know?"

"No."

"Do you plan to tell her?"

"Not sure it's necessary, though my aunt certainly thinks it is. Elizabeth had wonderful, loving parents, every advantage imaginable. Missy said Elizabeth was never curious about—me."

"Are you going to tell Sam?"

"Yes. I know he's puzzled about my agreeing to take Elizabeth. I've always been adamant about not wanting children. He was all right with that since he already has a son."

"And now you have a daughter."

Charlie looked at her watch. "I need to get home in case Child Protective Services is knocking on the door. Anything else we need for *Othello?*"

Knowing the conversation was finished for now, Tessa shook her head.

Charlie picked up her phone, "See you tomorrow," and fled before Tessa could see how upset she was.

She stopped by her own office for her briefcase and left campus.

Elizabeth was sitting cross-legged on her bed, flipping through a magazine, her bedroom door open. Charlie leaned against the door jam, "Hi." She was always hesitant about entering Elizabeth's private space, not wanting to presume she was welcome. And Elizabeth never asked her to come in.

Elizabeth looked at Charlie with Andre's eyes. "Hi."

"Your Grandma called."

"Yeah. She wanted to talk about Grampa. I guess he's not doing

45

well. The doctors have him on oxygen all the time now. Why did she call you?"

"To give me trouble about you being home alone, fixing yourself a sandwich." Which had guilted Charlie into stopping at Safeway before coming home. "I have stuff for a salad and Stouffers Mac and Cheese. Still hungry?"

"Pretty much hungry all the time. Anyway, it was only half a sandwich. Do you think Grampa's going to die?"

"Maybe not right away. But full time oxygen would suggest sooner rather than later. He smoked for most of his life."

"I guess that's why Mom was always preaching against smoking."

Be casual. "Have you ever tried it?"

Elizabeth shook her head, "But someone let me take a couple puffs of marijuana last year. Really yucky."

Charlie was surprised how relieved she was.

The first time Charlie saw Andre was opening day of the Spring 1999 semester. She was one of a dozen Yale graduate students in his seminar on Seventeenth Century Literature. He was gorgeous. Thick dark hair, glasses that he pushed up onto his head when he was lecturing. Maybe six feet tall, fascinating hands. The kind a carpenter or maybe a fisherman would have, not what a literature professor would have. His lectures were at once profound and amusing.

She was instantly captivated.

While she was an undergraduate at the University of Virginia, she'd dated a series of guys, but none of the relationships were serious. Ted, a soccer player who was not the brightest of her boyfriends. Carson, who was rich and took her to elegant restaurants but was intimidated by her wanting to get a Ph.D. Simon, a frat guy addicted to weekend parties and binge drinking. A history of choosing badly.

Thirty-eight year old Andre Winslow was in an entirely different category. A visiting professor from Northwestern with several articles in literary journals to his credit. A rising star in the academic world. Sure of himself, charismatic, and immediately interested in Charlie—though he always called her Charlotte. *Charlotte is a royal name; Charlie's a boy's name. You are definitely not a boy.* He encouraged her to let her hair grow. *It's the color of taffy. I love the way sunlight dances over it.* Sitting in his class listening to him lecture, she could feel the way his fingers caressed the back of her neck when he kissed her. That sensation did not help her concentrate on the lecture material.

Their first *meetings*—ostensibly conferences to discuss her research project—were in his office. During the second conference, he kissed her, a butterfly brush on her lips; after their fourth conference, he invited her to his apartment for a drink—and their affair raced ahead after that exquisite evening. Charlie had thought she knew all about sex until Andre showed her how much she didn't know. Once or twice a week, he took her to expensive restaurants, always someplace other than New Haven. *It's against the rules for professors to date students. I don't want to meet someone from the campus.* One night, they flew to Boston for dinner on the wharf and flew back in time for classes the next day.

She knew he had a family, two sons and a wife from whom he was separated. Whether he was or wasn't free didn't interfere with her feelings. She was besotted with him. There were bed and breakfast weekends in Vermont, quick trips to Manhattan to see Broadway plays. When her parents called because she didn't come home over Spring Break, her roommate made excuses for her. Andre had taken her to Bermuda.

Charlie had always prided herself on having a cast iron stomach—strange food combinations and exotic spices never bothered her—so the nausea that became part of her mornings finally sent her in search of pregnancy test kits. After three tests assured her she was pregnant, she made an appointment with an ob/gyn recommended by Student Health Services. He confirmed she was five weeks pregnant. Compliments of the Bermuda trip.

In spite of being sick every morning, she was elated. She was carrying Andre's baby. Her baby. Theirs. She imagined him tenderly touching her baby bump, holding the baby in the delivery room. They were going to share this child. She spent hours choosing names, though if it was a boy Andre wasn't an option. He already had one son by that name. The wonder of this gift made her feel valuable. She was not just his lover, but also the mother of his child.

There were of course unanswered questions. Would she have to withdraw from the doctoral program, would he ask her to move to Chicago with him? Most important— would he finally get around to divorcing his wife?

It took her several days to work up the courage to tell him about the baby. On a rainy Friday afternoon, she asked him to meet her at a coffee house near her apartment. He'd arrived first—his rain slicker on the back of his chair—waiting at a table near the windows. He'd already ordered two lattes. As she reached for hers, he gently took her hand and lifted it to his lips. "Hi beautiful."

She felt her bones liquify.

"Why are we here?"

Taking a sip of her latte, she smiled at him and spoke the words she'd been practicing.

I'm pregnant.

An ominous silence surrounded the table. He set his cup down with exaggerated care, his dark eyes hardening, now nearly black.

"Are you sure?"

Hesitantly, "Yes. I've seen a doctor—I'm six weeks along."

The silence expanded—the sound of the espresso machine and customers' voices receded. He didn't move a muscle. This was not the conversation Charlie had been imagining.

Sharply, "You have to get rid of it. There isn't much time."

It.

A shiver slid over her skin and invaded her heart. Though she'd been anxious about his reaction, she hadn't expected he'd tell her to get an abortion. To kill their child.

"You want me to kill the fetus?" She could scarcely get the words out.

His body had a strange rigidity. His voice was cutting. No hesitation. "God yes. Of course I do. I'll find a safe clinic and give you the money." The succulent voice that caressed her dreams was icy. "I already have two children and a wife. If anyone finds out, I could lose my job."

"But this is—*ours*." Only later did she realize the naivete in that sentence, how foolish she must have seemed to him.

He pushed his cup to one side and stood up. As though she hadn't spoken, "I'll get the money to you as soon as I can." Grabbing his slicker, he hurried out of the shop.

His melodramatic exit left Charlie frozen in place, all her joy about the baby stripped away. She was pregnant, had been dumped by the man she was in love with, and was sitting alone in a nondescript coffee shop. A scene from a 1940's B movie.

She had no idea how long she'd been staring at the door he'd closed behind him.

"Are you okay?" One of the male baristas was standing next to her.

Startled, Charlie looked up into his worried face.

"Not really." It was getting dark, the rain had stopped. "Sorry to stay so long." She stood up slowly, retrieved her purse and umbrella from the floor, and walked into the street, not entirely sure where she should go. At this time of day, she was usually waiting for Andre near his office. They would drive somewhere for dinner and go back to his apartment; sometimes she stayed all night.

She'd been so willing and so stupid!

After a few minutes, she turned left and forced herself to walk the two blocks to the student apartment she shared with a biology student named Fran.

Charlie wept her way through the next two days—barely able to get out of bed. Now she was sick all day, not just in the morning.

At some point, she would have to tell her parents. They would not understand but probably wouldn't abandon her. Fran wouldn't be shocked. She'd dealt with all kinds of crises in her dysfunctional family. Her response would be something like *What made you think sleeping with your married professor was a good idea?*

Thinking hadn't been involved. Charlie had never before felt such an overwhelming physical attraction to any man. His hands had molded her into a woman, and she'd enjoyed the transformation.

She had not, however, enjoyed their coffee house conversation.

Fran's questions were straightforward. "How far along?"

"Six weeks."

"Are you keeping it?"

"He wants me to have an abortion." Her voice cracked over *abortion*.

Fran shrugged. "Figures. He has a wife who would not be happy about you and certainly not a baby."

Charlie bit into a soda cracker—the only food that would stay down. "He's separated."

"That qualifies as married. Don't be a fool. He was just looking for a fling while wifey was safely in Chicago."

Charlie finished the cracker and waited to see whether her stomach would rebel. "I'm not having an abortion." Where her certainty came from, she didn't know. But having someone callously scrape away the beginning of a child seemed impossibly wrong.

Four days after the coffee house disaster, the cash from Andre—he was careful not to leave a paper trail—and the name of an abortion clinic arrived at her apartment via registered mail. Cold and final. Not caring enough about her to deliver it himself. Too worried about his precious job.

It took months to understand that, for Andre, their affair had only been about conquest and sex; for Charlie it had been about love. She was embarrassed and broken-hearted. The emotional damage done had never entirely healed. She'd learned that if you loved, you were at risk. Better to give only as much of yourself as you were willing to lose. Always keep something back. You might need it.

Because she couldn't bring herself to return to Andre's class, she asked another student to deliver her final research project.

She received an A.

The irony wasn't lost on her.

The morning sickness disappeared in the second trimester and her energy returned. She enrolled in summer school and, as a second year doctoral candidate, was eligible to teach a basic composition class that fall. Her first teaching assignment. The last weekend in August, her parents celebrated their silver wedding anniversary with a party at their golf club. Charlie screwed up her courage and said she'd attend. She was beginning to show and she had gone up a bra size. Her mother noticed the changes the moment Charlie got out of the car.

"When were you planning on telling us?" A mother-tone designed to foster guilt.

"Today."

"Who's the father?"

"He wants no part of this. Or me." The ugly truth, but she refused to let her mother see her sorrow.

"Are you going to put it up for adoption?"

Once again—it.

"I don't know yet. There's time."

"When are you due?"

"Late January."

On January 25th, after twelve hours of labor, Charlie gave birth to Elizabeth. A cap of dark hair—compliments of Andre—7 lbs. 6 ounces. By that time, all the arrangements for the baby's adoption by Missy and Rick were in place. Charlie held the baby for a few minutes after the delivery, then placed her in Missy's arms.

Missy gazed lovingly at her daughter. "I'm naming her Elizabeth, after our grandmother."

Charlie closed her eyes against the threat of tears. She'd spent countless sleepless nights convincing herself she was doing the best thing for the baby and herself. She would not let her emotions change that decision.

Missy offered to send pictures.

"Please don't."

For months afterwards, Charlie dreamed she could hear Elizabeth crying. Remembered her tiny, minutes-old face.

A week after giving birth, Charlie returned to campus. She was teaching two Freshman Comp classes that spring, taking one class toward her doctorate, and ready to choose a topic and a committee for her Dissertation. She retreated into the cocoon of academia and got her figure back. She was grateful no one at Yale asked where the baby was or who the father was. Whatever love she'd felt for Andre had effectively been scoured out of her the moment she handed Missy the baby. It was four years until she slept with another man, a meaningless encounter followed by other meaningless encounters.

Until she met Sam, who cared for her, held her close while giving her space. He didn't ask what baggage she had, and she didn't tell him.

She loved teaching. Lectured at Yale, spent a few years teaching at a community college near Sacramento, and finally landed the job at Humboldt. Her parents had attended a few Enright celebrations when Elizabeth was a toddler. After all, Charlie's mother was Missy's aunt and lived only twenty miles away. Once, when her mother mentioned Elizabeth, Charlie stopped her mid-sentence. *Don't. She belongs to Missy,* and hung up. Since her mother's death, her father and Missy's parents had been the only other persons who knew who Elizabeth's birth mother was.

The plan had been perfect.

Until the plane crashed.

CHAPTER 7

Elizabeth's story would have to be told, but Charlie hadn't found the right time to sit down with Sam—or Elizabeth—to explain the affair with Andre, explain giving Elizabeth up for adoption. There was, of course, no completely acceptable reason for giving your child away. No reason that would satisfy the child. Thus the procrastination. On simple issues like paying bills or cleaning house or correcting papers, Charlie was rarely given to procrastination. The Elizabeth issue was, however, not simple because it involved mistakes—hers. And feelings—everyone's. Charlie wasn't good with feelings. She preferred reason to emotion, a preference that, to the casual observer, sometimes made her seem cold.

Every day she promised herself she would confide in Sam, sure that he would understand, he always understood, always had her back. He might even help her tell Elizabeth. A comforting possibility.

But each day, she found compelling reasons to postpone her confession. Sam was in D.C. for three days, she had a mountain of papers to correct, rehearsals for *Othello* were beginning, and Elizabeth was preparing for a performance with the choir.

Charlie and Sam arrived late for the choir's Friday afternoon performance at North Coast Assisted Living in Eureka. They'd planned to meet at the complex a few minutes before 3 o'clock—Sam was taking a late lunch—but both were running behind, so the choir was already singing its second piece when they slithered along the back wall of the rec room and found two empty seats. Besides parents, there were about two-dozen residents, some with walkers, two in wheelchairs, and several staff members.

Elizabeth was on the far left of the second row, probably because she was tall. Charlie hadn't told her they planned to come in case something got in the way. It was Sam who'd suggested they attend. *She has a two-line solo in one of the pieces. We need to show her we're interested in what she's doing.*

Wearing their uniforms and red bow ties, the students were crowded onto a small stage, Bill Hannigan standing to the side, directing but not blocking them. They were good. Surprisingly good. Especially since they had only a pitch pipe to start each piece and were singing everything from memory. The tenor with bright red hair and a self-conscious grin could hit beautifully clear, high notes. Elizabeth's two lines went well and, when she finished, she looked so relieved.

She'd begun letting her hair grow out. Charlie liked it longer. The pixie look she'd had when she arrived was too harsh for her features. Unlike several of the girls who had clearly spent a lot of time on their makeup, Elizabeth wore only lipstick and a little dark blue eye shadow. Charlie was surprised she didn't seem much interested in wearing makeup. By the time Missy was thirteen, she knew her way around a cosmetics counter and was always dressed stylishly to show off her size 2 figure. When she was older, even her gardening clothes were coordinated.

Charlie, on the other hand, put lipstick on in the morning and often forgot to re-apply it during the day. She typically wore slacks and brightly colored tunics or sweaters while teaching. She wanted to be comfortable. Very little jewelry, never dangly bracelets because they got in the way when she was lecturing. Watching Elizabeth this afternoon, it occurred to Charlie that they both kept things simple.

Something in common.

Charlie tried not to let herself think about Elizabeth as her daughter. Safer to be Missy's cousin and Elizabeth's second cousin. No guilt, no repercussions. She didn't really want to tell Elizabeth the truth—not yet. Preferably not ever. It could spoil the tiny steps of trust that were beginning to grow between them.

For the choir's final selection, they sang *Wade in the Water*, always a crowd pleaser, and got a standing ovation—at least from those able to stand. It wasn't until then that Elizabeth spotted Charlie and Sam, and almost smiled. Smiling still didn't come easily to her. She made her way to where Sam and Charlie were standing, "You came. I didn't see you at the start."

More comfortable than Charlie at expressing affection in public, Sam leaned over to kiss Elizabeth's cheek. "We wanted to surprise you."

"Did we sound okay?"

"Wonderful." Charlie couldn't decide whether she should hug her or not. "Your solo was perfect," and passed on the hugging.

"When we're singing, I can't tell how we're doing because the sound is all around me."

Over the chatter of the audience, a male voice called "Elizabeth, we're leaving now."

"Oops. I have to ride back on the bus—it's a rule—see you later," and she hurried away almost like a normal teenager instead of a girl who'd been orphaned and displaced. A bit of progress.

Charlie and Sam walked out to the parking lot, "What time will you be home?"

"About seven. Don't wait dinner."

"We'll keep yours in the oven," Charlie kissed him. "I'm glad you suggested we come." She wished she'd thought of it. Though his ex had a low opinion of Sam's parenting abilities, he had a better handle on what to do for Elizabeth than Charlie did.

The choir sang at the nursing home. Mr. Hannigan said we hit every entrance straight on. I didn't make any mistakes in my little solo, though I was super nervous. Charlie and Sam came late, but they came. I kind of liked that there was someone in the audience for me. Like I had a family. A few of the kids at school have asked why I don't have parents. Sometimes, it makes me sad that they see me as different. They have differences too. Some of them only have one parent, and Jimmy in my Calculus class has a father who's in jail. And Martha's parents are seldom home at the same time because they own a bakery and work really odd hours. Mine's just a different difference. Hard to figure out what a normal family is. I mean, mom and dad and I seemed normal, but I wasn't their biological child. So what makes normal? I was pretty naïve about what a family is.

As fate would have it, when and how to tell Elizabeth about her birth was conveniently shelved the minute Sam's ex, Diane, called to tell him she'd been offered a promotion that required her to move to the company's headquarters in Spain. Diane had readily accepted but, because the English language school near the company's headquarters did not accept new students in the middle of the school year, Sam would have to take Greg for the remainder of this school year. Nothing resembling *Would you please help me out?* Just—*Greg will have to stay with you.* All of a sudden, Sam became an acceptable parent, the one who would oversee Greg's homework—he wasn't the best of students— get him onto a soccer team, and cope with a thousand other details. He loved his son, had wanted more time with him, but fitting him into his life with Charlie and Elizabeth would be complicated. Overwhelmed didn't begin to describe Sam's reaction.

There'd be room for Greg at Charlie's only if she gave up her office in the third bedroom. Four people living in the house. Two children who were strangers to each other and, face it, to Charlie. A makeshift family.

In hushed conversation—not wanting Elizabeth to overhear their uncertainty about this new development—Sam and Charlie sat on the back porch steps, their jackets zipped against the October chill. Elizabeth was still cleaning up the kitchen.

Sam reached for Charlie's hand. "Can you manage without an office here?"

Though she said "Probably," her tone wasn't all that convincing. "Maybe I can move some of my things to one end of the dining room table. We eat in the kitchen most of the time." Thank goodness she had wifi and a laptop; otherwise there would be cords all over the place.

"That won't give you much privacy."

"I'll try doing most of my lecture preparations on campus; however, if I'm in my office, people assume I'm available for conversation. It's hard to accomplish much."

They sat silently, each turning the options over and over.

He sighed and let go of her hand. "Even though I've wanted more time with him, I never expected he'd move back here—with us—while we're adjusting to Elizabeth and Elizabeth to us. I'm sorry."

Charlie was sorry too, "You can't really refuse." And neither could she.

But the thought had crossed her mind.

"We need to tell Elizabeth he'll be living here."

Actually an easier task than telling Elizabeth about her birth parents. "When will he arrive? Does he come with furniture?"

"Diane's driving him down Saturday. I was so shocked by what she was asking—more telling than asking—that I forgot to ask about furniture. I'll call tomorrow."

Instead of Sam helping with Elizabeth, Charlie would be helping with Greg and losing her private space. A strange year.

Charlie just told me Sam's son is going to be living here and I'll have to share the bathroom with him. Just when I was beginning to get the hang of living here. I mean, Charlie sort of leaves me alone—not prying or telling me what to do. But now I bet I have to watch out for him cause he's only twelve. A boy! Yuck.

Though Charlie had never met Diane, she had briefly met Greg when he visited Sam for a weekend last Christmas. He and Sam had stayed in the Eureka apartment because Diane had balked at having *her son* at Charlie's, probably imagining nightly sex orgies.

Charlie had been annoyed. "Clearly she doesn't trust you to look out for your son. Does she have men in her life?"

"No clue."

Charlie decided not to pursue the topic.

The days following the phone call had not been easy for either Sam or Charlie. Now that Greg would be living under Charlie's roof without so much as *Is this all right with you?* from Diane, all sorts of things had to be rearranged. A whole new ballgame.

Again.

Charlie emptied her books from the floor to ceiling shelves and the contents of the desk drawers onto the dining room table so she and Sam could move the desk into the garage and, with the help of one of Sam's colleagues, move the guest room furniture into what was now Greg's room and put the bed frame back together. Diane had already made arrangements to rent her condo fully furnished, so no furniture was coming.

They bought more sheets and towels and another laundry hamper. Charlie was imagining mountains of laundry. How had this happened? As soon as she opened the door to Elizabeth, the universe—mistaking her motives—now believed she was willing to take care of Greg too.

After Friday afternoon's *Othello* rehearsal, which had not gone well, Charlie filled Tessa in on the Greg scenario.

Not surprisingly, Tessa laughed.

Charlie took issue. "It's not funny."

"I know, absurd rather than funny. In less than three months, you've gone from peaceful co-habitation with Sam to mothering two teenagers."

"One teenager and an almost teenager, and I'm a long way from *mothering*. I have no idea what that word really involves, except maybe more cooking and laundry. In a real family, there's time to grow into the relationships. But we're all being thrown together, sink or swim."

"It's not always any easier when a kid is with you from the beginning." A momentary frown. Jimmy was still in rehab. "Is there one good thing that's coming out of this reorganization of your life?"

"Ah, your famous half full glass. Well, since Sam won't be paying child support to Diane, he suggested getting someone to come in once a week to clean and do laundry."

"That's a plus. I can give you a couple of names."

"But when Sam has to go to D.C. or there's an emergency at the refuge, I'll have two kids to look after. Things with Elizabeth have been mostly okay up to now. But news of Greg's arrival has not been well received. They'll have to share a bathroom and, since I have late afternoon classes twice a week, they'll be on their own together. Sam's trying to find a soccer team for him, but that'll only take care of one or two afternoons after school."

"What grade is he in?"

"Seventh."

"So he'll be at Sunny Brae."

"I guess."

When Diane's mini van pulled into the driveway about dinnertime Saturday, Charlie stayed inside, letting Sam handle their arrival. He opened the car door for Diane, a slender redhead in wool slacks and a heavy sweater, while Greg came around the back of the van to unhook his bicycle. Greg had grown since Christmas, his auburn hair moussed into sticky blue spikes. Sam took notice but didn't react.

Elizabeth came up alongside Charlie. "Look at his hair. Yuck!"

"Agreed."

"Is his mother staying for dinner?"

Sam had fixed a pot roast and vegetables, spending most of the day in the kitchen. *Cooking calms my nerves.*

"We'll have to see. She may prefer to have dinner someplace with Sam and Greg. She's had a long drive and has to start back in the morning. Thank goodness she's staying at the Hampton Inn."

As it turned out, they all ate Sam's pot roast. An uncomfortable hour and a half during which conversation tripped and stumbled over everything that wasn't being discussed. Only the conversation about Greg's school records and which classes he should be enrolled in lasted longer than a few minutes. Whenever possible, Diane made it a point to leave Charlie and Elizabeth out of the conversation, giving Sam countless instructions about caring for Greg.

After dessert, Elizabeth and Charlie escaped to the kitchen, preferring cleaning up to being ostracized. Charlie rinsed the dishes and loaded the dishwasher while Elizabeth put the leftovers in the refrigerator and wiped down the counters.

"What did Sam ever see in her?"

"Hard to know. Sex interferes with logic." *And I'm the poster child for that behavior.*

"Did you hear all the instructions she gave Sam? If I were Greg, I'd be embarrassed to have people I don't know hear about my allergies and what time I go to bed; telling them to check on whether I brushed my teeth. Jeeesh. My mother would never have told strangers such personal things about me."

"Diane never thought Sam was a good enough parent, and she certainly isn't going to trust me."

"But now she wants her new job badly enough to dump Greg on Sam."

Like I dumped you. The conversation about that event was going to be terrible. Elizabeth would judge her so harshly. And Charlie deserved it.

Sam and Greg followed Diane's van to the motel to make sure she got settled in. Sam stayed in the truck so Greg could tell her goodbye in private and Sam could catch his breath. Stress was strewn everywhere. Diane's behavior during dinner was no surprise. She was an expert at dominating a situation. He needed to apologize to Charlie and Elizabeth.

Greg opened the passenger door and climbed in. "Let's go before she thinks of anything else."

Sam started the engine. "Good idea."

"She's so jazzed about her job that she doesn't care about my life. I was playing forward on the soccer team. And I have a lot of friends in Portland. I didn't want to leave."

Sam felt a surge of sympathy for his son and anger at his ex. Diane had chosen her career over her son. *Now who's the bad parent?* Greg had no other choice except to live with Sam. "Whatever the reason, I'm glad you're here."

Greg leaned forward and began fiddling with the radio. "Not much to choose from."

Sam smiled to himself. When Greg had last lived in Eureka, he hadn't been old enough to care about radio stations. "We only get two Eureka stations and the one at the university. Too far away from San Francisco for any of those stations to be clear."

Greg finally gave up and studied the screen on his phone. Sam was probably going to have to put Greg's phone on his plan. Sam and Charlie had been glad Elizabeth didn't seem as addicted to her phone as other kids, though she certainly spent a lot of time on her laptop. Was it possible to wean an almost teenager from his phone? Or video games? What kind of music did he like? Had Diane had THE TALK with him? Sam knew almost nothing about his son's world.

By the time they returned to Charlie's, Elizabeth was in her room and Charlie had gone for a walk, giving Sam and Greg space to begin unpacking Greg's clothes. They had emptied two of the suitcases and were pulling comic books and stacks of DVDs out of a large box when Charlie stopped outside the door. "Do you need anything?"

Sam smiled at her, "Hi, no. I don't think so."

"Okay. Greg, your towels are the dark blue ones. The white ones are Elizabeth's."

"Un huh" was all he said.

Sam was quick to step in. "Thank Charlie."

Grudgingly, "Thanks."

"You're welcome."

An hour later, Sam and Charlie were once again sitting on the back steps. Greg was showering and Elizabeth was in her room, working on her family album. Charlie's books and files had pretty much taken over the table where Elizabeth had been sorting pictures, so she moved everything into her room, spreading the pictures across the floor.

Sam stared into the darkness, "He didn't want to leave Portland. All his friends are there."

"At least Elizabeth could start school at the beginning of the semester. He'll be in the middle of everything, playing catch up."

"He's always liked sports more than school. His grades are barely average. Not like Elizabeth's."

After a minute, "I haven't actually talked to her about her grades or seen her homework. Am I supposed to sign a report card or something? There's so much stuff I don't know about high schools."

"And I get the joy of dealing with the middle school on Monday. Imagine how many mistakes I can make. On a positive note, I have a lead on a soccer team in his age group that's short on players. They practice Tuesday and Friday afternoons."

She leaned over to kiss him, taking it slowly until he relaxed and pulled her against him.

"Thank you for taking Greg on."

"You're taking Elizabeth on."

"I love you."

"I love you too."

They needed to find more time for each other. It seemed they hadn't had time to talk, really talk, for weeks. Parenting was filling their days and nights.

CHAPTER 8

Most wars begin slowly, the culmination of small wrongs that get out of hand.

However, the kid war at Charlie's moved with lightning speed.

The first battle was over Greg's wet towels dropped on the bathroom floor the first night. The second was Greg ranting about the amount of time Elizabeth spent showering on Sunday morning and how he NEEDED to pee. RIGHT NOW. So in the midst of shaving, Sam let him into the master bathroom. A late afternoon skirmish involved a sticky mess of peanut butter and jelly on the kitchen counter and, sometime around eight Sunday evening, loudly slammed bedroom doors finally pushed the adults into the fray. The escalating conflict could no longer be ignored.

Sam took on Greg.

Hesitantly, Charlie went into Elizabeth's room.

In pink pajamas, Elizabeth was propped against pillows with her music folder resting against her knees. Before Charlie said a word, "I'm not going to clean up after him." An attitude Charlie hadn't seen in her before.

Charlie ventured sitting on the foot of the bed and tried reason. "This is all really sudden for him," followed by gentle pleading, "give him a little time to adjust. He's probably upset with his mother for taking the job and leaving him behind."

"He's a slob and he leaves the toilet seat up."

So much for sweet reason. "That's a guy thing, but I find it hard to imagine Diane let him get away with it." Maybe she didn't, and Greg was testing his new surroundings.

Elizabeth dug her heels in. "Tell Sam to make him put it down."

"Perhaps you could ask Sam to talk to him." Charlie did not want to be the go-between. She'd always been terrible at conflict resolution. After just one weekend, she was, admittedly, on Elizabeth's side, ready to put Greg on the next flight to Spain. Adding Elizabeth to the household had, so far, been fairly simple. She took care of her own clothes and kept her room clean. After two months, she'd begun talking more—about choir or a teacher. Nothing about her parents or her feelings. But at least she was talking about the superficial stuff. Charlie hoped she wouldn't have to deal with deeper issues—but that was wishful thinking.

Greg was a different case altogether. It would help if Sam had had more contact with his son in recent years. But the weekend visits in Portland were too artificial. Going to movies or sporting events and playing laser tag had nothing to do with toilet seats and cleaning up after himself.

Having failed to bring Elizabeth on board with "understanding," Charlie retreated to the kitchen, wiping counters that were already clean, waiting for Sam to appear. She was afraid she would have to have his back this time.

When he walked into the kitchen, he looked beaten. "I've already been reduced to using threats." He sank into a chair, his eyes troubled. "I've never had this kind of behavior from him. He's sulking. Said he didn't have to take orders from a girl." Sam sighed, "When I was visiting Portland, we did what he wanted, the way he wanted to do it because I was trying to be the fun parent. I really haven't disciplined him for six years. I don't have a track record—or the skill."

You aren't the only one. "I never had brothers or male cousins so I'm really out of my element. At least you were once Greg's age. What worked with you and your brother?"

"Fear. My dad had no patience if we skipped chores or talked back."

"Did he hit you?"

"Never. But my chores around the farm would multiply. And *grounded* was almost my middle name."

"Greg has certainly pushed Elizabeth's buttons. I didn't know she could yell like that. She's been fairly quiet since she came. But I have to say, she's right. We shouldn't have to clean up after him. And then there's the whole toilet seat issue."

"Good luck there. My mother never quite solved that one either."

"What did you threaten?"

"Grounding. It didn't bother him. Informed me he didn't have anywhere to go anyway. Effectively took the sting out of that punishment." He found a bottle of beer in the refrigerator. "I've made arrangements for Herman to cover for me tomorrow morning so I can get Greg enrolled at Sunny Brae Middle. Diane always did the school stuff. Once again, I'm out of my comfort zone."

Charlie felt her stomach clench. What had happened to their well-managed life! She'd often felt sorry for her colleagues who had to juggle family emergencies and still meet their classes, go to meetings, design new courses. She'd always been able to build her days around the demands of her career. If she had papers to grade on the weekend, she stayed home to do them, and Sam gave her the space and time she needed. If he wanted to watch television, he used headphones so the house was quiet.

Now her schedule was falling apart. Tomorrow, she was giving the first midterm in the Shakespeare class. She always tried to do her grading as soon as possible to keep students from asking when they were getting their papers back. She preferred returning them in a week.

But tomorrow, she would have to hurry off campus to pick Greg up as soon as her exam ended because Sunny Brae was too far for him to walk home. She needed to find out whether he could ride the school bus so she didn't have to pick him up every day. Elizabeth wouldn't be back until dinner because the choir was planning its carnival booth. The high school carnival would take place on Halloween afternoon and evening. She had no idea what the middle school would be doing or what Greg was accustomed to doing on Halloween. Surely he was too old to go Trick or Treating. Maybe he'd be willing to go to the high school carnival. Kill two birds. The PTA president had roped Charlie into being a chaperone during the evening. *You don't have to do anything, just keep the peace.*

Very funny. She couldn't even figure out how to keep the peace in her own house.

Because Sam would not be home for dinner, she'd be on her own with the kids, probably no time to get started on her papers. And she had a set of Comp papers coming in on Thursday. She felt selfish and, at the same time, victimized. Her schedule was being rearranged without her permission. The only other time that had happened was when she was with Andre.

During the months she spent with him, she seemed to have no will of her own, but didn't care. They had sex when he wanted sex, ate at the restaurants he chose. She wore clothes that he admired, saw the foreign films he favored, read his favorite poets. At 23, that's what she thought love was—pleasing the other person. Though Andre pleased her with romantic words and powerful orgasms, he didn't pay attention to what foods she preferred, what movies she might like to see. She'd been embarrassingly willing to do his bidding—until he told her to get an abortion.

Only after Elizabeth had been turned over to Missy did Charlie try to figure out who she was, how she wanted her life to be, and how to keep herself from falling into another Andre trap. She vowed she would never again give control of her life away. By the time Sam appeared in her front yard, she'd already established a lifestyle she was comfortable with, and Sam hadn't challenged it. Yet this afternoon she was picking Greg up at school and worrying about how she was going to get her work done.

As soon as she turned the engine off, Greg was out of the car, heading for his room. Not even a thank you. She understood he was hurting, missing his school and friends in Portland. But he wasn't the only one dealing with the fallout from Diane's move. *Be mad at her, not us.*

Instead of letting him get to her, Charlie tried to grade a few papers. Compared to his sulking, reading papers from students who hadn't studied enough and had abysmal handwriting looked pretty good. She immersed herself in the exams, coming up for air long enough to fix macaroni and cheese—*thank you Kraft*. Claiming he didn't have any homework, Greg ate his dinner in front of the TV, watching ESPN. She suspected he was lying about his homework, but she'd let Sam check it out. She ate her dinner at the dining room table and listened to her iPod so she couldn't hear the TV.

Elizabeth arrived a little before seven. "Sorry. Mr. Hannigan wouldn't let Martha and me walk home in the dark, so we had to wait for him to lock up, and he drove us. Is there more mac and cheese or did *he* eat it all?"

Charlie went into the kitchen with her. "There's also salad in the fridge. His highness doesn't *do* salad." She filled a bowl with the pasta and put it in the microwave. "What do you want to drink?"

"Just water. We drank Cokes while we were working." When the timer went off, Elizabeth retrieved the bowl and sat at the kitchen table. "I'm famished. Mr. Hannigan brought snacks, but the guys gobbled everything up."

"How's the booth coming along?"

"So far we're just designing the outside. The school uses the same frames every year. The shop class will put them together next week; then we paint. The PTA gives us decorating supplies. Instead of running a game, we're selling cupcakes." Around a mouthful of salad, "I said I'd bring three dozen."

Charlie let the information sink in, hoping her face didn't register her thoughts. It had been years since she'd baked cupcakes. Never that many at the same time.

"Don't worry. You don't have to help." Elizabeth could read her all too well. "Martha has to make three dozen too, so we'll make them together here. If that's okay."

Too late to say no. At least they'd clean up after themselves and be on hand to look after Greg that afternoon. A useful trade off. Somewhere in the baking project was a hint that Elizabeth felt she didn't have to ask if she and Martha could use Charlie's kitchen. *I hope that's a good thing.*

Besides the bathroom skirmishes, there were the homework battles— Sam taking point on those. Charlie was trying to stay below the radar. It turned out Greg really did have math and science homework his first day of classes and had lied. Sam checked with the school and found out how to access the daily homework assignments Greg's teachers posted on line—a convenience for students who had been absent and parents, like Sam, who were checking on their children's schoolwork. If Sam was going to be late getting home, he'd go online, then call Greg and remind him about his assignments and that Sam would check the work later. As a result, most of Sam's evenings were spent with Greg at the kitchen table.

He made sure Greg understood that unless he made passing grades, Sam would pull him out of soccer, probably the most effective threat so far, but the tension in the house was interfering with Charlie's sleep.

It took Martha and Elizabeth two afternoons to make the six-dozen cupcakes needed for the carnival booth. Charlie had purchased two yellow cake mixes and two red velvet mixes, along with a variety of packaged frostings.

Though Elizabeth had initially wanted to make everything from scratch, Martha and Charlie voted for easy rather than complicated. Baking on Thursday, frosting on Friday.

When Charlie came home late Thursday, the house smelled wonderfully sweet with cupcakes lined up on the racks cooling. Fortunately, Sam had picked up cartons of Chinese food on his way home. No one felt like cooking.

November roared in with an early winter storm, compliments of Oregon, dumping rain on California's north coast for four days straight. Fall had been dry and even warm, so the shift in weather took everyone by surprise. Both Elizabeth and Greg needed new rain boots. A shared shopping trip that did not improve anyone's mood; not even pizza at the food court could lighten the tension.

In order to be home to keep an eye on Greg and the homework, Sam traded schedules with Herman, which meant Sam had to be at work by 7 a.m. If it was raining hard in the morning, Charlie drove Elizabeth to school. The middle school bus stopped at the corner for Greg and two sisters living down the street. The house was empty by 8:30, giving Charlie time to catch up on housework and laundry and paying bills before going to her own classes.

CHAPTER 9

Overseeing Greg's homework every night, as well as adjusting to the new Superintendent at the refuge, filled Sam's days. So far he'd been able to keep his early work schedule.

Charlie was spending two evenings a week at the *Othello* rehearsals—helping the students with character interpretation so Tessa could concentrate on directing and the thousand other details involved in putting on the production. The Madrigal Choir was gearing up for its Christmas programs: one at an elementary school, another at the Rotary Club and, most important, their performance at Humboldt Plaza on Christmas Eve afternoon.

The Ames/Ledger household had its hands full.

Because Charlie's schedule was more flexible than Sam's, either she or Elizabeth tried to be at the house in the afternoon so Greg wasn't unsupervised. Fifty years ago, a twelve year old staying at home alone wouldn't have raised eyebrows. Today, Sam might be hauled in for neglect.

Trying to create order in the midst of what felt like chaos, Charlie purchased an erasable wall calendar and, with magnets, put it on the side of the refrigerator. She bought markers in four different colors so each person could put commitments and times on the calendar. The squares were full and running over.

It had been three months since Elizabeth arrived in Arcata, and Charlie still hadn't told Sam she was Elizabeth's mother. He wasn't angry about her silence—he was rarely given to anger, though Greg's schoolwork was testing his patience—but he was disappointed she didn't trust him enough to explain.

The Saturday before Thanksgiving, Charlie and Sam had the house all to themselves. Elizabeth and Martha had gone to the mall in Eureka to look at Christmas decorations. *We're just going to window shop. Martha doesn't have much extra money.* But Martha did have her driver's license and occasionally had the use of her older sister's car. Greg was attending a soccer clinic at the high school.

While Charlie was at the kitchen table making a grocery list, Sam decided to get the Elizabeth issue into the open. He sat across from her and, as he'd done with Tessa, opened the picture of Elizabeth and Charlie that was on his phone and pushed the phone over to her.

She glanced at it, "Is that the one you took when Elizabeth first arrived?"

"Yes."

"Nice. Can you send it to my computer?"

"That's not the reason I'm showing this to you."

She looked up, puzzled.

"The smiles." He took a breath, "they're the same."

Charlie laid her pencil down. It suddenly felt heavy.

"Honey, please, let's talk about whatever the story is. No kids to interrupt."

She studied his face, read his eyes. Knew he was going to put her on the spot.

"Okay."

"Am I right? She yours?"

He'd known almost from the beginning. Now he'd encourage her to tell Elizabeth.

Softly, "Yes." She should have been the one to bring this up. "Sorry. I didn't know how to—Tessa figured it out too."

"You don't want Elizabeth to guess or have someone else call the resemblance to her attention. That would be," he searched for the right word, "unfair to her."

He waited.

"You're right, of course. At first, I told myself she was already coping with a new place and school—and didn't need any more changes. But mostly, I'm just plain scared."

More waiting.

"I, well I don't know when I should tell her. She's going to hate me. And she should. I gave her away." She stood up, "You need to read Missy's letter to me."

In a few minutes, she laid the envelope in front of him, returning to her chair.

Sam unfolded the single sheet of paper.

Dearest Charlie: The fact that you are reading this means something terrible has happened to Rick and me. And Elizabeth is alone.

When we were setting up this trust and writing our wills, the lawyer asked who should take care of Elizabeth if something happened to both of us. I knew it had to be you (we did not tell him why you were our choice) and, even though taking care of Elizabeth will change your life, once again she belongs to you. She was, after all, yours for nine months before she was ours.

Please, please don't refuse, no matter how inconvenient or frightening this seems. She's a remarkable child with some of Rick and me, and surely some of you and her birth father in her personality. She must have his coloring; she certainly doesn't have yours.

She has never asked about her birth parents. So you don't have to tell her yourself, I've written a letter for her too. You can choose to give it to her or not. A thousand thanks. I love you. Take care of our girl, Missy

He refolded the letter and carefully returned it to the envelope, sliding it across to her. "That must have been devastating to write even though she had no idea it would ever be used."

Charlie picked up the envelope. "Missy was a class act. When we were children, we were best friends even though she was all girl and I was all geeky, arms and legs, and no boyfriends."

He smiled at her description. She always made jokes about herself though the geek had become a beautiful woman. "Let's sit on the couch so I can hold you while you tell me."

It was easier with his arms around her.

"Andre Winslow was a visiting professor from Northwestern my second year in the Yale doctoral program."

"I'm guessing he has dark coloring."

"Yes. Elizabeth has his eyes too. They catch me by surprise sometimes." Not necessarily a good thing.

"She has your smile and figure."

"Yes."

"Is he still alive?"

"I've never checked." She hadn't. Afraid of repeating the mistake of Lot's wife.

"Married?"

She nodded. "Supposedly separated. Two young sons."

"How long were you together?"

"Four months or so."

"And—" Getting her to talk about herself was always a struggle.

"He wanted no part of a baby and mailed me money for an abortion and the name of a clinic. I never saw him again." Her voice trembled at the memory of that rainy afternoon in the coffee house. Sam's arms tightened around her, and she let the silent tears come. She hadn't cried about him and what he'd done since Elizabeth's birth. She'd spent the intervening years telling herself that she'd put Andre and Elizabeth behind her. She was no longer that naïve girl who believed her handsome professor loved her. Now she had her career and Sam.

Safety.

But Elizabeth's plight had shaken that safety.

Sam interrupted her memories. "How did Missy fit into the story?"

"Missy'd always wanted a big family, but she couldn't get pregnant. She and Rick tried everything—*invitro* a couple of times—and were on a very long waiting list with an adoption agency in Virginia. My mother became the go-between. I knew I wasn't ready—maybe willing is a better word—to have a baby in my life. I'd have to take whatever job I could find and be a single mother needing childcare, wondering whether another man would take on my child. It's probably unnatural not to want your child but, when my mother made all of us sit down and talk about the possibility of the baby being adopted within the family, it made sense to me. No question they'd be good parents. I don't think I was cut out to be a parent." When other little girls were carrying their favorite dolls around, Charlie carried a copy of *Charlotte's Web* and had a library card.

"And yet here you are." Trying to lighten the story.

"Here I am."

"I wish you'd told me everything when you came home from London." *You should have trusted me. But you have trouble with trust. Is that his fault—this Andre who turned his back on you?*

"Are you upset with me?" *Stupid question. He is. I can see it in the set of his mouth.*

"Yes and no."

She really wanted him to say *No*.

For almost sixteen years—so many years—she'd pretended Andre never happened, compartmentalized the fact that, in Virginia, a dark-haired little girl was having birthday parties and sleepovers. Charlie was a mother in DNA only. Elizabeth wasn't part of her life and Charlie wasn't part of hers. That had been okay because looking back got in the way of the present. Though if someone had asked, she wasn't at all sure where her present was going. A life measured by semesters filled with students who could never remember the difference between *its* and *it's* or why reading the English Romantic poets and Shakespeare mattered in their lives.

Even after a year of living together, Charlie had no clue where she and Sam were going. Mostly taking their life together a day at a time. No long range plans. She needed him, not just physically but in ways she couldn't articulate, even to herself. Without her asking, he'd made Elizabeth welcome, treated her with kindness. Not every man would do that.

"Will you help me tell her when I work up the nerve?"

He kissed her, tasting the salt of her tears. "You know I will."

Charlie's story about Andre, about giving Elizabeth away, explained her preferring not to talk about her past. Sam's parents had told each other everything, even things they probably shouldn't have. When ten year old Sam wondered why they did that, his dad had laughed: *Fewer nasty surprises.* Then more seriously: *Keeps us close.*

Once he and Diane were married, Sam tried telling her everything, encouraging her to do the same. To no avail. Like Charlie, she wasn't given to sharing and, more than once, suggested she didn't need so much information about him. He'd assumed married meant close. Diane was puzzled by the concept. *I need my space.*

They'd married soon after they discovered she was pregnant. Sam was fresh out of graduate school, frantically interviewing for jobs in his field, not sure where they would end up, so they had a small wedding at his parents' house in rural Iowa. Not until the chaos of their divorce, six years later, did she confess she'd simply stopped taking her birth control pills. An intentional accident. He might not have rushed to the altar if Greg hadn't been on the way. It had taken Sam time to realize that, in too many ways, he and Diane weren't a good match. She was always complaining that Sam should spend more time with Greg, complaining about Sam's twelve hour workdays, his trips to Washington. All that complaining kept him at work more hours than necessary. The divorce was inevitable.

As soon as Greg started kindergarten, she began submitting her fashion designs to a women's clothing company headquartered in Portland. The owners were impressed by her work and offered her a job. Once she had the job, she filed for divorce and Sam's son disappeared from his day-to-day life. Now the Portland company had been bought out by an international firm headquartered in Spain. And they wanted Diane to move to Madrid to work with the European designers. No small thing.

Woefully ignorant of kid music, videos and movies, Sam was scrambling to learn what music Greg listened to, what video games he played. At the same time, he tried to monitor the TV shows Greg had access to—not so easy now that tablets and streaming had arrived on the scene. Gone were the days of setting parental controls on the family TV.

Connecting with his son was a matter of two steps forward, one step back. Sam was never sure whether Greg missed Diane or whether he was glad to escape her oversight. Greg more or less accepted Charlie's presence as a necessity, ignoring her whenever possible.

Elizabeth was another matter. Greg made every effort to annoy her and, as mellow as Elizabeth was when left to her own devices, he could set her off. Almost like he needed someone to fight with. Fighting with Sam or Charlie only got him in trouble.

Thanksgiving night: I've been hoping the holidays wouldn't come but they did anyway. All the ads on TV and the sappy Hallmark Channel movies are about families and traditions and happy ever after. Even Martha's busy family closed the bakery for the weekend and went to Crescent City to visit her grandparents. My family and our traditions are gone.

We had dinner at Tessa's. Sam contributed a huge cranberry salad with marshmallows, nuts and grapes, everything slathered in whipped cream. Probably a thousand calories a bite. Tessa and her husband Harold fixed everything else. Their son Jimmy was there for dinner. He had to leave right after because he's in rehab for drugs. He has a curfew. Tessa drove him back. He's really cute.

It was an okay day. Greg watched football with Sam and Harold and stopped being a pain in the butt for a few hours. When I first met Martha, I felt sorry for her having to look after her brother, and then sulky, stupid Greg shows up. I think he acts like he can't do his homework just to get Sam to pay attention to him.

CHAPTER 10

The weeks between Thanksgiving and Christmas would be full and running over. In other years, those weeks were more manageable because the hardest part of Charlie's semester was over. It was the students' turn to prove themselves and, despite mountains of final exam grading, she was usually more relaxed. Time to take her foot off the teaching accelerator.

She'd never made a big deal out of Christmas—a fresh green wreath on the front door—she loved the smell of it—a red poinsettia plant in the front hallway. A few cards to friends. A gift for Sam, a book for Angela—she loved mysteries—and jewelry for Tessa. Charlie and her father had stopped exchanging gifts when he remarried. She'd have no idea what to get him. In truth, she was always glad when holiday expectations and marathon gifting were over and life returned to normal.

Christmas this year had many more layers. Sitting in the monthly English Department meeting, pretending to pay attention to a discussion about the new electronic equipment in one of the lecture halls, she roughed out what she remembered of her December schedule on a yellow pad. Seeing it in print was daunting.

The *Othello* performances were the Friday and Saturday nights of the first two weekends in December, immediately followed by finals week. Classes ended for her and the kids on the eighteenth. Thankfully, student grades didn't have to be in until the first week of January. One of the perks of the campus computer system—she could send them from home. She'd promised to attend all four *Othello* performances, staying backstage in case Tessa needed help with something. Charlie had purchased two tickets for Elizabeth and Martha for the first Friday performance. Elizabeth had studied Shakespeare at the academy, so Charlie figured she wouldn't be totally bored. Including Martha would give Elizabeth someone to sit with since Sam voted against subjecting his son to Shakespeare: *You've got to be kidding. Greg doesn't sit still all that well unless he's playing a video game.*

Charlie and Sam, and probably an unwilling Greg, would attend Elizabeth's choir performance at the plaza. Charlie typically avoided local celebrations but, since Elizabeth and Greg had lost their usual Christmas traditions, she was determined to make their holiday as pleasant as possible. Martha and Elizabeth were planning an all day cookie bake in Charlie's kitchen. *Mom and I always baked mountains of stuff at Christmas.* On the twenty-second, Greg's soccer team coach was hosting party for the boys. Greg needed to bring a gag gift. Charlie hoped Sam would take him shopping. Greg took forever to make up his mind about everything: what he wanted on his pizza or what shirt to wear to school. Her patience usually ran out quickly.

Both Greg and Elizabeth had already shopped for the gifts that had to be mailed. Greg's gift to his mother—a pair of earrings that Sam picked out—had been mailed the day before Thanksgiving, though the Post Office couldn't promise it would get to Spain in time for Christmas. Elizabeth sent gifts to her grandparents and Julie. Unlike Greg, she was amazingly good at making decisions about such things. The allowance from her parents' trust seemed to cover most of what she needed. Bigger items, like her clothing, came from Charlie's stipend.

Though Charlie was beginning to know what her daughter liked, deciding what to buy her for Christmas wasn't easy. Just as Charlie was ready to chicken out and give her a Macy's gift card, the gift puzzle was solved when Elizabeth told Charlie and Sam that she wanted to learn to drive and was ready to take the test for her Learner's Permit. Could Charlie find out if the trust would cover the cost of a car? Charlie's first reaction, which she kept to herself, was *You're too young* but, since the State of California obviously didn't agree, she had no case. A whole new nest of snakes was on the doorstep.

After Elizabeth's announcement, Charlie and Sam took a walk, ostensibly to pick up something at her office, but actually to regroup. He took Charlie's hand and tucked it into his jacket pocket. "I saw her reading the DMV book; I should have known driving was on the horizon."

"And a car of her own?" Charlie couldn't hide her dismay.

"Will Missy's trust foot the bill for a car?"

"No idea. I can ask, but I'm not sure I want her to be on the road by herself. She doesn't know much about this area."

Good heavens. I sound like an overprotective mother. Where did that come from?

Admittedly, there probably weren't as many dangers in Arcata as there would be in Virginia. There was however the residual hippie culture, the "travelers" who hung out downtown; the transients who weren't as transient as Charlie would like them to be. But they weren't much of a driving hazard.

"The other option is letting her drive one of our vehicles. Which means adding her to your insurance. Probably wiser to let her drive your car than my Rover."

Charlie sighed. Until now, she hadn't worried about Elizabeth's activities since most were with the choir or Martha and her family. A driver's license opened up all sorts of new things to worry about. But Charlie didn't want to play bad cop and lay down rules right now because, gradually, she and Elizabeth were finding things to talk about—trying out different coffee flavors, sharing their problems with Greg, and discussing Missy's family photos. They'd already sent Grace the ones Charlie couldn't identify. She was hoping for a comfortable connection before she had to sit down and tell her about Andre and herself.

Sam, as always, was practical. "How about we pay for driving lessons for her Christmas present? That buys us some time to deal with the car issue."

"Better that a professional teaches her."

"Agreed."

"What about Greg's present?"

"Against my better judgment, he wants a skateboard. Best guess, Diane wouldn't let him have one, so he's hoping I'm a softer touch. If I buy it, he's also getting a helmet and protective padding, which he will hate."

"Talk about dangerous transportation!"

"Yeah. Makes the car look a lot better, doesn't it?"

"Remember when all we had to decide was whether to eat in or go out for dinner?"

They stopped walking and Sam turned her into his arms. "We're still us." He kissed her. "I love you."

"And I love you, but everything else feels difficult." She rested her face against his jacket. "It's all happened so fast and I haven't even gotten to the really hard part yet."

"Let's get through Christmas first."

She nodded and tightened her arms around his waist.

Greg's phone rang just before 6 a.m. Christmas morning.

"Merry Christmas, darling. Have you opened your present yet?"

His mother.

He rolled onto his back, the phone against his ear, struggling to make himself wake up. "What time is it? It's still dark."

"It's three o'clock in the afternoon in Spain. I've been invited to have Christmas dinner with some of my new friends. I wanted to talk to you before I leave. What about the present?"

"It's under the tree." By the weight and shape of the box, he'd already guessed it was clothing, never his favorite gift.

"Can you go open it now?" He was all too familiar with that tone of voice. She always thought her gifts, usually clothes, were perfect, and so he would have to tell her that. Otherwise, life would be ugly. One year, when he really, really hated a jacket she bought, he had to go with her to return it and spend an afternoon shopping for another one. At least this year he could return the gift without having to shop with her.

"Please open it now so I can enjoy it with you." Grudgingly he pushed back the covers. Nothing to be gained by arguing. Because Charlie kept a tiny nightlight in an outlet in the hall, he didn't have to turn the lights on. The Nordstrom's box was wrapped in red and white candy cane paper. Inside—a pale blue, long-sleeved, v-neck sweater and a dark blue plaid shirt. Dorky.

Honesty would only prolong the conversation. "They're great, Mom."

"I'm glad you like them. They are definitely your colors."

He cringed. *Colors* were for girls.

"Did you get my present?"

"Not yet, but deliveries are slower here. How are things going?"

"Okay."

"How's school?"

"Okay."

"How are your grades?"

"Okay." Not entirely true but not the moment to explain his failing grade in Algebra.

"What are you going to do today?"

"Regular Christmas stuff."

"I need to run, darling. Luis is waiting for me. Have a good day. I'll call next week."

Before Greg went back to bed, he turned his phone off.

Charlie was making coffee when Elizabeth came into the kitchen. "Merry Christmas. Want some coffee? It's the hazelnut we bought last week."

"Sure. Merry Christmas. Did you know Greg already opened one of his presents? And left a mess."

Both kids had taken to ratting each other out. Charlie wondered whether that was good normal or not. She poured a half-cup of coffee for Elizabeth, so she could add milk, and a full cup for herself. "Is he up?"

"Don't think so."

"It doesn't matter. Which present was it?"

"The one from his mother." Elizabeth stirred in the cream and sugar. "It doesn't feel like Christmas even though it's cold today."

"I suppose it doesn't. I had to get used to warmer holidays too. What did you usually do on Christmas day?"

Elizabeth concentrated on stirring her coffee—and stirring. Finally, "Dad made pancakes before we opened our presents, and we'd do the stockings last. My friend Julie's family does their stockings first." She took a swallow of the coffee. "Maybe I'll just have cereal this morning."

"I can make eggs. Sam's going to do a roast for dinner."

"Cereal's okay. It's sorta what I eat now." She sounded resigned. "Today doesn't need to be special."

Charlie's throat tightened. At Elizabeth's age, Christmas should be special. She worried that Elizabeth was almost too strong—though maybe she cried privately. A month from today, she'd be seventeen—still childhood. Guilt raised its ugly head. Charlie reached across the table and placed her hand over Elizabeth's. Until now, Charlie hadn't tried to hold her daughter's hand—or hug her. But today it seemed okay.

For a few minutes, Elizabeth didn't move her hand. And then went to the cupboard for a cereal bowl.

Christmas night: Today hasn't been so bad. I got really bummed a week ago, with Christmas carols all over the place and lights and people being ho-ho-ho jolly. Nothing felt right. I was really grumpy. Even the choir singing carols in the plaza bothered me.

In Virginia, we sometimes got a little snow around Christmas, making everything look like a Christmas card. I doubt they ever get snow here, just damp and cold. Snow would be better.

Mom loved Christmas and started shopping before Halloween. Then we'd decide how we were going to decorate the house—we never did it the same way twice, and Dad ordered plenty of logs for the fireplace. His excuse for avoiding the house decorating was that he had to split kindling.

Everything always seemed magical. We baked cookies by the dozens to give away to the neighbors, and my grandparents always came to help us decorate the tree. Grandma Grace loved to string popcorn and cranberries.

I was afraid this year would be awful. I don't think Charlie ever did much about Christmas because Tessa was totally shocked we had a Christmas tree. It's like Charlie wasn't interested in family type stuff. Sam and Greg shopped for the tree, and Charlie and I bought decorations—funny to have everything new. Mom had kept decorations from her childhood. But at least *Charlie had a tree and a wreath for the front door. My best present is driving lessons next month at a driving school in McKinleyville. I also got a fleece jacket from Charlie and Sam, and perfumed bath salts from Greg. Charlie probably picked that out. My grandparents sent me a check to buy whatever I want because Grandma can't leave Grampa alone at home to go shopping. I called to thank them and tell them I love them. Grampa sounded really weak. For a moment, I don't think he remembered who I am.*

Julie and I always buy each other t-shirts. I got her one from the Humboldt Wildlife Refuge and she sent one from Wolf Trap. I miss going to Wolf Trap.

Greg got his stupid skateboard and rode it from noon till dark. The house was positively peaceful until he fell off and scraped his chin. Blood and hysteria everywhere. Boys are such babies.

So that's my first Christmas without parents. I'm glad it's over. When I left Virginia in August, Grandma hugged me hard and told me I was going to have to grow up quickly and figure out how to parent myself. I thought it was weird for her to say something like that, but I'm beginning to understand. I don't think Grandma likes Charlie much. Wonder why. I had great parents and Charlie has been okay, not a friend exactly and not a big sister—someone asked me if we were sisters. She doesn't push or boss me around, but I guess if I needed help, she would help me.

CHAPTER 11

The Monday after Christmas, Sam and his boss flew to D.C. to present the report on Castle Rock's status to the bigwigs at the Department of the Interior. "I hate to leave you with all the kid stuff."

"Good thing I'm still on break until the end of January. The kids go back next Monday." Once they were busy at school, she'd have more time to work on her Spring classes: two writing classes and one on Shakespeare's Women, which she hadn't taught since her first year at Humboldt. All her notes and handouts needed updating.

She drove Sam to the airport for the 10:15 flight to San Francisco, kissing him goodbye before he went through security. There was never much of a line in the McKinleyville airport.

"I'll call tonight." His fingers brushed her lips briefly, "You'll be fine. Don't worry."

Good luck on that.

She missed him already.

Turning off teaching-mode during the semester was impossible but, once the semester was over, Charlie was usually able to stop delivering classroom lectures in her head. Down time for her brain.

This year however, in place of her lectures, she found herself creating dialogues for telling Elizabeth the truth. Experimenting with opening lines:

Elizabeth, there's something I need to tell you—about your adoption.

Elizabeth, your mother said you never asked about your birth parents.

Elizabeth, I'm your birth mother.

Or the coward's way out—*Elizabeth, this envelope was with your parents' wills.* Then wait for her reaction. Charlie had no idea what Elizabeth's dialogue would be. Or whether there'd be any dialogue at all.

Every scenario sounded worse than the last. When Charlie had decided to give her child up for adoption, she hadn't looked at her decision as being irresponsible. She saw it in practical terms: a good home for the baby that Andre had wanted her to destroy and the only way for Charlie to get back to the life she envisioned for herself. Seventeen years later, she knew that not keeping your child qualified as selfish. Her daughter had every right to hate her for what she'd done. And not telling her the truth for the four months they'd lived under the same roof wouldn't earn Charlie brownie points either. Just when she was beginning to appreciate Elizabeth's poise and strength—to connect with her on simple things—she'd have to ruin everything with *the conversation.*

But none of her hypothetical scripts included someone beating her to the punch.

On her way home from the airport, she stopped for groceries. These days, food entered and left the house incredibly fast. Either she or Sam went to the grocery store almost every day. Today, it was milk, lots of it, sandwich makings, bananas.

As she was lifting the milk jugs into the refrigerator, the front doorbell rang. "Elizabeth, can you get the door?"

The bell rang again before Elizabeth got there.

Then a man's voice. Familiar.

"Hello, you must be Elizabeth."

Charlie closed the refrigerator door and ran into the hallway just in time to hear her father saying "Is Charlie home? I'm her father. Your grandfather."

The last two words hung in the air.

Charlie and Elizabeth froze—for entirely different reasons.

Pandora's box had been opened. After Charlie's mother died, John Ames had moved his construction company to Los Angeles, eventually marrying the company's office manager. Charlie's stepmother, Nora, was standing slightly behind John, her hair professionally blonde, her clothes casually expensive.

She smiled. "Hi, Charlie. Good to see you again." Charlie didn't know Nora well. There had only been brief encounters, mostly dinners, when Charlie was in L.A. Nothing lasting long enough to get past superficial conversation.

Her father stepped into the hall. "Hi darling. I had a Christmas card from Grace, telling me about Missy and that you had Elizabeth with you. Since we spent the holidays with Nora's family in Marin, we thought we'd drive up and surprise you and Elizabeth."

Surprises all-round.

Charlie's gaze was fixed on Elizabeth, who had backed up a few steps, her face instantly ashen. She turned abruptly and headed toward her bedroom. Charlie followed. Over her shoulder, "Give me a minute. The living room is in there." She pointed.

By the time Charlie got to the bedroom, Elizabeth had emphatically closed the door behind her.

"Elizabeth, may I come in? Please."

No answer.

"Elizabeth?"

Charlie stood outside the door, her heart racing as though she'd sprinted a mile. It was tempting to blame her father, but she had only herself to blame. She'd waited too long. Maybe Missy's letter for Elizabeth would help. She went into the kitchen, unlocked the small household safe she kept at the back of the pantry, and returned to Elizabeth's door with the envelope. "I have something for you. Please open the door."

No sound.

"A letter your mother left for you—explaining."

More silence. Then the knob turned and the door opened part way. Elizabeth's eyes were dry and oddly sunken. She extended her hand for the envelope.

"May I come in while you read it? So you're not alone." Charlie's voice wavered.

Elizabeth shook her head and closed the door again.

Tears of frustration slid over Charlie's cheeks. There was no way to fix what had just gone horribly wrong. When it came to her teaching, she always wanted to be ahead of whatever curves might occur. In this case, however, she was months behind the curve. Ironic that it should be her father, who had not wanted her to give up the baby, who was the one to tell Elizabeth the truth.

"Sweetheart," her father's voice was behind her, "I take it I said the wrong thing. Can I help?"

She shook her head slowly and let him put his arms around her. She wanted to be five years old, to let someone else make everything better. She longed to hear Sam's voice, but he would be unreachable until evening.

John finally coaxed his daughter into the living room, sitting beside her on the couch, waiting for the tears to stop. Nora was perched on the edge of the armchair across from them. After a few minutes, she went into the kitchen. Charlie could hear the teakettle being filled.

With effort, she straightened. "Do you have a handkerchief?"

John shifted so he could get the neatly ironed cloth out of his pocket. "I'm so sorry, Charlie."

"Not your fault. How could you have known I hadn't told her yet? Grace has been nagging me to tell her. It's the penalty for you and me not talking often enough." She folded and refolded the handkerchief.

When Nora returned, she was carrying the bamboo tray Charlie kept on top of the refrigerator. Placing it carefully on the coffee table, she handed one of the mugs to Charlie, one to John, and took the last one herself. "I thought we needed cups to hold and tea to drink. I couldn't find any cookies."

"It's the kids. We're always out of everything. I don't plan food for four people very well. Sam does better." Her voice was scratchy from crying.

"You're doing a lot of parenting all of a sudden." Her father pulled the sugar bowl closer and stirred a heaping spoonful of sugar into his cup. Like Tessa, he loved sweet tea. He was still handsome. Construction work provided a year-round tan, but there were more lines around his eyes, more gray in his hair than when she'd last seen him. He'd always made a good living but, as his housing developments got bigger, she guessed he was now making very good money. He and Nora lived in the Hollywood Hills, did a lot of entertaining, and had probably flown to San Francisco first class.

"Where's Sam?"

"In D.C. till Friday. His son had a sleepover at a friend's last night."

"His son?"

Ignoring his confusion, Charlie glanced at her watch. "Heavens. I need to pick him up. Would you mind sitting here until I come back? I won't be long. I don't want Elizabeth to come out and find the house empty."

"We'd be glad to."

It took only twenty minutes to collect an exhausted, cranky Greg from Justin's—the sleepover hadn't included much sleep—and get back to the house. When she introduced him to her father and stepmother, all he said was "I really need to go to bed" and walked away. She let his rudeness pass. No sense trying to discipline Greg in front of others. He rarely paid attention to her unless Sam was in the vicinity.

Besides, Elizabeth was a much bigger concern.

Elizabeth was sitting on her bedroom floor, her back against the door, not entirely sure what she should do next. She had the envelope in her hand, her mother's handwriting on the front: *For Elizabeth*. Oddly, she didn't feel like crying or yelling. She didn't feel like—anything. Suddenly she had a grandfather she hadn't known about—sort of good looking. And Charlie was her birth mother. It was all like a play within a play. A family to replace a family

It took almost an hour for her to work up the courage to open the envelope.

My Darling Girl: You know that Dad and I love you more than anything else in the world. You have been our greatest gift. What you don't know is that you were a gift to us from my cousin Charlie. When she gave birth to you, she wasn't able to provide you with the kind of life and family that we could and, since Dad and I couldn't have children of our own, we were so happy to include you in our lives.

If you are reading this, then you are already with Charlie, missing us as we are missing you. Don't judge her for giving you to us.
All our love forever, Mom and Dad

Don't judge jumped off the page. Elizabeth didn't know how she could *not* judge. A mother shouldn't give her baby to someone else— even a favorite cousin—and walk away as though that baby wasn't important. And since Charlie hadn't wanted Elizabeth in the beginning, why would her mother hand Elizabeth back to Charlie? Of course her parents hadn't known they would both die. If the plane had gone down after Elizabeth turned eighteen, she would have been considered an adult. No need of a guardian. No Charlie in the picture. Elizabeth would probably never have known who her birth mother was. It would have been better that way.

Elizabeth remembered the summer afternoon in the lawyer's office. Her Aunt Rowena had told her they were going to meet her guardian and that she would soon be living in California. Elizabeth had been so lost, moving when she was told to move, eating whatever food was put in front of her, as though she were in some sort of parallel universe. Everything looked real—but wasn't. All she remembered of the lawyer's office was crying and then Charlie crying too. Why had Charlie cried?

Elizabeth was in the fifth grade when she first saw her parents' wedding pictures, eager to have each person named. "And that's my cousin Charlotte—we've always called her Charlie." When Elizabeth asked why she'd never met this cousin, Missy explained, "She lives in northern California."

"Why?"

"She teaches there, and her father lives in Los Angeles. Her mother, my Aunt Arlene, died a few years ago."

Elizabeth had studied the picture. "Charlie's tall."

"By the time she was twelve, she was five foot six and really hated it."

"So Arlene and Grandma Grace were sisters?"

"Right."

"But since I'm adopted, I'm not a blood relative of theirs."

"No."

"I wonder who I look like."

"I don't know."

And that was pretty much the end of the discussion about Charlie.

By the time Elizabeth started kindergarten, her parents had explained about adoption. They'd done the whole *We chose you* story, and Elizabeth had been proud to be chosen. But maybe she hadn't been chosen. Maybe her parents had simply done Charlie a favor, taking Elizabeth off her hands. Now Elizabeth wasn't sure about being *special*, though she'd certainly felt loved, felt like she was the most important person in her parents' lives.

Her entire existence was being realigned. What she'd believed her whole life wasn't true. She was a totally different Elizabeth.

When she could no longer ignore her hunger, she opened the door, half-expecting Charlie would be in the hall, anxious to talk. But she wasn't. The house was silent. Had everyone left? Greg-the-grump's door was closed. Maybe he'd come home. She peered into the kitchen. On the table was a freshly prepared sandwich covered with plastic wrap. A post-it on top: *For Elizabeth.*

No sign of Charlie. Elizabeth took a bottle of water from the refrigerator, picked up the plate and scurried back to her room. She closed the door and devoured the ham and cheese sandwich. As miserable as she felt, she was starving.

From the living room, Charlie heard Elizabeth go into the kitchen. A few minutes later, the bedroom door closed. She was glad she'd left the sandwich with the post-it. Giving Elizabeth space but fixing her lunch.

Charlie was simultaneously wired and emotionally drained. Her father and Nora had retreated to their hotel in Eureka. *Having us here might interfere with you talking to her.* Charlie agreed, even though she was afraid to talk to her alone. Afraid of—*face it*—Elizabeth's reaction. It might have been slightly better if Charlie had initiated the conversation, but that advantage was gone.

Should she apologize? But how did she apologize for almost seventeen years? How did she say *Sorry I didn't want you.* Truthfully, Charlie probably never would have been part of Elizabeth's life if Missy were alive. She still wasn't sure why she'd agreed to the guardianship. It wasn't pity or guilt or some sort of latent maternal pull. Maybe it was that Child Protective Services was the only other alternative for Elizabeth.

Charlie had turned her back on Elizabeth once. Twice would border on cruelty. The two of them were trapped by two deaths and a legal document.

In the time Elizabeth had been in Arcata, Charlie had begun to relax—a little. Taking care of Elizabeth wasn't all that difficult, especially with Sam's help. Gradually, Charlie and Elizabeth were easier with each other. Maybe like college roommates forced to fit into each other's lives. But now, their fledgling connection might have been wrecked forever.

Her father and Nora would return this evening, bringing dinner for the five of them. "What do the kids like?"

"Pizza's a safe bet. I can fix a salad."

"What time?" It was nearly 3:30.

"Six?"

"Done." Her father kissed her cheek.

Waiting for whatever was next was tortuous. After Elizabeth returned to her room, Charlie left a message on Sam's cell and decided to clean out the pantry. Busy hands.

CHAPTER 12

Charlie resisted knocking on Elizabeth's door until a little after four o'clock. When she didn't get an answer, she opened it enough to look inside, needing to know that Elizabeth was all right. Her daughter was sitting in the upholstered chair she'd brought from Virginia, staring at Missy's letter.

"May I come in?"

Though Elizabeth didn't answer, Charlie stepped inside. There had to be some sort of conversation. She sat in the swivel chair at the desk. And waited.

Elizabeth had hung two metal-framed posters over her bed, one with *Shenandoah National Park* printed across the bottom, a spring scene, dogwood adorning the leafless trees. The second poster was of the 2014 Fourth of July Fireworks display on the National Mall. Elizabeth and her parents had attended the festivities every summer until she started going to camp. Charlie guessed the posters had been in Elizabeth's Virginia bedroom, but she'd never talked to her about them. The bed had a patchwork quilt in bright oranges and reds—the only strong colors in the room. Probably one of Grace's quilts. The setting suited Elizabeth. No teenage clutter, only her schoolbooks and notebooks piled on the desk beside her laptop.

A sharp contrast to the midden that was on the floor of Greg's room. Walking into his bedroom was risky. Tired of nagging about the mess, Charlie let Sam take on the unending tussle about which clothes were clean or dirty and where his homework was.

After a few moments, "Do you know who my father is?" Elizabeth's voice was low, not quite accusing.

"Of course I do."

It wasn't a one-night stand. He meant everything to me—until he walked away from us.

"Is he still alive?"

"Probably."

"What's his name?"

"Andre Winslow."

"Is he French? Andre sounds French."

"No idea." He never talked about his past or personal details because that would have gotten too close to his Chicago life, his Chicago family. Not asking questions made it easier for Charlie to believe Andre belonged to her. He loved talking about literature, reciting poetry, ever the professor impressing the starry-eyed student he was sleeping with. He was a very good lover, not something she needed to share with Elizabeth.

"What does he do?"

"He was a visiting Literature professor at Yale when I was doing my doctoral work. He had tenure at Northwestern University in Chicago. He's probably still there."

"Do you have a picture? I don't look like you, so I must look like him." There was a hint of sarcasm in her voice.

"You have his coloring and his eyes. But no, I tore up the few pictures I had." Not only tore them up—but burned the pieces.

Five minutes of silent tension. Then, "I'd like to be alone."

"Okay." Charlie glanced at her watch. She didn't want her to be alone too long. "Dinner will be at six o'clock. My father and Nora are bringing pizza."

Elizabeth didn't respond.

While Charlie was in Elizabeth's room, it had begun raining. Because the house was as gloomy as everyone's mood, Charlie turned the lights on in the living room. If only Greg had another sleepover tonight, but no such luck. She decided to set the kitchen table for four. Greg was usually happier eating in front of the TV whenever Sam was gone. If Sam was home, he didn't let Greg get away with ignoring everyone.

Still nothing on her phone from Sam.

Desperately needing to talk to someone, Charlie finally called Tessa, who answered on the first ring. "Hi. What's up?"

Charlie rattled off the abridged version of her day.

"Do you want me to come over?"

"No," she hesitated, "No," more firmly. "I just need to tell someone. I can't reach Sam."

"What did she say when your father let the cat out?"

"Nothing. And he didn't tell her as in *tell*. He introduced himself as my father and her grandfather. She's been in her room ever since. When I couldn't stand it any longer, I went in and she asked me a few questions. Like did I know who her father was?"

"Ouch. Straight for the jugular."

"Yeah. The other questions were less punishing, but there'll be more. Then she asked me to leave. Tessa, I'm scared she'll—oh I don't know—run away or get drunk or—"

"Very creative worrying. You are officially a parent."

Charlie sighed. "What do I do? My father and his wife are coming back for dinner. Do I make her sit with us at the table? I've really never had to force her to *do* anything."

"It's better to have her come to the table—a bit of normal."

At six sharp, John and Nora were at Charlie's front door. Two large pizzas, one with everything, one with just pepperoni. And two bottles of wine. At this point, Charlie could have drunk one of the bottles all by herself.

John kissed Charlie's cheek. "Is she in her room?"

Charlie nodded. "I talked to her for a few minutes, then she asked me to leave."

"Let me try."

Not something she would have expected from her father. He'd never been one to deal with emotional issues, leaving that sort of thing to her mother. This was a new father-feature. Maybe Nora's influence.

"Sure. I'm letting Greg eat in the living room. He's better off watching TV. No need to have him asking awkward questions. He pushes Elizabeth's buttons just for fun."

Sitting in the dark, listening to the rain against the window, Elizabeth heard the doorbell. Charlie's father. Which meant someone would soon call her to come for dinner. She didn't want to do anything but sit here and hold her mother's letter, as though it possessed some latent warmth. If she went out there, *they* would expect something from her. An acknowledgement that suddenly—inexplicably—she'd been turned into part of the Ames family. A blood relative of people she didn't want to be related to. She was an Enright. With grandparents and aunts. That's who she'd always been. No one could force her to be someone else. She refolded her mother's letter and slid it into the envelope. Where should she keep a message from the grave? She needed to find a safe place.

A light rap on her bedroom door interrupted her ruminating. "Elizabeth?" Charlie's father. "May I come in?"

Refusing wouldn't do any good. There was no lock on the door. "If you want."

John Ames stood in the doorway. Tall, maybe over six feet. Graying hair, an expensive, long-sleeved blue shirt. Charlie had said he owned his own construction firm and was fairly successful.

He moved inside the room, closed the door, and reached for the light switch that controlled the lamp beside her bed.

"Have you been sitting in the dark all this time?"

"Doesn't matter."

He crossed the room to sit on the desk chair. His eyes took in the room, coming to rest on the posters. "Have you been to Shenandoah?"

"Yes."

"It's a beautiful area. Even better when the rhododendrons bloom."

No response.

He waited. "I'm sorry I threw the whole grandfather thing at you. I didn't know you didn't know—the story."

Nothing.

"Charlie wanted to be the one to tell you."

"Then why didn't she?"

"I don't know. Scared perhaps." He waited a moment, "Sometimes, it's hard to talk about, about things like this. About the past."

"Hard to talk about me?"

"No. No, I didn't mean that. About the adoption, about, well, the adoption."

"About not wanting me."

"More about not being at a point in her life where she could take care of you by herself."

"Did you know him? My birth father?"

"No."

"Why not?"

"He'd returned to Chicago by the time we found out," he took a deep breath, "that you were on the way."

"So he didn't want me either." Not a question.

Before John answered, the door opened and Nora stuck her head inside, "Dinner's on the table."

Without looking at Nora, Elizabeth mumbled, "I'm not hungry."

Slowly, John stood up and reached his hand toward Elizabeth. "Please. It looks like terrific pizza. You need to eat something." His voice was comforting.

After a moment, she stood up, still holding the envelope.

He smiled, "Good girl," and took her free hand.

Charlie was surprised when her father and Elizabeth walked into the kitchen hand-in-hand. What kind of magic had he worked?

She willed herself to act as though the only thing different was the presence of her father and Nora. After Nora put two pizza slices on each plate, Charlie added a helping of the salad she'd thrown together. She handed Elizabeth a glass of Diet Coke, then poured wine for herself, Nora, and her father. Instead of letting what no one wanted to talk about dominate the meal, Nora regaled them with stories of her twin two-year-old grandsons. "They don't talk much yet, but they understand each other perfectly. As they get older, they're going to be dangerously clever at outwitting the adults. It was fun seeing them open their Christmas presents."

John smiled at the memory. He was getting a second shot at grandparenting.

Greg came back for two more pizza slices and milk. Diane had laid down the law about carbonated drinks, and he hadn't tested that rule, though he'd certainly tested almost all the others.

Elizabeth ate her pizza, picked at the salad, then, "May I be excused?"

Charlie tried to make eye contact and failed. "There's pecan crunch ice cream." Elizabeth's favorite.

"No thanks," and she disappeared into her room.

Sam called a little after eight.

His voice washed over Charlie and crowded her throat. How could he be a continent away when she needed him so much?

"Charlie, are you there? What's wrong?" His voice was worried.

"Umm—" she swallowed, "she knows. Elizabeth."

A long pause, "I thought we were going to tell her together."

"Yeah, well my father showed up and accidentally put his foot in it."

"Is she okay?"

"I doubt it. She's not talking."

"You?"

"A mess."

"Tell me."

She appreciated the offer but decided it was too early to put her feelings into words. She was never good at explaining how she felt. Even to Sam.

"Can't—" her voice cracked.

After a few moments, "Charlie, remember I love you and you can do whatever you have to do. Elizabeth's a sensible girl. It's just a shock right now."

For the next few minutes, she listened to his counsel and eventually found enough of her voice to outline what she wanted to tell Elizabeth, then said she loved him and hung up so she could cry before she went in to talk to Elizabeth again. She didn't cry often or easily. What she didn't understand was why she wanted to cry now. It was like the afternoon in Donovan's office. Watching Elizabeth cry, Charlie had cried for both of them. She wasn't sure she'd cried this much since Andre left her, not even the day she gave Elizabeth to Missy. Lately, it was like sixteen years of tears were pushing their way to the surface.

This time, Elizabeth's door was open. She was at her desk, her music folder open, and the envelope with Missy's letter alongside.

"May I come in?"

A shrug. She closed the folder.

Charlie took the upholstered chair this time and gathered her courage. She was glad she'd run her thoughts by Sam first.

"Elizabeth, nothing about your life here has to change. We were doing okay until this morning. I'd like to keep the *okay* part. I'm not trying to be your mother. Missy is your mother. You don't need another one, and I'm not in the running for the job."

She paused, in case Elizabeth wanted to say something. When she didn't, "You don't have to like what I did, and you'll probably never understand why I did it, but the problem is—until you're eighteen, you need a place to live and someone to be responsible for you." Sam had vetoed saying *take care of you.* "And I intend to honor your mother's request that I be responsible for you."

Her knees were shaking as she left the room.

CHAPTER 13

The next morning, Nora and John stopped at Charlie's to say goodbye. They'd initially planned to stay another day but, after yesterday's debacle, John decided to return to San Francisco. *I don't see how we can help the situation right now.* Nora agreed.

Elizabeth was alone at the kitchen table, eating cold cereal with banana slices. Charlie was in the small utility room, folding laundry, giving Elizabeth privacy. John sat across from his granddaughter and took her hand. "I'm so glad we've had a chance to meet. Maybe sometime you could come down to stay with us over a long weekend," he paused, but Elizabeth didn't respond. "We have great beaches."

Finally, very quietly, "Maybe. Thank you."

Charlie was always impressed by the way Elizabeth's good manners surfaced, even when she was in a bad place. It had been the same in Donovan's office that first day—politeness seemed to smooth the rough edges that life was handing her.

"Good. We'd love to have you," he leaned over and kissed her cheek. Nora briefly touched Elizabeth's shoulder and followed her husband to where Charlie was waiting.

"Thanks, Dad."

"Are you okay?"

"Not really."

He put his arms around her. "When is Sam coming back?"

"Late Friday." She walked them to their rental car, wishing she were wearing a sweater. "It looks like more rain. Have a safe trip." She returned Nora's hug, grateful that her stepmother could be supportive without saying much. A useful quality in times of stress. Long after their rental car disappeared from sight, Charlie stood on the sidewalk, avoiding the heaviness that had taken up residence in her house. By the time she entered the kitchen, Elizabeth had returned to her room, and Greg's door was still closed.

The whole day lay before her. If only Elizabeth would ask more questions, let Charlie explain. In all the time since Elizabeth's birth, no one, not even Charlie's mother, had encouraged her to talk about that part of her life—the man, the baby, and her embarrassment about allowing herself to be sucked into thinking Andre really loved her. She'd never talked about the fear that her life had been irrevocably destroyed. That she was damaged goods.

Nowadays, the stigma of an illegitimate birth, of single parenthood, was less. And since she'd never been asked about her feelings, Charlie had successfully ignored them, burying them and herself in books and students and classrooms. She seemed to lack whatever skills were necessary to purge the past.

Instead of cooking dinner, she took Greg and Elizabeth to the McDonald's in Eureka, any excuse to get out of the house for a while. She made them leave their phones at home—nothing more annoying than being ignored while they flipped through emails.

It wasn't a comfortable hour but, when one of Greg's soccer teammates came in with his father and stopped at their table while his family's take-out order was being filled, the elephant that was following Charlie around stayed out of sight.

It was raining hard when she pulled into her driveway. Once inside, Greg headed for the TV and Elizabeth, predictably, vanished into her bedroom. Charlie hung her dripping raincoat in the utility room and decided to make herself some tea. It was probably too late to call Sam. He had an early meeting tomorrow. As she removed the teabag from her cup, the landline rang.

"Charlotte? It's Rowena." Richard's sister had always avoided Charlie's nickname.

"Yes?"

"There's a problem."

Not the word Charlie needed to hear. "Is it Kevin?"

"Yes. Grace called me this morning; he passed on last night."

Charlie's uncle had been a sweet, somewhat reclusive accountant—more comfortable with numbers than people. "Thanks for letting me know. I'll call her."

"Wait, there's more. Grace asked that I get a plane ticket for Elizabeth. The memorial service is Friday. She wants Elizabeth to be with her, so I made a reservation for tomorrow morning. I've sent the confirmation number and itinerary to your email. I know it's short notice. And I explained to the airline that she's sixteen so they will look after her between Arcata and her arrival at Reagan. She has to bring her ID to get her boarding pass at your airport. I'll pick her up here and take her to Grace's."

Charlie's brain raced in a thousand directions. "School begins on Monday. She doesn't like missing classes." Probably not the right response. "I'll talk to her and call you back."

Another loss for her daughter.

Softly, Charlie knocked on Elizabeth's door. When there was no answer, she opened it. "Elizabeth, that was your Aunt Rowena. Can you come into the kitchen? I need to talk to you." Even more than before, Charlie didn't feel welcome in Elizabeth's room.

"Is it Grampa?"

"Yes."

On the way to the kitchen, Charlie picked up her laptop and was searching for Rowena's email as Elizabeth sat down at the table; her eyes were full, a few tears already on her cheeks.

"Is he dead?"

"Yesterday." She found Rowena's message and opened the attachment with the flight itinerary. "Your grandmother would like you to come back to be with her. The memorial service is Friday afternoon."

"So soon?" For the first time since yesterday, Elizabeth was actually looking at Charlie, instead of looking down or off into the distance.

"Well, his death wasn't a surprise. Probably everything had been prearranged. Rowena already bought your ticket." Charlie scrolled through the itinerary. "The plane leaves at 8:25 tomorrow morning, with an hour layover in San Francisco. You get to Reagan just before 5 o'clock."

Charlie hit the print button and heard the printer start in the dining room. The magic of wifi. She retrieved the pages and handed them to Elizabeth. "Do you need help packing?"

Elizabeth shook her head. "What about school?"

"I'll see to it. There shouldn't be a problem."

Elizabeth pushed back her chair. "I need to call Martha."

And Charlie needed to call Rowena to tell her that Elizabeth would be on the plane and that she knew about her birth parents.

Charlie had never liked getting up before sunrise, but airline schedules were no respecter of personal preferences. At 5 a.m., Elizabeth was in the shower and by six she had rinsed her breakfast dishes and was waiting for Charlie to get Greg in gear. Loud complaints from his room. "Why do I have to go too?" With his jacket over his pajamas and wearing bedroom slippers, he crawled into the back seat and went to sleep. Charlie envied his ability to sleep anytime, anywhere. Once they got to the airport, he refused to get out of the car.

"Fine. Keep the doors locked." Charlie didn't really want to bother with his attitude while getting Elizabeth through check-in. They picked up her boarding pass and, once they checked her suitcase, the flight attendant was contacted. In San Francisco, Elizabeth would be turned over to another attendant.

At security, "Do you have enough cash? And your ATM card?" She should have asked earlier.

"Yes. And phone numbers. I know how to do this." Irritation.

"I know you do." Charlie was sure there were things she should have done, should have said. The security line moved forward and Elizabeth handed the boarding pass and her learner's permit to the guard. Before Charlie could say goodbye, Elizabeth turned around, "I want to meet him," entered an open TSA lane, and placed her shoes, purse and laptop in the container that would go through the scanner. In a few minutes, she passed through the gate, retrieved everything, and walked straight ahead. No backward glance at Charlie.

I want to meet him.

Not a request.

And Charlie had thought that Elizabeth getting her driver's license would be difficult.

Tracking down Andre and presenting him with a daughter he knew nothing about would not be easy. Charlie would have to take Elizabeth to meet him. Stand in front of him while maintaining her composure. In all these years, she had never wanted to see him again, never needed closure because his telling her to get an abortion was enough closure for one lifetime. And yet she owed Elizabeth a meeting with her biological father. In August, Charlie had been uncertain about taking responsibility for Elizabeth; that uncertainty was nothing compared to the fear of confronting Andre.

He wasn't where she thought he'd be. When she pulled up the names of Northwestern's current faculty, he wasn't listed. He'd been thirty-eight when Elizabeth was conceived. Now he'd be fifty-four or fifty-five. Too young to have retired. And so she googled him. There were several entries reviewing the two books he'd written: a 2005 collection of criticism on Jonathon Swift and a 2015 biography of John Donne. In that review, she discovered he was currently the Chairman of Georgetown University's Humanities Department, practically on Grace's doorstep.

She was suddenly short of breath.

On Friday afternoon, the Presbyterian Church sanctuary was only half-filled for Kevin Fiello's memorial service. Wearing the new black dress Rowena had helped her buy yesterday, Elizabeth sat alongside her grandmother in the front pew, their hands clasped. Her grandmother's cold hand felt small, more fragile than Elizabeth remembered. The service lasted only half an hour. Afterwards, they stood at the church door, greeting the mourners as they left. At a moment like this, Missy should have been with them. Elizabeth was only too aware that she and her grandmother were all that was left of that side of the family, other than a few second and third cousins who lived in Ontario—and Charlie. Three members of her family gone.

There was no graveside service as Kevin's ashes would be scattered at sea so, when the church was empty, Rowena drove Grace and Elizabeth home. Even though Missy had always been just a little afraid of her husband's sister, Elizabeth was beginning to appreciate Aunt Rowena who, in times of trouble, was willing to help in any way she could. Like last summer when she'd driven to Maine to pick up Elizabeth as soon as she'd heard about the plane crash and her brother's death. Since Kevin's death, she'd done a little of everything for Grace: turning away people Grace didn't want to talk to, overseeing last minute arrangements for the memorial service, answering the phone, and making sure there was food in the house. Though neither Elizabeth nor Grace was eating much.

It was getting dark by the time Rowena parked her van in the Fiello driveway. She went inside with them, turning on lights, adjusting the thermostat setting, and putting the kettle on the stove. "Maybe some tea?" Since Rowena didn't like coffee, no one got coffee if she was in charge of beverages. Grace thanked her and sank gratefully into the upholstered rocking chair she preferred. Elizabeth went upstairs to change into a pair of fleece slacks and a heavy sweater. She slipped into her Ugg boots and rejoined her grandmother. On the coffee table, Rowena had set out two cups of steaming tea and slices of banana bread a neighbor had brought over.

Rowena buttoned her coat. "I need to take care of a few things at my place. Willow needs to be fed and walked or I'll have a mess to clean up. Are you two going to be all right? I can come back later if you want me to."

Grace shook her head. "We'll be okay. You've done so much already."

Elizabeth walked Rowena to her car. "Thanks for helping Grandma."

Never especially good at giving or accepting compliments, Rowena focused on practical matters. "What day do you want to go back to California? I can make the reservation."

Elizabeth hesitated. "I feel awful leaving Grandma alone right now." Rowena waited.

"What would happen if I stayed here?"

"Until?"

"I don't know." Though the idea of staying longer had followed her around all day, Elizabeth hadn't really thought the possibility through. She only knew she didn't want to think of her grandmother sitting alone in this big house without her grandfather or Missy or herself. Watching her grandmother's grief reminded Elizabeth of how she'd felt when her parents died. How she still felt when she let the sadness get the better of her, the piercing emptiness that couldn't be explained or chased away by doing homework or singing in the choir or fighting with Greg.

"Charlotte said your school starts on Monday."

"I know, but I can't just—leave my grandmother here. You're working and there isn't any other close family that would help keep her company."

"But you have to be in school someplace."

"Could I go to school here? I know it costs a lot."

"I have no idea. Charlotte's your guardian, so she's the only one who can legally make that kind of decision. And you should ask your grandmother first."

The more Elizabeth thought about the possibility of staying in Virginia, the better she liked it. "I will, I will." She ran back into the house before Rowena could talk her out of this new, wonderful plan. If she stayed, she could spend time with Julie and her other school friends. She would miss the Madrigal choir members and Mr. Hannigan. And of course Martha.

On the plus side, staying in Virginia would send Charlie a clear message.

CHAPTER 14

Though they'd long ago agreed that Charlie didn't need to pick Sam up when he flew back from his frequent trips to the East Coast, she was standing near the McKinleyville baggage claim when he walked into the airport late Friday. Bundled into her heavy jacket, her hair tucked behind her ears, puffy eyes, and no lipstick. Not the usual put-together Charlie. He waved as he came through the doorway and headed for the circling carousel. As soon as he retrieved his dark green duffle bag, he hurried to where Charlie was standing.

"Hey," he set the bag down and pulled her against him, "Thanks for coming. Is Greg with you?"

"No, he's at Henry's till tomorrow morning." Her voice was muffled against his jacket, her arms tightening around him.

"What's wrong? Is it Elizabeth?"

He felt her nod.

"Was the memorial service today?"

Another nod.

"Charlie," he moved her away so he could look at her, "talk to me." Why was it always so hard to extract information from her?

"She's not—coming back." Her words stirred the tears that had been waiting in her eyes.

"Come on," he kissed the top of her head, "let's go home." She reached into her jacket pocket for the car keys and handed them to him. He kept an arm around her as they crossed the parking lot. This had been the wrong week for him to be out of town. First John Ames' misstep and now Elizabeth defecting.

The house was cold because Charlie always turned the heat down when she left. Sam adjusted the thermostat and slipped out of his jacket. "Have you eaten?"

"No."

"Come sit in the kitchen. I'll throw something together."

"I'm not all that hungry." She was still wearing her jacket, her hands jammed into her pockets.

"Food will make you feel better."

"I doubt it."

The refrigerator didn't offer much inspiration, but there was plenty of fettuccini in the pantry, a bag of mixed frozen vegetables in the freezer, and the ingredients for an Alfredo sauce. He found a half empty bottle of Chardonnay and poured her a glass. She let it sit for a few moments, then took a sip. "Aren't you having any?"

"That bottle's all we have. I suspect you need wine more than I do."

Sipping the wine, she watched him fix dinner, eating only half of what he put on her plate. Still not saying anything.

Sam let her eat in silence, afraid to push for fear she might crumble.

By the time they finished eating, the house was warmer and Charlie took off her jacket. As she closed the door to the hall closet, Sam was behind her and turned her into the living room, keeping an arm around her shoulders.

On the phone, she'd told him about Kevin's death and the story of her father telling Elizabeth she was Charlie's daughter, so Sam decided to fast forward to the *not coming back* issue. "When did she call?"

"After the memorial service this afternoon."

He waited.

Finally, "She doesn't want to leave Grace alone."

"What does your aunt think?"

"I haven't talked to her yet." Knowing Grace thought Charlie should have told Elizabeth the truth as soon as she accepted the guardianship, Charlie wasn't ready to hear her *I told you to tell her* speech.

"Will Grace be completely alone if Elizabeth leaves?"

"Mostly yes. My mother and Missy and now Kevin are gone. Elizabeth and I are her only close family. And Rowena, sort of."

On the surface, it looked like Elizabeth was being a loving granddaughter, but the degree of Charlie's distress suggested more was involved.

"But?"

Charlie let his arm pull her tighter. "I suspect it's a way of avoiding me. She hates me. She's barely spoken to me since Monday. The way she found out was all wrong. I should have initiated the conversation about her birth months ago."

"She probably doesn't hate you." He hoped he was right.

Charlie pulled away, on the defensive. "You weren't here when it happened. You don't *know.* I've tried to apologize, to explain about— everything and now she wants to meet him and I don't know what to do about any of this. I understand that she's curious and angry and confused. She's still hurting from Missy and Rick dying and now this. She's only sixteen and she has to be in school and she's my responsibility and I don't think forcing her to come back will help anything but I don't know what Donovan will say. And I'll have to take her to meet *Him.* He's at Georgetown—too close to Vienna. It's like I'm being punished all at once for—for what I did." As her misery spilled out, she began trembling as though she were freezing.

Afraid for her, Sam gripped her shoulders, "Shh, Charlie, shh." But when the shaking continued, he picked her up and carried her into their bedroom, set her on the bed, and went to turn on the shower. He took off her watch, her shoes, her slacks and sweater, then walked her into the shower, still in her underwear, and closed the shower door behind her.

The shock of the hot water had the desired effect. She yelped, then stood still, letting the water soothe her. After almost ten minutes, she turned the shower off. Sam was waiting to wrap a bath sheet around her, holding her against him.

"Better?"

"Uh huh, but I need to take off my wet underwear."

She put on a flannel nightgown and crawled into bed, asleep almost instantly. Sam turned off all but his bedside lamp and went back to the kitchen. In the midst of Charlie's distress, he hadn't wanted to add Diane's new email message to the chaos.

He was exhausted—partially because he was still on East Coast time, mostly because Charlie's meltdown had scared the crap out of him. Never before had she fallen apart like that. Having children injected into their lives was taking a toll on her and on their relationship. He'd been hoping that, after the holidays, they could find more time for themselves. To talk about their future. Greg was finally making friends and had stopped being such a pain in the butt. But the outside world seemed intent on delivering obstacles to their doorstep.

Yesterday brought Diane's unexpected email. Before leaving for Spain, she'd met one of the Madrid-based owners of the fashion house she was now working for. Two weeks ago, Luis de Leon proposed to her. Because they were getting married this summer, she was flying into McKinleyville week after next to tell Greg and also put her Portland condo on the market. As soon as Greg's school year ended, he would fly to Spain with Diane's mother to meet his new stepfather, who already had grown children, start a new school, and learn about a country half a world away from his childhood. Sam foresaw having to renegotiate the custody arrangement with Diane and work on accumulating frequent flyer miles.

Before he turned into a zombie, he showered in the kids' bathroom so he wouldn't disturb Charlie and slid in beside her. She never moved.

Greg called Sam's cell just before ten. "Hey Dad, I'm at Henry's. I need a ride to soccer practice. Charlie said she'd tell you."

"Give me the address." Henry was a new friend.

He filled his thermal cup with fresh coffee and drove across town to collect his son. On the drive to the soccer field, Sam casually mentioned that Diane would be visiting.

Greg was instantly worried. "Why? Am I going to have to go back to Portland?"

Diane had specifically asked that Sam let her break the news to Greg, so Sam lied. "I don't know." Sitting on the weathered bleachers at the middle school soccer field, Sam watched the team practice. The coach had Greg playing defense. Seeing his son go through drills and practice plays, Sam was impressed with how he had improved in the last few months and that the other team members seemed to have accepted him. Taking him to Spain was a disruption Greg did not need.

Monday, Sam needed to contact his lawyer to get ahead of whatever curve Diane was going to throw at him. The conversation with her was not going to be pretty.

The sound of Sam's Rover pulling out of the driveway woke Charlie. It took her a few minutes to remember she'd forgotten to tell him about Greg's soccer practice. Yesterday's emotional crash had left her feeling bruised.

Hoping coffee might help, she put on the same Levi's and sweater she'd worn last night, found a pair of heavy socks and shuffled into the kitchen. Sam had left the coffeemaker on, the pot half full. She poured herself some, added milk, then added more milk. The coffee was much too strong.

When Sam and Greg returned, it was just after one o'clock. Greg headed for the shower, and Sam found Charlie sitting on the floor in Elizabeth's room, going through the photo album Elizabeth had been compiling. Sam held out a Burger King sack, "We brought you lunch, super size fries"—Sam knew her weakness—"and a chicken sandwich. We ate lunch with Justin and his father. I bet you didn't eat breakfast."

She looked up, "You'd win."

He extended his free hand, "Come eat, French fries are no good cold."

Charlie had to admit eating helped clear her head a little. She devoured all the fries. "I need to pack up Elizabeth's things. Do we have some boxes left in the garage?" Elizabeth had been very firm about Charlie sending all her clothes, the picture album and the books stacked on her desk.

"Shouldn't you wait until the schools and the lawyer give their okay?"

"So long as I give my permission, they will." Right now, having something to do might help steady her.

She spent the rest of the afternoon putting the contents of Elizabeth's closet and dresser drawers into the boxes Sam brought her, discovering her daughter was something of a neatnik. Her underwear folded, socks matched. That must be Missy's influence. Charlie was inclined to stuff underwear in the drawer any which way and struggle to find matching socks at the moment she was ready to wear them. She took her time packing, carefully folding dresses and tops, sweaters and leggings. Charlie hadn't realized the extent of Elizabeth's wardrobe, as she'd unpacked the moving company boxes gradually. There were still clothes in the garage, her school uniforms, ski clothes, swimsuits.

She needed another box.

Emptying Elizabeth's bedroom of everything but its furnishing and posters felt surreal. When Donovan's office caught up with Charlie in London, she'd wanted no part of the guardianship. Did not want to be part of Elizabeth's life and had gone to Vienna intent on refusing. Charlotte Ames might have given birth to a child, but she wasn't a mother in any sense of the word.

A little at a time, she'd lost her initial resistance, had begun to feel more comfortable as Elizabeth's cousin/guardian, finding ways to connect without treading on Missy's role as mother. Elizabeth was easy to like and up to the moment when John Ames appeared on the doorstep, easy to get along with. Her battles with Greg were exceptions, but even that explosive situation had calmed as Greg got used to his new living arrangements and stopped baiting Elizabeth.

Charlie would not have expected she'd feel Elizabeth's absence so strongly, to feel like a failure. In most other parts of her life, she'd seldom failed, and cleaning up after this failure would involve Andre. Elizabeth wanting to meet him was probably the trigger to last night's meltdown.

Charlie was afraid of seeing him, of how he might hurt Elizabeth. Or even worse he might decide he wanted a relationship with his daughter. Charlie did not want Elizabeth to like him. He didn't deserve her. Hopefully, Charlie was just borrowing trouble. She did that sometimes. After a few hours of packing and ruminating, she lay down on Elizabeth's bed and fell asleep.

By Sunday, she'd worked up the courage to call Grace to make sure her aunt wanted Elizabeth with her. An uncomfortable conversation, though Charlie was certain Grace was pleased Elizabeth had chosen to keep her company.

The rest of the day was devoted to Sam and Charlie discussing the bombshell that Diane was going to drop on Greg. It was easier to worry about Sam's parenting problems than hers.

Monday, Charlie arrived at the high school mid-morning to talk to Principal Severin, explaining Elizabeth's decision and that the provost at The Vienna Academy would be calling to formally request Elizabeth's fall semester records. Both Donovan and the provost had called Charlie early that morning to discuss the formalities of Elizabeth's move back to Virginia. Donovan would be overnighting legal documents giving Grace temporary custody of Elizabeth, transferring the trust money that had been going into Charlie's account into Grace's. The provost would be sending enrollment documents for Charlie to sign. Classes weren't beginning until next Monday, so Elizabeth wouldn't be missing any school days.

Before leaving campus, Charlie wrote a note to Bill Hannigan, thanking him for giving Elizabeth a chance to sing in the choir, explaining the reasons for her sudden departure.

Charlie moved through the rest of the morning in a self-induced fog. Everything was happening too fast, but then Elizabeth's arrival in Arcata had happened quickly too. Four plus months ago. Last July, Charlie would never have imagined missing Elizabeth.

But she did.

She'd gotten used to the sound of Elizabeth in the house. Puttering in the kitchen, her bedroom door closing, the thud of her backpack hitting the floor when she came home from school. Her absence was louder than Charlie expected.

Before Sam left for work, he loaded the five boxes going to Elizabeth into Charlie's car. Fortunately, she found someone to help her unload them at the UPS store. As usual, she'd put too much in each box and couldn't manage them herself. When she left the UPS store, she sat in her car for a while, not sure what she should do. She considered calling Elizabeth to tell her that the boxes were on their way, but she wasn't feeling up to hearing Elizabeth's cold voice. The voice that hated her. Taking the low road, she texted her daughter, then drove to the university. She had plenty of prep work to do for the next semester. Immersing herself in writing new syllabi would keep her thoughts off Elizabeth and off Sam's new crisis.

Monday night: It's a done deal. I get to stay with Grandma for this semester. Grandma cried when I told her what I wanted to do. The provost called Charlie and the principal at Arcata. My records at Arcata will be faxed here tomorrow, and I can start school next Monday. The lawyer that has my trust is sending Charlie forms that will give Grandma temporary custody. Charlie didn't say much when I called to tell her what I want to do. Maybe she's relieved I won't be back. Aunt Rowena said I had to make the call. I was hoping she or Grandma would call her, but I suppose Aunt Rowena was right even though I'm still angry with Charlie.

Grandma and I spent the weekend writing thank you notes to all the people who sent flowers and brought food. There are four casseroles of some kind in the refrigerator. I've been fixing dinner but haven't used the casseroles because they don't look all that appetizing. I walked to the mini mart for fresh fruit and vegetables. There certainly isn't much to choose from. California has lots more, even in the winter.

In the evening, we watch Grandma's TV programs, like Jeopardy and Downton Abbey. Better than the sci-fi stuff Greg watches.

CHAPTER 15

Though Elizabeth had been in and out of her grandmother's house most of her life, she'd never slept there even one night, so unpacking the boxes Charlie had mailed felt a bit strange. It seemed just yesterday that she was unpacking at Charlie's. This bedroom was totally different. Old-fashioned wallpaper with large pink roses and pleated drapes over sheer curtains at the windows. She preferred the shutters in her Arcata bedroom.

An hour ago, Julie called for directions to Grace's house, which was only seven miles from the house Elizabeth and her parents had lived in. Julie had her driver's license and was allowed to drive her mother's car. Elizabeth was envious. If she were still in Arcata, she'd already have had one driving lesson. Charlie had undoubtedly canceled the appointment. Elizabeth really wanted to be able to drive but, since her Grandmother had a lot on her plate right now, driving lessons wouldn't be on the agenda. Instead of spending money on lessons, she might ask Rowena to teach her. The downside to that idea was Rowena's impatience with other drivers. She'd probably be impatient with Elizabeth too.

The doorbell interrupted that train of thought, and she could hear her grandmother telling Julie which room Elizabeth was in. A moment later, Julie appeared, her smile wide and her squeal familiar. "Oooh Lizzie, I've missed you." They hugged and then hugged again.

Elizabeth, minus the squeal. "I missed you too."

She shut the bedroom door. One thing she'd learned since her arrival was that her grandmother had excellent hearing.

Julie sat on the bed, piling pillows against the headboard. "Tell me everything. How come you're back? Where's your cousin?"

Elizabeth pulled a straight-backed chair alongside the bed and propped her bare feet on the mattress. "She's in California. Her semester starts next week."

"So she let you come back?"

"Only for the memorial service but, after I got here, I decided to stay."

Julie sat forward, "What's going on? Was it awful there? Was your cousin mean?"

"No and no. It was just—well, I didn't think my grandmother should be alone right now," Elizabeth hesitated, "and I'm really upset at Charlie."

"Because?"

So far, Elizabeth hadn't talked about the whole birth mother thing with anyone. Not her grandmother. Not Rowena. Even though she knew they knew about Charlie's father telling Elizabeth the truth.

But maybe she could tell Julie. "You have to promise not to tell anyone. And I mean anyone. Not even your mom."

"I swear."

"Charlie's my—birth mother." Hard words to say.

Julie was uncharacteristically silent.

Elizabeth decided to get the story over with. "Charlie's father came to visit a couple days after Christmas and introduced himself as my grandfather. He thought I knew."

"So Charlie hadn't explained?"

Elizabeth shook her head.

"Jeez, it's like you've got a new mother that you had all along. What a great story! Are you glad you know?"

"Not sure. Maybe simpler not to know. It's—uncomfortable. We aren't talking about it."

"What about your real father?"

"He's an English Professor at Northwestern University. His name is Andre Winslow."

"Sexy name. Are you going to get to meet him?"

"I told Charlie I wanted to. I didn't give her a chance to tell me no."

"So you'll go to wherever Northwestern is?"

"It's in Chicago."

"Wow. That's huge."

"Yeah." Elizabeth could feel her stomach tightening. The subject needed to change. "What's going on with you—and at school? Distract me."

Waiting for Diane's arrival was akin to expecting an invasion from a foreign power. Sam felt rather sorry for this Luis, who was so eager to marry her. Did he know what his life was going to be like?

She parked in the driveway just as they were finishing dinner. Since Elizabeth's departure, Greg's job was rinsing dishes, filling the dishwasher, and making sure the counters were clean. Elizabeth had done it better, but he was trying, and the threat of being dragged off to Portland or Spain had, not surprisingly, improved his attitude around the house. Sam was hoping it might eventually improve his schoolwork. Too early to measure that.

Diane had called from San Francisco. "My plane lands at McKinleyville at 6:30. I'm renting a car so I can drive to Portland tomorrow."

At least she wasn't staying long.

Sam sent a reluctant Greg out to meet his mother. "Do I have to?"

"Time to be the good son." Sam gave him a nudge out the front door. *You might be able to talk yourself out of going to Spain.*

When they came inside, Diane had her arm around Greg's shoulders. His face registered discomfort, but Diane was all smiles. The good mother. As she entered the hallway, "Our son is so grown up."

"Taller certainly. He's outgrowing clothes and shoes." Sam had been shocked at the price of Greg's shoes—one pair for soccer, one for everyday. "Come into the living room. Have you had dinner?"

"Yes, but I could use some tea. Herbal of course."

Of course

Sam left Greg and Diane in the living room and retreated to the kitchen where Charlie was pretending to be busy. He put the teakettle on and rummaged in the battered can holding a collection of tea bags.

Charlie watched him nervously fumbling with the teabags. "Do you want me to come with you?" She didn't really want to be there; her presence would only annoy Diane.

He chose Calm Mango and laid the bag on the saucer. "Yes I would, but you'd better not. Likely to be a difficult conversation. Stay safe." He reached for her, held her until the teakettle began whistling. "I promise to come back alive."

She laughed, loving the lightness he could find when all she could see was darkness. If Greg went to Spain permanently, Sam would be struggling to find the time and money to visit his son.

Sam carried the cup and a napkin into the lion's den.

Living in Virginia again almost felt normal—whatever normal was these days. Elizabeth's classes had been matched with those she'd been enrolled in at Arcata—except for the choir. Her grandmother drove her to school in the morning and, since the city bus was convenient to both her grandmother's house and the school, Elizabeth bought a bus pass and took public transportation back home. That way, if she needed to stay late for any reason, she wasn't inconveniencing Grace. On days when Julie had access to her mother's car, they went to the mall in Tyson's Corner and Julie drove her home.

It was on one of those trips that Julie offered to teach Elizabeth to drive. "It's not all that hard to learn, and then you could drive your grandmother when she doesn't feel like driving herself."

"But my learner's permit is for California."

"Maybe the California permit works here. People drive with out-of-state licenses. I still have the DMV booklet for Virginia. You could study that and get a learner's permit for here. Or we could just practice and then you could take the written and driving test at the same time. Easy peasy."

Elizabeth was tempted. "I was supposed to have driving lessons after Christmas."

"I work cheaper. Just cokes and French fries."

It's my seventeenth birthday: Aunt Rowena and Grandma took me to dinner at Café Renaissance and gave me a gift certificate for TJ Maxx. It

was the first time Grandma's been out of the house for something social.
She's doing a little better. I'm glad I'm here with her, but it's pretty boring.
If it weren't for Julie and my other friends at school, it'd be worse. But
then mostly everything's been hard this year. Changing schools again hasn't
helped.

Charlie sent me a pink cashmere cardigan. It has a shawl collar and
patch pockets. She also called, but we had trouble talking because we don't
talk about what she did and how I feel about it. I guess Greg's going to stay
in Arcata until June and then move to Spain. His evil mother is getting
married to a rich Spaniard. Charlie said Sam is not happy about Greg
moving so far away.

Julie and I drove by my old house last week. Weird. The people in it
must have little kids. There was a plastic wagon and a tricycle in the front
yard. The grass needs cutting and there aren't any flowers in the borders.
My dad always loved working in our yard. It made me really sad.

Julie's going to give me my first driving lesson next week. Something to
look forward to.

Even though school is familiar, being away last fall, I missed stuff and,
when someone talks about a game or a dance, I feel left out. I felt left out in
Arcata too. If I have to go back there, I'll be on the outside all over again.
Maybe I shouldn't have come back, but it was the only way I could put
space between me and Charlie. I don't want her to be my mother. I could
deal with her when she was a cousin, but her being my "mother" makes me
uncomfortable. Like she might want me to love her. I won't do that. I can't
ever love someone who gave me away like an unwanted object. I don't feel
like I belong anywhere.

Julie decided to use one of the country roads near Vienna for
Elizabeth's first driving lesson. A straight, two-lane road paralleling
colonial-style houses surrounded by white rail fences. The best part—
very little traffic in the middle of the afternoon. Julie had learned to
drive in her mother's red Corolla so she guessed teaching Elizabeth in
the same car shouldn't be too hard. Once Elizabeth was comfortable
driving on the quiet two-lane road, Julie would take her into one of
the nearby towns to get used to light traffic, then venture into Vienna.

In truth, Julie hadn't yet driven on any of the major arteries near the Beltway. Fortunately, her driving test had been given within the confines of Vienna.

They started on the Monday after Valentine's Day. Elizabeth in the driver's seat, Julie alongside. "First adjust the seat. You're taller than me. You'll want it moved back a bit." Elizabeth moved the lever. "Okay, now all the mirrors, side and rear. Can you see?"

"How do I know how much I should be able to see?"

Explaining that was harder than Julie had counted on, so she decided not to deal with the side mirrors for the moment. Once they were ready to drive in traffic, she'd worry about that part of the instruction.

For the next half hour, Elizabeth dutifully signaled as she pulled from their parking spots onto the road, gradually increasing her speed to the 35 mph on the road signs, then slowing and pulling back onto the shoulder. Repeat and repeat. When Julie took over to drive back into Vienna, both of them were tense. Elizabeth rummaged in her backpack for her bottle of water and took a deep swallow. "It's harder than I thought. There's a lot to think about all at the same time, and we didn't even meet one car."

"It gets easier." At least it had for Julie.

By the end of February, Elizabeth was gaining confidence. They'd tackled roads with more traffic, practiced turns and backing up, and agreed that Julie's parallel parking didn't qualify her to teach it to Elizabeth. After three days of Julie not being able to park parallel even once, both girls were on edge.

"How did you pass the driving test if you can't park?"

"I did everything else well, I guess. So failing that part didn't make me fail the whole test."

"Well, I can't be sure that would happen for me. Maybe I'm going to have to ask Aunt Rowena for help. I really hate to. She's so impatient."

They were on the outskirts of Vienna. "Do you want me to take over or do you want to drive a few blocks in town?"

Elizabeth surveyed the street ahead. "Sure. I've got to try sometime."

She stayed in the right lane, slowing as she came to a busy intersection. "Is this where we turn?"

"No, it's the next block."

When Elizabeth reached the next corner, she stopped at the red light, checked for oncoming traffic, and turned carefully into the lane closest to the curb, her hands tense as cars sped by in the other lanes. Then, behind her, flashing blue lights and the sharp *blip, blip* from the police car framed in the rear view mirror. For a moment, she felt as though she would faint. She was going to be arrested and in BIG trouble. Trouble happened to other kids, never ever to her. She pulled over and stopped.

"What did I do wrong?"

"I don't think you did anything wrong. You stopped before you turned."

Elizabeth's hand was shaking as she pushed the button to lower the window. The frowning officer leaned over. "May I see your license?"

"I just have a learner's permit."

He put out his hand while Julie handed Elizabeth her purse.

He studied the permit. "This is for California, not Virginia."

"I know. But if I had a California license, I could drive here."

His eyes narrowed. "Not the same thing. How old are you?"

"Seventeen."

He looked at Julie. "Let me see the car registration and your license. I assume you have one."

Julie nodded, digging in her purse, handing him her wallet. She found the registration in the glove compartment.

"Please take the license out of your wallet and give it to me."

He gave it a cursory glance, handed it back to Julie, and turned his attention to Elizabeth. A pen in one hand and a pad in the other, he began to write. "You made an illegal right turn. The signs clearly say *No right turn on a red light*. And you are driving without a Virginia permit." Looking at her permit again, "You are Elizabeth Enright?"

"Yes sir."

"What is your Virginia address?"

She gave him Grace's address.

"And that's your parents' address too?"

"My parents are dead. It's my grandmother's. Please don't call her. My grandfather just died and she's having a hard time."

"Is there another adult relative I can call? I need to have someone responsible pick you up."

Elizabeth took a deep breath and recited Rowena's cell number. Her aunt was going to be furious. And once her grandmother found out, Elizabeth would probably be grounded for the rest of her life. She listened as the officer explained the situation to Rowena and that Elizabeth needed a ride home with someone other than another teenager.

Fifteen minutes later, Rowena's van pulled in behind the police car. She was wearing a tailored tan jacket with expensive denim slacks. She'd probably been at work. Her expression was predictably thunderous. Elizabeth watched in the rearview mirror as Rowena and the policeman walked to the back of Julie's car. The policeman talked. Rowena listened. When he finally walked back to Elizabeth, he had her sign the ticket and gave her a copy. "You will need to report to court on this date," he pointed, "with your aunt. She will take you home now." He looked at Julie. "And you are to go straight home. No more driving lessons. Ms. Enright will call your parents."

Elizabeth retrieved her backpack from the rear seat, slipped her purse strap over her shoulder and walked to Rowena's van, wishing she could disappear. Rowena didn't say anything until they pulled into Grace's driveway. Other than the drive from Maine to Virginia last July, this was the worst ride of Elizabeth's life.

After Rowena turned the engine off, Elizabeth ventured a question, "What's going to happen to me. Am I going to jail?"

Rowena stared straight ahead. "No, but there will be a hefty fine and you may not apply for a driver's license until you're eighteen. There might be community service. I'll put up the money for the fine, and you will have to pay me back out of your allowance."

"Do you have to tell grandmother?"

"Of course. She's the one responsible for you while you're here."

"And Charlie?"

"Yes."

A voicemail message from Rowena did not bode well. When it arrived, Charlie had been in class. She was always careful to turn her phone off because she required that all the students' phones be turned off during class. No exceptions. A tough stance, but anything softer led to disruptions of all kinds.

Once back in her office, she hit voicemail and listened to a very annoyed Rowena explain what Elizabeth and Julie had been up to.

Charlie waited to tell Sam about Elizabeth's plight until Greg was in bed. No sense letting Greg in on Elizabeth's fall from grace. He'd be ready to pile on.

Sam's first question was "Will this go on her driving record if and when she does get a license?"

"I have no idea. I'll text Rowena so she can ask that question when she goes to court with Elizabeth next Tuesday." Texting would be easier than having another conversation with Rowena. Throughout the first conversation, Charlie had the feeling Rowena believed that Elizabeth's behavior was somehow Charlie's fault. "Rowena's canceling her appointments to take Elizabeth to court."

"Are you going to call Elizabeth?"

"I will. It's too late tonight. I need to decide what to say and how to say it. I gather Grace fell apart and cried and, of course, Rowena played bad cop." Charlie explained about the community service and the fine. "I suspect that not being able to drive for another year will ultimately be the worst part."

"What'll happen to her friend?"

"Legally nothing, but Rowena called Julie's parents. I gather Julie's not going to have the use of her mother's car any time soon." She rubbed her neck, trying to ease the tension. "Thanks for listening. I need to enter some grades before I come to bed."

"I'll be awake," he kissed the top of her head.

Once Greg left for school the next morning, Charlie poured herself and Sam more coffee. "Let me know what you think of my idea."

"The one that got you up at dawn?"

"Yeah, that one. Sorry."

"I went back to sleep, no worry."

"Well, there's nothing I can do—directly—about what happens to

Elizabeth in court. Rowena can probably go up against a judge better than I can. The judge doesn't know what he's in for. Anyhow, I should talk to Elizabeth face-to-face about the adoption and her father—and, of course, the driving fiasco. I should've talked to her about everything before she left, and I need to introduce her to Andre." She hesitated. "And Andre to her. I can't hide from this any longer. My Spring Break is week after next," she stopped, "will you be here for Greg?"

"Yes, no trips planned."

"I guess I need to get all of this off my agenda. Though dealing with Rowena and Grace will not be fun, and the prospect of facing Andre with Elizabeth is—scaring the hell out of me."

Charlie was not so much afraid of Elizabeth's reaction to Andre, as what Andre's response would be. Then there were her long buried feelings about him. Would she revert to the twenty-three year old who let him take over her life? Or tell him how rotten he'd been.

"Will you tell her about his paying you to have an abortion?"

"I don't know."

"Are you staying with Grace?"

"No. I made a motel reservation. Neutral ground. It's a hard time for Grace right now. She doesn't need a guest. I'll put my itinerary on your phone before I go."

"Are you going to call him first?"

"Not sure. I don't have any clue what he's like now. I hope he's polite to her. I don't want him to hurt her like he hurt me."

She was afraid of that meeting. Not sure about Elizabeth's reaction or Andre's or her own feelings about him. Could she confidently confront him? For years, she'd convinced herself the entire episode was over, but injecting the teenage Elizabeth into Charlie's world had reopened feelings that proved she hadn't reached anything resembling closure.

"Do you want him to apologize?"

"To me?"

"And Elizabeth."

"I doubt he thinks he did anything wrong." Probably not the answer Sam was looking for.

CHAPTER 16

Tuesday night: After standing in front of the judge, I feel like the worst person on the planet. Aunt Rowena went to court with me after school. I was so nervous I couldn't think about anything else all day. The strange part was the judge didn't yell at me or anything. He seemed sort of bored about my case. Maybe he's had his fill of people who break the law. He just shook his head about me thinking the California Learner's Permit would be okay here; thank goodness he didn't give me any community service. That would be super embarrassing. There's still the fine for making an illegal right turn, a really expensive fine, and I can't apply for a driver's license until I'm eighteen.

Since all this happened, Grandma just looks at me and sighs, like I'm a disgrace to the family, but I'm really not part of her family anyway, so she doesn't have to worry what people will think.

Charlie's coming on Sunday. It's her Spring Break. I don't have time off until the week before Easter. She didn't sound mad, mostly concerned. Julie's parents won't let her hang out with me after school any more. Like their daughter can't have a friend who had to go to court or something. I know I was wrong but it was Julie's idea about the lessons. And Julie's halfway mad at me because she can't use her mother's car for two months. The way she's acting, I guess I won't be her cabin mate at camp this summer. Maybe I just won't go at all. Something else gone.

Once again, Charlie was at the McKinleyville airport. Since Sam was driving Greg and two other soccer players to a game in Ferndale, Tessa drove Charlie, parked in an open slot at the Departures curb and pulled the trunk lever. Charlie lifted her suitcase onto the sidewalk and raised the handle. "Thanks for the ride. I owe you."

"No problem. I have errands to run his morning. Jimmy's coming for a visit tomorrow."

Charlie was pretty sure Tessa was looking forward to Jimmy's visit more than Charlie was anticipating her days with Elizabeth, Grace and Rowena.

With a quick wave, Tessa drove off, and Charlie was on her own. She had no clear idea what she would say to Elizabeth or how they would confront Andre. Her mind refused to slow down, creating a variety of possible dialogues and responses. His *Facebook* site provided only minimal personal information: a fairly recent photo of him and his sons, Elizabeth's half brothers. An older Andre. Andre Gilbert Winslow, Ph.D., Born, May 8, 1961. Divorced. Degrees: BA from Yale, Ph.D. from Rutgers and a list of his publications. The comments the students posted were mostly positive. Not surprising. He was a compelling lecturer. Much too compelling.

Because Georgetown's break was two weeks away, he should be on campus now. She'd decided not to warn him. Blindsiding him would be more interesting. She'd always told herself she didn't want revenge, never wanted to look him in the eye and tell him he'd been cruel, but she'd been wrong. She wanted to see him squirm, if only for a moment.

The flight to Reagan National seemed endless. Sleeping was impossible, given the issues facing her once she landed. She'd told Grace she'd rent a car at the airport. *I'll eat on the way and check into the motel before coming over.*

It was close to eight o'clock when she reached Grace's house. Elizabeth answered the door, wearing leggings and a pink sweater that was perfect for her coloring. "Hi." No smile included.

"Hi. Sorry to be late. I forget what a mess the roads are around here."

"Grandma's in the living room."

Charlie hadn't seen Grace since her mother's funeral the summer Missy's family was in Provence. Grace was sitting in a dark blue rocking chair, a magazine in her lap, the TV tuned to the Food Network. The chair was almost too large for her. Charlie leaned over and kissed her cheek. "Thank you for looking after Elizabeth."

Grace studied Charlie, "Your hair is darker than it used to be. Are you coloring it?"

Not what Charlie expected but Grace always said what was on her mind at the moment. Her opinions, like Rowena's, unfiltered. A wonder that they tolerated each other.

"No color. I'm not out in the sun as much as I used to be. It rains a lot where I live." She really shouldn't have to apologize for her hair. Other crimes, yes. Awkward start.

"Maybe you should get some streaks."

Charlie chose not to respond. Grace could beat an unimportant subject to death.

"Is it okay if Elizabeth and I talk someplace—so we don't disturb you?" Better to talk without Grace putting in her two cents worth. Charlie had already decided not to discuss the driving episode with Elizabeth. Rowena had probably been hard enough on her.

Confronting Andre was more important.

Elizabeth half smiled, "Let's go to the kitchen," and turned into the hallway that led to the back of the house.

Following her, Charlie was once again grateful for Elizabeth's innate poise.

Over her shoulder, Elizabeth asked, "Do you want something to drink?"

The kitchen looked the same as it always had, stuck in the sixties—tile counters and yellow ochre cabinets—though the refrigerator was new. Charlie sat at the rectangular kitchen table, its finish showing wear. "Just water. If I drink any more coffee, I'll be awake all night."

Elizabeth pulled two bottles of water from the refrigerator and sat across from Charlie.

Waiting.

The ball was definitely in Charlie's court. It seemed to be there a lot lately.

She retrieved her iPad from her purse, turned it on, found Andre's *Facebook* page, and turned the tablet so Elizabeth could see it.

Finally, "I already looked at this." Of course Elizabeth would have thought to check Andre out online. "His sons look like him. How old are they?"

"Not exactly sure. Maybe 22 and 24."

"So they were in elementary school when you had sex with him."

"Yes."

"So he's divorced."

"Apparently."

"He's very good looking, even now."

Charlie had thought the same thing and was annoyed at herself for noticing the shape of his mouth, the lips that had been capable of making her lose all reason. She shouldn't notice or remember how those lips had felt on her skin. She loved Sam, who was everything Andre wasn't. Faithful, caring, supportive. With Andre there had been fireworks, drama. In cliché terms, she had been head over heels in love and lust—until the afternoon in the coffee house.

Elizabeth turned the iPad toward Charlie.

"What time do you get out of school tomorrow?"

"Ten after two."

Charlie mentally took a deep breath. "I thought we could go to Georgetown, find his office, and you can meet him."

"Are you going to tell him we're coming?"

"No."

"Oh."

"I don't want him to find an excuse to avoid us."

"Would he?"

The odds are good.

"Maybe."

"Okay. I'll be in my school uniform though."

"You don't need to be anyone but who you are."

Elizabeth sat with her hands folded on the table, chewing on her lower lip. "I think I'm scared."

"Yeah, me too."

"Does he know about me?"

"No."

Charlie could see Elizabeth processing that information, then "Did he want you to have an abortion?"

Elizabeth was too smart sometimes. No sense lying. "Yes."

"Why didn't you?"

"I couldn't do that."

"Then why didn't you keep me?"

Oh Damn. I don't have an answer that will make her feel better or hate me less.

"I was afraid."

And selfish.

"I don't think I could give my baby away."

"Let's hope you never have to make a decision like that. At your age, I would probably have felt the same way."

A dead end. *What ifs* were irrelevant. Charlie couldn't undo that part of her life—wasn't sure she would want to if given the chance for a do-over.

There was nothing to be gained by saying *I'm sorry. I'll try to make it up to you.* Because she couldn't make up for sixteen years. Besides, Elizabeth would probably never understand or forgive. Charlie just had to live with that. Right now, she needed to have the Andre soap opera scene behind her.

Driving back to the motel, she decided she'd make a dry run to Georgetown tomorrow before she met Elizabeth. She hadn't driven in D.C. for years and had never been on the Georgetown campus. She needed to know where his office was and what his office hours were.

Andre Winslow was not having a good Monday. Because his two-year old BMW had been rear-ended on Saturday while he was waiting at a stoplight, he'd spent half an hour on the phone with the insurance company. And then his ex-wife's lawyer had called to tell him Lee Ann was taking him back to court to make him pay for her medical insurance. The legal snarl of their divorce was at four years and counting. To reduce the alimony that Lee Ann had asked for, he'd given her his share of their Arlington home, which she promptly sold at a handsome profit. *It's too big for one person.* Because freelancing as a web designer did not provide her with medical benefits, they'd be back in court again. Andre's sons were pretty much on their own. His older son, Nick, was graduating from Georgetown Law School in June and had been offered an internship in North Carolina; Andre junior enlisted in the Marines right out of high school. Not a career choice Andre senior approved of, but he hadn't been consulted. And hanging over his own future was surgery on his left knee. Too many years on the tennis court.

Though his personal life was less than perfect, his professional life was solid. He was in his second year as Chairman of the Georgetown Humanities Department and, as a result of his critically acclaimed biography of John Donne, he had been invited to be the keynote speaker at the International Literature Conference in London in mid-June. His knee surgery would have to wait until he returned.

He'd left his tenured position at Northwestern six years ago when Georgetown came knocking on his door, following the publication of his Jonathon Swift book. Lee Ann had not welcomed the move. For years, she'd ignored, and even occasionally forgiven, his infidelities, but moving the family to the D.C. area, away from her own extended family, had finally eroded what was left of their marriage. Two years after the move and a week after Andre junior graduated from high school, Lee Ann moved out and served Andre with divorce papers. The process had been irritating and expensive but, at the same time, a relief. Though the rents in D.C. were high, his one bedroom condo was less than the mortgage on the Arlington house.

Ironically, once he was free to pursue women, the chase wasn't as intriguing as it had been when he was younger. His hair was threaded with gray, thinning a little. His beard completely gray, and his bad knee gave him a slight limp. Now that he was in his fifties, female students weren't all that interested in him, and women his age were—his age.

Being Department Chair had its perks: a designated parking space as well as an assistant to keep track of the paperwork, remind him of meetings, and deflect student complaints about their instructors. The downsides of the job were the endless administrative meetings, which typically accomplished little or nothing, having to fight for the Humanities' share of the budget or a new teaching position, and the idiosyncrasies of the other professors. It wasn't just the wrangling over specific classes and class times, *I can't teach before 10 a.m., I don't want to teach on Fridays,* it was also classroom issues. Because Dr. Sheridan couldn't tolerate drafts, he kept his classroom so warm that his students were constant visitors to Andre's office, complaining. Dr. Knudsen's time spent with New Age ideas during her graduate school days had made her overly sensitive to a classroom's *vibe* and only Room 114 passed her vibe test. Making up the semester schedule had all the charm of negotiating peace in the Middle East. Nevertheless, he didn't regret the move to Georgetown or the divorce. He was now free to do as he pleased.

One benefit—his relationship with Nick had improved since both were at Georgetown. Schedules permitting, they met for drinks late Friday afternoon. During the upcoming Easter Week, Nick was going skiing in New Hampshire. He'd invited his father but, until Andre's knee was repaired, skiing was a bad idea. At least he'd been invited.

The Humanities Department Meeting was scheduled for the second Monday of every month, typically starting at 3 p.m. and ending at 4 p.m. Today, the meeting had run late because of a disagreement over the criteria for evaluating the Graduate Assistants. At 4:20, Andre adjourned the meeting, which had turned into a shouting match, and headed for his office. He could expect more conversation about the evaluations tomorrow. Right now, all he wanted to do was pick up some paperwork and go to the gym to swim off the effects of the meeting and loosen up his bad knee. His assistant, Marjorie, was waiting for him outside his office door, wearing her coat and carrying her purse.

"You have two visitors in your office. A woman and a teenage girl."

"Did they have an appointment?" He'd checked his calendar before going to the meeting. It had been blank.

"No. But the woman says you'll remember her. Dr. Charlotte Ames. She's a Professor at Humboldt State in California."

Charlotte Ames.

Time stretched.

He remembered.

What in God's name was Charlotte doing here with a teenager?

Then he did the math and felt his mouth go dry.

"Do you know her?"

He only thought he'd been having a bad day.

"It's okay, Marjorie. Go on home." He didn't want anyone else witnessing this meeting.

When he walked into his office, Charlotte looked up quickly—her expression uncertain. At the same moment, the girl next to her looked at him deliberately, her wide-set eyes missed nothing as they scanned his face. If his math was right, she was probably sixteen or seventeen—slender, with dusky skin and rich black hair that tumbled around her shoulders.

He knew why Charlotte was here. Once he left Yale, he'd erased her and the pregnancy. During that semester at Yale, there had been plenty of willing female students, but Charlotte was special, worth risking the wrath of the university if they were caught. And Lee Ann was safely in Chicago. He wasn't exactly proud of the affair with Charlotte. Not apologetic either.

He didn't pause between the office door and his chair, needing to put the desk between him and his suddenly resurrected past as quickly as possible.

"This is unexpected." Total truth but not a particularly effective opening line.

"I suppose it is."

Andre couldn't decide what to say next, so he simply looked at Charlotte. She was still pretty, high cheekbones, the same amber eyes that had attracted him all those years ago. The sweet, slightly quizzical smile—though right now she was not smiling. He noticed her the first day of the spring semester class he'd taught at Yale. She sat in the back row, her hair much longer then, a single braid down her back. It was the intensity of those eyes, their total concentration as he explained the course content, that had captured his interest. All those years ago, neither of them could have imagined this moment.

After a few seconds, Charlotte sat up straighter, "Andre, this is Elizabeth. Our daughter. She asked to meet you."

At a loss for words, Andre moved his eyes to Elizabeth. What was there to say to someone who, he believed, had never been born? Did the girl know he'd sent Charlotte the money for an abortion? Just how much did she know about—everything? And why was she asking to meet him now?

If he said *Nice to meet you,* he'd be lying. This moment was anything but nice. It was profoundly disturbing. Did they want money? Which he had little of since the divorce. Did they want help enrolling Elizabeth at the university? That he could do.

"You're here just to meet me?"

Elizabeth answered calmly. "Yes. I've recently learned that you and Charlie are my birth parents. I wanted to see you in person."

Well-spoken. A bit of a Virginia accent. No hint of coming after him. He relaxed slightly.

"Where do you live?"

"Vienna, Virginia. For this semester, I'm living with my grandmother. Or who I thought was my grandmother. She's actually my great aunt. My adoptive parents died last summer."

So close to Georgetown. "Where do you go to school?" A safe go-to question when he didn't know what else to say to students.

"The Vienna Academy, except for a semester in California."

Which meant she'd been with Charlotte. He was trying to piece together the scenario.

"How did your parents die?"

For the next twenty minutes, Elizabeth calmly explained about the crash and the guardianship, Arcata, her discovery that she was Charlie's child, and her move back to Virginia.

A lot for him to digest.

Charlotte had brought Elizabeth's birth certificate and the adoption papers in case he didn't believe that Elizabeth was his. This morning he'd been the father of two; this afternoon he was the father of three.

If he and Lee Ann were still married, she'd have a field day with this revelation. Still might.

CHAPTER 17

In spite of herself, Charlie had to admire the way Andre adjusted to the sudden reality of having a teenage daughter—without losing his balance. His poise mirrored the poise Elizabeth often displayed. She certainly hadn't learned equanimity from Missy, who had never been smooth or calm in unsettling situations. Was there a DNA marker for staying cool when your world was reconfiguring itself?

Several years ago, someone coined the term *boomerang kids*. Charlie, Andre and Elizabeth were a *boomerang family*. They'd spent all of Elizabeth's life going their separate ways, only to end up together in Andre's office at 5 p.m. on a Monday in March.

Charlie stayed out of the conversation between her ex-lover and their daughter, preferring to watch and listen. All of them were in uncharted territory—a nuclear family that had never been a family. Never would be. Andre was still charming and handsome, even with creases in his face and gray in his hair. Seeing Elizabeth with him, no one could miss the resemblance. Their hair, eyes, and skin tone.

Other than her family, no one had known Charlie's secret—that she'd borne a child and willingly given her away without looking back. How had she done that? Was she so cold-hearted that she could walk away from Elizabeth and get on with her plans as though the nine months she'd carried her had had no effect on her. She was afraid the answer just might be *yes*.

As though things weren't complicated enough, Elizabeth's reappearance in Charlie's life was fraying her relationship with Sam. He'd believed he knew her—but once he figured out who Elizabeth was, knew some of what had happened, he retreated a little. He still had Charlie's back, and they were working together to manage their new, cobbled-together family, but she knew her secret had shaken his trust. If she could keep so enormous a secret from him, from the man who loved her, what other secrets did she have?

She'd never trusted anyone with her past because she hadn't trusted herself to confront it.

Now she was confronting it anyway.

From far away, "Charlotte, did you hear me?"

Andre and Elizabeth were looking at her. "Would you and Elizabeth have dinner with me tonight?"

Charlie turned to Elizabeth. "What about homework?"

"Just calculus. Maybe an hour's worth. I did some of it in class."

Andre didn't hide his surprise. "You're taking calculus?"

"I like math and music."

"Amazing. You certainly didn't get the math gene from me or Charlotte."

Charlie was briefly grateful he hadn't said *your mother*. Elizabeth wasn't ready for that phrase. "Maybe we could find someplace close. We have to drive back to Vienna."

Andre stood. "The roads will be clearer in an hour or so. There's a good diner a block from campus. We can walk." Though his knee would not be happy.

Charlie hadn't expected that this meeting with Andre would be anything more than one meeting. Yet the three of them were going to dinner. Elizabeth seemed comfortable with his invitation. Charlie, however, wasn't at all certain she should be letting Andre take charge of this—this situation. But that's what he'd always done. Like some sort of Pied Piper. He led while she—and now Elizabeth—followed. The scenario Charlie envisioned had already been rewritten.

It was nearly dark as they crossed the Georgetown campus spread along the bluff above the town itself; the massive gray stone buildings imitating European architecture were silhouetted in the twilight. Walking ahead of Charlie, Andre was giving Elizabeth an abridged history of the university. His charisma had not dimmed. Here she was, a reluctant third wheel as father and daughter were tentatively connecting with one another.

Neither Charlie nor Elizabeth said anything during the forty-five minute drive to Vienna. Each processing *the Andre encounter* but neither willing to share her thoughts. As Andre predicted, the traffic had cleared out, and they arrived at Grace's just before eight o'clock. Charlie parked at the curb. "You'll need to tell your grandmother about tomorrow. She may not approve."

"I'll just say that you'll pick me up at school so I can visit his class and that he'll call her to make arrangements to meet her soon. She'll be okay as long as you're taking me."

Clearly Elizabeth had no clue that Grace was not Charlie's biggest fan.

Phone numbers and email addresses had been exchanged during dinner. This whole connecting process was racing ahead too quickly. Andre and Elizabeth seemed eager to spend more time with each other. Admittedly, the dinner had been okay, and Charlie had relaxed a little. But giving Andre easy access to Elizabeth, once she returned to California, frightened her.

Elizabeth unlocked the passenger door. "Thanks. For taking me."

"You're welcome."

"He's quite easy to talk to and didn't seem bothered when he found out about me."

"He was always charming." Now he's charming you. Dangerous territory.

"Did he charm you?"

Elizabeth wasn't afraid to ask hard questions.

"Big time. You're here, aren't you?"

After s few seconds, "Same time tomorrow?"

"Yes. We'll have to get directions to the lecture hall."

Charlie waited until Elizabeth was inside the house before driving away, eager to get back to her room and stand in the shower for an hour or two until her brain stopped deconstructing the evening. And then call Sam.

After Charlie's call, Sam wasn't sure whether he should be worried—correction, more worried than he already was—about Charlie's reunion with Elizabeth's father. His reasonable side understood that Elizabeth's request had set this encounter in motion. Charlie had promised to make the introduction and, if Charlie promised something to a student, a friend, or Sam, she did everything she could to fulfill that obligation. However, this promise involved the bastard who'd seduced her and then dumped her when she got pregnant.

Sam had assumed there'd be one meeting. *Hello/goodbye, have a nice life.* But now they'd also had dinner and there would be a second meeting so Elizabeth could watch him lecture. Charlie hadn't mentioned whose idea that had been. If it was Elizabeth's, Sam could see that she would be curious, wanting to see him in action. If it was Andre's, then he probably wanted to show off, which fit the picture Sam had of him. Sam told himself he was not jealous. Just worried.

And because they were meeting again on Tuesday, Charlie had changed her Wednesday flight to Thursday so, on Wednesday, Andre could be introduced to Grace and Rowena. Elizabeth arranged the meeting and wanted Charlie to be there.

Charlie sounded exhausted. He'd wanted to ask how she felt about seeing Andre. The *felt* was important. Had her attraction to him resurfaced. A spark maybe? As much as Sam's heart needed her to tell him about her feelings, he knew full well how difficult it was for her to share them.

He also knew his distrust of Andre was connected to his own past with Diane. Her pregnancy had set Sam on a path he hadn't been ready for. A path Andre sidestepped without penalty. A dozen years later, Sam was sure he hadn't loved Diane, but the fact of a child had pushed the marriage, as Diane had known it would. And he, fool that he'd been, had fallen into a trap older than time. She'd pulled him into marriage and, when marriage no longer suited her, pushed him out. And Greg was paying the price of a broken family. Since Greg had been in Arcata, Sam was learning he was actually a fairly good father, albeit out of practice and, little by little, he and Greg were learning to be father and son. Letting Greg teach him how to play *Quantum* something-or-other had helped. They at least had something to talk about other than Greg's homework and soccer.

Friday night: It's been a strange and amazing week. I met my birth father on Monday. Andre Winslow, Dr. Winslow. Instead of being Elizabeth Enright, I might have been Elizabeth Winslow. Even though he's in his mid-fifties, he's very good looking and charming and interesting. Monday we went to a funky diner full of university students and had hamburgers and fries. We both like hot mustard and ordered our hamburgers medium rare. He puts ranch dressing on his fries. Gross. He drank some sort of beer called Guinness. It's really weird to be sitting at a table with a new set of parents.

On Tuesday, Charlie and I attended his Seventeenth Century Literature class. He was lecturing on John Donne. I have no idea who that is. I need to google him. Charlie and I sat in the back of a lecture hall that was half full—maybe 70 students. He's like a performer and yet he provides lots of information. My dad's job had something to do with finance and I couldn't ever see what he did because it was mostly on the computer or meeting with clients.

After class, we went to dinner again. An Irish pub. He has expensive clothes. Slacks and tweedy sport jackets. Charlie came with me both times, but I bet she's not happy about being with him. They don't say much to each other.

And on Wednesday evening, he came over to Grandma's to meet her and Aunt Rowena. Charlie was there too. I sort of felt sorry for her because no one said much to her. She has dark circles under her eyes like maybe she's not sleeping. I'm glad she hasn't given me trouble about the driving thing or about staying here with Grandma. But I'm still mad at her. Grandma was polite to Andre—that's what I call him—but I could tell she doesn't exactly trust him. When he asked if he could maybe see me on Sundays when we are both free, Rowena told him yes but that she and Grandma would want to know where we're going and how long we'd be gone. No one asked Charlie what she thought.

So this Sunday, we're going to the Holocaust Museum and maybe my half brother Nick will come too. I've never been there. Mom said I was too young but that was a couple years ago. Having a brand new father is okay so far. If I'd stayed in Arcata, I wouldn't have had the opportunity to spend time with him and his sons. I now have two brothers. How neat is that!

Charlie left yesterday. I overheard Rowena telling her that Grandma is thinking about selling her house because it's too much to take care of. I don't know what that means for me. But right now, I'm studying for the SAT test and getting to know my new family.

During Andre and Nick's regular Friday meeting at *il Canale* in Georgetown, Elizabeth was the primary topic of conversation. Understandably, Nick was shocked that he had a half-sister.

"Does Mom know?"

"God, no. And please don't tell her." Infidelity was one thing, an unexpected daughter was an entirely different thing.

Nick rolled his eyes, Andre's eyes. "I'm not stupid. So what's she like? How old?"

"Seventeen." Andre guessed his son was doing the math.

"Was that the time you were teaching at Yale?"

Andre nodded. Nick had been seven, Andre junior almost five.

Again, "What's she like? Pretty?" A major requirement for Nick's girlfriends.

"In a teenager kind of way, yes. My hair, my eyes, dusky skin. Tall. Her mother's smile. I gather she's smart. Except for last semester, she's attended The Vienna Academy since first grade. It has a good reputation."

"So you thought the mother had an abortion?"

Andre nodded. "I gave her the money but never checked to see whether she had gone to the clinic."

"And?"

"She let her cousin adopt her. Those parents died in a plane crash last summer. In their wills, they made Elizabeth's birth mother her guardian." Andre filled in the few details he had about why Elizabeth was back in Vienna and then ordered more beer. It had been a stressful week, and pretending it wasn't stressful had taken a toll. At the same time, he was pleased with Elizabeth. A daughter who wanted to get acquainted. Pretty and smart. Not a giggly airhead.

"I had to go make nice with the great-aunt and a younger aunt on her father's side who, I bet, is going to be watching me very closely."

Nick finished his beer and signaled the waiter for the check. "I can tell you're enjoying having a grown-up daughter who probably thinks you're wonderful. All the tiresome, basic parenting is done. You get to be the fun parent."

Not a compliment.

Andre eyed his son. "You know me all too well."

"True."

"I let your mother be the bad cop with you boys and look how well you turned out."

Nick laid cash for his share of the bill on the table. "I have a date in an hour."

"Who?"

"Someone new. Her name's Jessica; she's a paralegal."

"Serious?"

"You know better than that. Too soon."

"Just don't be me."

"Too late. And yeah, I'll meet you and Elizabeth at the museum Sunday. I'm curious."

CHAPTER 18

For the time being, nobody was parenting Elizabeth.

Grace was gradually reevaluating what she should do with her life. Without question, she missed Kevin, but she didn't miss being his caregiver. It had been a long, long year. She was finally able to sleep through the night and didn't have worry whether he'd be okay on his own if she went to the grocery store for an hour.

Except for the driving episode with Julie, Elizabeth was no trouble. She mostly took care of herself and enjoyed cooking for the two of them but, now that Grace was feeling better, she was re-thinking the future, and Elizabeth's presence was a bit of a problem. One of Grace's long-time friends had recently moved to a senior housing complex on Florida's Gulf Coast and was encouraging Grace to join her. *You'll love it. You can go back to playing golf.* So the weekend Elizabeth went on the school-sponsored ski trip to New Hampshire, Grace flew to Pensacola to visit her friend and, even though Rowena had lectured her about making any rash moves so soon after Kevin's death, decided to put herself on the waiting list for one of the two-bedroom condo units, then applied for a membership at the golf club.

As soon as Grace returned from Florida, she hired her neighbor's grandson to help clean out the attic and garage, while she and Elizabeth concentrated on the kitchen and closets. Time to get rid of a lifetime of possessions she no longer had use for. Downsizing felt good.

Andre didn't see the time he spent with Elizabeth as actual parenting. Genetically, he was her parent, but true parenting involved more than a matching DNA. He liked her, enjoyed impressing her. They'd spent two Sundays together, first at the Holocaust Museum, along with Nick, and the next Sunday at a Wolf Trap matinee. The third weekend, she'd gone skiing with school friends and the weekend after that she took the SAT. He called her late that Sunday to ask how she felt about the test.

"I can't tell. My brain is fried."

"How about lunch next Sunday? We could take a look at possibilities for colleges."

"That would be great." Some of her friends already knew where they wanted to go. Elizabeth had no idea.

The next morning, Andre put Marjorie to work researching scholarships and entry requirements for top-rated, four-year institutions. Elizabeth's high school grades would be a plus and she would probably receive good SAT scores. This kind of parenting he could handle. At least on a temporary basis.

Rowena had never been interested in parenting or, for that matter, taking care of a husband. She preferred being the family watchdog, keeping an eye on Grace and advancing Elizabeth the money to pay the traffic ticket. She disapproved of Grace's rush to sell the house and move to Florida. Much too soon. Grace was, of course, stubbornly ignoring her advice, yet Rowena had to admit she was looking better and had more energy. Last summer, Rick and Missy's sudden deaths had forced Rowena into mini-parenting to get Elizabeth settled. But Elizabeth hadn't stayed settled, and Rowena was probably going to have to alert Charlotte about Grace's plans to move to Florida.

Charlie was parenting at a distance—if exchanging a few texts per week with Elizabeth qualified as parenting. On the other hand, texting was better than not communicating at all. To fill the gaps between texts, there were emails from Rowena, telling her that Grace was heading for Florida as soon as the house sold. A condo had become available. Emails from Andre alerted her that he and Elizabeth were discussing topnotch East Coast universities. No surprise. He was still an intellectual snob.

Strangely enough, Elizabeth didn't seem to be angry with him—just with Charlie.

The weeks following her return from Virginia had been a mixed bag. There was a brief flurry on the Humboldt campus when it looked like the CSU professors statewide would go on strike because the contract talks were at an impasse. Fortunately, both sides resumed negotiations, and the flurry subsided. At the end of April, Tessa's son was released from rehab and promptly disappeared. Tessa and her husband drove to San Francisco to see whether he'd returned to the life that had originally put him in rehab, but none of those friends knew where Jimmy was or they were covering for him. Tessa was understandably distraught and not in the mood to listen to Charlie's problems with Elizabeth. *At least you know where Elizabeth is.*

In the plus column, Greg had turned thirteen and, instead of being victimized by his teenage hormones, he'd begun to settle into Arcata. He and Sam had been planning to hike fifty miles of the John Muir trail the last week in July, but Greg's pending move to Spain in June canceled their plans. Greg seemed sincerely disappointed. Sam was not only disappointed but ready to give Diane a piece of his mind. Not that his ranting would change anything.

The biggest cloud on Charlie's horizon was the state of things between her and Sam. Not open conflict, more an intangible distance, going through the motions rather than really enjoying each other's company. And sex. When she came back from Virginia, Sam had asked a lot of questions about Andre, which she had tiptoed around even though she had nothing to hide. She simply felt strange talking about him. She wasn't attracted to him, at least not sexually. But he was still handsome and interesting, and he was paying attention to Elizabeth. Now Rowena wanted Charlie to come back to discuss Elizabeth's living arrangements because Grace would soon be in Florida.

Another trip that might involve Andre would not set well with Sam.

Sam was in full parenting mode, grateful that he and Greg were on better terms. Eager to keep it that way. He missed Elizabeth though he'd been her friend, not a parent. He worried that her birth father might capture her affections and keep her in Virginia.

The one time he'd asked Charlie if she thought Andre would want Elizabeth to live with him, she'd quickly dismissed the idea. *I wouldn't let that happen. He has a short attention span. Right now he's on a parenting honeymoon. At the first sign of real responsibility, he'll run for the hills.*

And now that Charlie was planning to go back to Virginia when the semester ended, Sam's discomfort moved up a notch.

Because Missy and Rick's parenting had been at once supportive and open-handed, Elizabeth didn't see that she needed much more parenting. Once she turned eighteen, she would be considered an adult and would be given a small portion of her trust. She believed she knew right from wrong, knew that she'd soon have to make her own way in the world. Scary but inevitable. She felt older and wiser than her friends, most of whom still lived with one or both of their parents. None of them came with a new set—albeit the original set—of parents. At this point, Andre and Charlie seemed extraneous, but pragmatism dictated that she needed a place to live. And someone legally able to sign documents for her.

May: The semester is almost over and I've hardly had time to write in this diary since I've been at Grandma's. When I bought this notebook, I thought I'd write in it all the time.

I'll start with the most important stuff. I like my birth father though, if he were truly fathering, I might not like him as much. My half-brother Nick (I like the idea of a brother, even half a one) told me that Andre hadn't spent much time with him and his brother when they were young. They see one another more now since they're at the same university. I wonder what Andre's ex-wife is like. It's hard to think of Charlie as the other woman. And I'm the product of that. Puts a strange spin on my story. Are girl babies bastards?

Andre and I have been looking at the information on colleges and scholarships. The trust my parents left will cover a lot but not everything. College is really, really expensive. And there's the whole in state and out of state thing with public universities. I have to establish residency someplace. Andre looks down on public institutions like the University of Virginia or Humboldt, where Charlie teaches.

Until I get my SAT results, I can't do much. I'll need to apply for scholarships before I do anything else. I think I'd like to major in music education or maybe math. Andre can't imagine any other major than something in the liberal arts. I like to read but that would be reading on demand. No fun.

I emailed Mr. Hannigan to find out about schools with good music programs. My voice would be my instrument. I'd need to learn to play something else, probably the piano. Mr. Hannigan sent back a list. Most of the schools he suggested are private, like Pepperdine in California or the University of Miami, which is where he went. I sent off for information on both of them but didn't tell Andre. He only wants me to look at important East Coast schools.

The good news is that Julie has stopped hating me, maybe because she couldn't find anyone else to room with at camp this summer. We're both going to be counselors this year. I'm doing little kid crafts and Julie's teaching beginning swimming so we probably won't see much of each other anyway. I can't believe she's been so mean.

Camp runs from mid-June to mid-July. Then I don't know what I'm going to do. Grandma is listing the house next week and Charlie is coming the last of this month to talk about—everything. I'm pretty sure Andre doesn't want me to live with him, and Rowena would drive me as nuts as I'd drive her. So that leaves boarding at the academy or going back to Charlie's. I guess I'm not as mad at her as I was. I'm not angry with Andre and, let's face it, he tried to kill me so I probably don't have much of a case against Charlie.

CHAPTER 19

The last Sunday in May, Andre picked Elizabeth up just before ten o'clock. Each time he came for his daughter, he brought Grace a small bouquet of spring flowers. Nothing elaborate, just pretty and grandmotherly. Grace always beamed when he handed them to her. He had that effect on women of all ages, and he wasn't averse to using it.

At Elizabeth's request, they were driving to Charlottesville to look at the University of Virginia campus. Because all their college research had been online, she wanted to see a campus in person, imagine herself as a student living there. Andre wasn't in favor of UVA but, since that was where Charlie did her undergraduate work, Elizabeth was adamant about visiting it. He was discovering that, on some topics, his daughter could be very determined. He stopped short of using the word stubborn.

They ate lunch a few blocks from the campus. While they were waiting for their hamburgers, Elizabeth reached into her purse and laid a sheaf of papers in front of him. "This month it's free to go on *Ancestry. com,* so I researched your family tree.

I did it for Charlie's family too. I want to know where I come from. Charlie and my mother's backgrounds have some similarities, but yours is brand new. I asked Charlie if you were French, because of your name, but she didn't know. Now I know. You're French-Canadian so that makes me French-Canadian too. Do you speak French? I've been studying French in school. My parents, my other parents, rented a time share one summer in Provence."

Reading from the chart she'd printed out, "Your mother was named

Emilie Marie Devereaux. She was born in Montreal in 1939, and she died at Saranac, New York, in 2005. Do you have pictures of her?"

He shook his head. "My sister Renee might. I've never kept mementoes like that."

"Even though he's American, does your father speak French too?"

"No. My mother spoke to us in French when we were little, and my father spoke to us in English. Renee and I were totally bilingual for a while. My French is rusty, but I can still read and understand it so long as the person speaks slowly. Canadian French is a little different from Parisian French."

"Where does your sister live?"

"In some god-forsaken west Texas town. Instead of finishing college, she married a cattle rancher. They have three sons who live for football."

"Where's your father?" Elizabeth was rather pleased to have a new aunt and another grandfather. And three cousins.

"Still in Saranac. He didn't remarry after my mother died."

"Do you see him often? Can I meet him? What does he do?"

"He owns a bar." Andre rarely admitted that to any of his university colleagues. Not exactly ashamed of his beginnings—not proud either.

Her enthusiasm was pushing him in ways he wasn't ready for. Spending time with Elizabeth was one thing, pulling in the whole family quite another. Driving to upstate New York was not enticing. He'd never been much on family and all the required togetherness. When he and Lee Ann were living in Chicago, her large family had cluttered up their lives, constantly in and out of one another's houses.

"I always wished I had a large family. Cousins and siblings. My mother, Missy, was an only child and my father has two sisters, one lives in Europe and has a daughter older than me. I hardly know them. Rowena never married. I don't think she likes men. Maybe she's a lesbian." She stopped to take a bite of her hamburger. When Andre didn't respond, she continued with her mouth full. "Now I have another family," she sighed, "but I wish I still had my parents too."

When Grace inquired about the visit to the University of Virginia, Elizabeth's only comment was "Too many columns."

"What do you mean?"

"The buildings all look like the architect was frightened by a Greek temple."

"So you don't want to go there?"

"No, I just wanted to see a campus other than Georgetown and see where Charlie went." Elizabeth wasn't sure why she was interested in seeing something from Charlie's past. She'd hinted to Andre that she'd also like to see Yale, see where her new parents had met, but he said the drive was too far for an afternoon.

"What do you and Andre have planned for next Sunday?"

"Don't know."

"Charlotte called an hour ago. She'd like you to call her back tonight. She's coming here next week. I told her she should stay with us this time. It seems Rowena's been emailing her about your college finances and your living arrangements after I move."

Elizabeth took a handful of grapes from the bowl on the kitchen table and went up to her room. She wished her grandmother had waited another year to move. But of course the universe currently governing Elizabeth's life refused to cooperate. She was enjoying her Sundays with Andre, though he'd be in London the middle of June and then he'd be having knee surgery. She'd be at camp anyway. And by the end of July, she'd probably have to go back to California. She consoled herself with the fact that she'd survived this difficult year. One more year and she'd be an adult. Allowed to choose for herself.

When the call from Elizabeth ended, Charlie joined Sam in the garage where he was installing new brakes on his bike. As she entered, he laid the small wrench he was using on the workbench. "What'd you two talk about?"

"Her schedule for the next week or so. She's leaving for the camp in Maine the second Sunday in June. Julie's mother is driving them up."

"How long does the camp last?"

"Four weeks. And since she and Andre don't have anything specific planned for next Sunday, I'll go Friday, maybe come back Wednesday. I need to set up an appointment with Donovan to talk about the trust. Unless Elizabeth gets scholarships, there might not be enough to cover her college fees. I haven't paid enough attention to the trust finances. Her return to Virginia was an unexpected expense. And I have no idea what this camp costs."

Sam washed his hands in the small laundry tub. "Any ice cream left or did Greg inhale all of it?"

"There's some of the Peach Parfait. He avoids flavors with *things* in them—like peach bits." Back in the kitchen, she placed the half-gallon on the table between them and handed him a spoon. "Not often we're able to do this anymore since we aren't supposed to teach the younger generation our bad habits."

Sam wanted to stay on topic. "If Andre and Elizabeth do something on Sunday will you join them?"

Charlie shrugged, "Depends on whether I'm invited. They seem to be enjoying their outings, though Elizabeth wasn't impressed with the UVA campus. Too many columns."

Sam chuckled, "She's good at calling 'em as she sees them. I've never been there."

"Actually, she's right but I didn't tell her that."

"Did Andre like it?" Sam kept pulling him back into the conversation.

"Probably not. He's big on Ivy League schools. Right now, he's not pushing her, but I bet he will when it's closer to decision time."

"So if they go visit another campus, will you go with them?"

Charlie heard subtle worry in his question. Maybe jealousy. She licked her spoon clean and set it on a napkin. "I don't know." She suspected Sam wanted her to say *No*. "If Elizabeth wants me to, I will. The fact that we just had a civilized phone conversation is a sign of progress. I don't want to step on that. If she comes back here next year, we need to be able to get along."

"I understand that, but I'd rather you didn't spend time with him." If she could fall in love with Andre once, what was to prevent her falling again? And this time he was single.

Charlie felt a twinge of annoyance. Sam wasn't usually given to telling her what to do—not so directly anyway. "I'm not about to jump into bed with him. The first time I did that didn't end well." Her response was probably too snappish.

He pushed his chair back just a little. "I didn't say you would." But the possibility kept wandering around his thoughts.

"What then?"

"He hurt you once. I don't want that to happen again. It's kept you from trusting people, trusting me. Not telling me you'd given a child up for adoption. Waiting months to tell me Elizabeth was yours."

Now she heard irritation, not quite anger. It wasn't that he was wrong; he wasn't. But hiding from her mistakes was an old habit—a safe haven—and Sam was calling her on it. Not telling him had been a major miscalculation.

"I apologized."

"I know."

"But it wasn't enough?"

He didn't answer.

"Why are you still upset with me?"

"Because I love you, I love the way we were. But we're not in that place anymore."

He made it sound like the change was all her fault.

He was studying his spoon as though it had an answer. Sam was clearly having trouble talking through the problem. Now of all times!

To end the uneasy silence that settled over the table, she returned the ice cream carton to the freezer and went to make her plane reservation. Maybe she'd stay the whole week. It might be more comfortable there than here. She could help Elizabeth get ready for camp or help Grace.

And yes, she was avoiding the problems between her and Sam.

No sooner had she made the plane reservation, than Sam was notified he was again needed at Merritt Island.

"When?"

"A week from Monday, the day after Greg leaves for Spain." A good thing Diane's mother would be accompanying Greg; otherwise Sam would have been making the trip. It was too far to send Greg by himself.

"How long?"

"Through July, maybe longer. I'll be evaluating the restoration project, and I'll be overseeing the wildlife count so they know how successful all the work has been. Summer is busier at Merritt than it is here because of tourists visiting the Space Center."

Charlie couldn't think of anything to say or anything else to ask. They'd be apart for two months. Last summer, her trip to London had kept them apart five weeks. And with each of them flying back and forth across the country this year, it seemed as though they'd been apart more than they'd been together. Assuming she and Sam could spend more time together this summer, she'd passed on teaching a Summer Session class at the university. Now she'd be alone until August. Before Sam entered her life, she'd never minded being alone.

Eleven days later, Sam flew to Florida and, the same afternoon, Charlie flew back to Arcata. Not seeing him before he left wasn't intentional—that was what she told herself anyway. They'd talked every day but weren't talking about what each of them was thinking, worrying about. She was careful not to mention her Wednesday dinner with Andre because Sam had sounded annoyed about her and Elizabeth accompanying Andre to the Sunday matinee at Wolf Trap.

As it turned out, she had a valid reason for staying in Virginia beyond Wednesday because the only time she could get an appointment with Donovan was late Friday afternoon. They reviewed the year's expenditures and speculated about what would be necessary for the coming year. If Elizabeth chose to do her senior year in Virginia, she'd have to board at the school because Grace's house would undoubtedly sell before summer ended. If Elizabeth returned to Arcata, expenses would be much lower so, when she turned eighteen in January, there might be money for a used car.

Since Rick and Missy had begun saving for Elizabeth's education, the cost of attending college had exploded. There was perhaps enough in the trust for a public institution, but certainly not enough for a private one. Hopefully, she'd receive a scholarship or two. If she had to resort to student loans, she'd be in debt when she graduated. Charlie didn't have much in her savings; buying her house had pretty much cleaned her out. Even with Sam sharing the mortgage payments, rebuilding her savings was a slow process.

Saturday, Charlie and Grace spent the day getting Elizabeth ready for camp. Last minute shopping, packing, and fielding phone calls from Julie. Early Sunday morning, Julie and her mother collected Elizabeth for the drive north. On Monday, Charlie drove herself to Reagan, turned in the rental car, and spent most of the flight to Arcata revisiting the events of the previous week.

Especially the oddly pleasant evening with Andre. On Wednesday, Elizabeth and Julie had been invited to a birthday party for a classmate, so Andre suggested Charlie join him for dinner to discuss Elizabeth.

Charlie's *Yes* was admittedly tentative. Andre frowned, "It's just dinner, Charlotte."

Good point. What was she afraid of? The worst had already happened years ago. Her second *Yes* was firmer. She wanted to show him he hadn't hurt her, that he had no power over her. But each time they were together, she wasn't certain about the whole power thing. She dressed carefully, choosing a long white cotton skirt and a sleeveless teal tunic. The rain had ended and the evening air was heavily warm, the dampness making her hair curl slightly.

Sitting across the table from him was more *déjà vu* than she expected. He held her chair, ordered a bottle of the house red—once her favorite, though it wasn't now—and waited patiently while she read the menu. His charm was still hard to ignore. The young hostess had blushed prettily when he greeted her by name and asked for a table by a window. Clearly, this wasn't his first visit to the restaurant.

Once they'd ordered—veal parmesan for her, pasta primavera for him—Charlie wasn't sure what to say. She sipped her wine and took one of the bruschetta from the basket the waitress left on the table when she brought the wine.

Andre finally asked, "How far is this camp she's going to?"

"It's west of Bangor. In miles, I'm not sure. According to Julie, it's an all day drive. Her mother will stay overnight in the parents' quarters and drive back Monday."

"Do you know anything about the camp?"

She shook her head. "I'm sure Missy checked it out thoroughly. I wouldn't know what questions to ask." In truth, it hadn't occurred to her to check on it. She wasn't good at getting ahead of the parenting curve.

That topic was going nowhere. He tried again, "Tell me about your cousin, Elizabeth's other parents."

Interesting. He was thinking of himself as Elizabeth's parent. That hadn't taken long. Charlie was still having trouble with the word *parent*. And *mother* wasn't in her vocabulary.

"Fairly comfortable financially. Not wealthy, though Rick's parents owned a successful stud farm near Appomattox. Rick and his sisters sold it when Rick's father passed away. Maybe a decade ago. Rick worked for a major mutual fund, so there was plenty of money for a private school and summer camps and vacations abroad. Elizabeth had advantages I probably couldn't have managed. Missy was a stay at home mom."

"No other children?"

"They couldn't conceive."

"Did you know Elizabeth joined *Ancestry.com* and is researching my ancestry and yours. She knows more about my parents and grandparents than I do."

"When she was in Arcata, she was putting the pictures Missy and Rick had saved into a scrapbook. I guess she's trying to figure out who she is."

"Did she know she was adopted—before?"

Charlie nodded. "Missy said Elizabeth wasn't curious about—us."

"It feels strange to have a grown daughter I didn't know about. Not bad, mind you. Just strange."

Their meals arrived to fill the silence that kept returning. Charlie wondered whether she should point out that he had known about the baby but didn't want it. And she then did.

He didn't respond, so Charlie shifted to easier topics.

"She's quite self-possessed, unlike Missy, who was given to flying apart. Did Elizabeth tell you about her traffic ticket? I think it's the first time she's ever been in trouble for much of anything."

"She did. I laughed. Let's face it wasn't much of a stumble, but she was quick to tell me it wasn't funny at all. I guess her aunt came down a bit hard."

"Not surprising. Rowena's tough but she's at least helped with Elizabeth this last year."

"Did you have contact with Elizabeth before last summer?"

"No. I wanted it that way."

"Were you ever curious?"

Charlie considered the question. Then. "No. I didn't let myself think about the adoption. I buried everything from that time." She added wine from the carafe to her glass. The conversation was entering difficult territory.

"And me."

"Especially you." Her voice was suddenly firm.

"Probably good that you did."

For a moment, she thought he was going to apologize. But of course he didn't.

"Do you mind my seeing her?"

She did, but was reluctant to admit it. "As long as she's comfortable."

"If she goes back to California, could I visit? Or could she come here?"

"Not California, but maybe Rowena would let her visit."

"I'm guessing your boyfriend wouldn't be too happy having me in town."

So Elizabeth had told him about Sam.

"He would not." No sense lying about Sam's discomfort.

Twilight was softening the city as they drove to Grace's. More silence. He parked in front of the house and walked around to open her door.

When they were on the front porch, "When do you leave for London?"

"Next week."

"Quite an honor."

"Yes. And two weeks after I return, I'm having surgery on my knee."

"Thanks for dinner."

"Thanks for letting me get to know Elizabeth." He sounded sincere.

"Her choice." *Not mine*

Before she could stop him, he leaned in to kiss her cheek. "Stay well."

As the car drove away, she was still standing on the porch, her cheek remembering his touch. Not necessarily a good sign.

CHAPTER 20

Because texting to and from Spain was cheaper than calling, Sam had revised the phone plan he and Greg shared. And within the first forty-eight hours that Greg was in Madrid, he'd sent a dozen messages.

"It's 2 hot."

Living in Northern California and Oregon had not prepared him for non-stop hot and dry.

"G and Mom arguing."

No surprise. Diane argued with everyone.

"Nothing 2 do. Internet slow."

Perhaps Arcata was looking better.

For the most part, Greg hadn't been exposed to cultures or countries other than his own, so strange food, a language he didn't understand, and having a new stepfather were probably stretching his coping skills. Sam could sympathize about the weather. The heat and humidity of Florida's east coast were already making him long for the temperate breezes in Arcata.

He missed Charlie but was no longer certain about their relationship. Where it was going. The summer she was in London, he'd bought an engagement ring and was ready to propose. But after Elizabeth and Greg arrived, the time to give her the ring hadn't been quite right. Especially once doubt and jealousy showed up.

Their daily phone conversations tended to focus on practical rather than romantic matters. Forwarding his personal mail, the bills, shared and separate, most of which were paid online. She told him about Elizabeth's departure to Maine. The meeting with Donovan. The possibility that Elizabeth would come back to Arcata. The three offers on Grace's house.

The phone conversations didn't allow Sam to look into her eyes, to read her face when she talked about Andre so he could gauge her feelings about Elizabeth's father.

Much of his world was out of joint. He'd just begun to have a decent connection with Greg, only to have him a world away and, once again, under Diane's influence. And he and Charlie were not in sync. Admittedly, he was jealous. They needed to be in the same place at the same time—alone. Instead, he was stuck in Florida. He missed touching her. Waking up with her.

The permanent staff at Merritt Island was finishing up the restoration of the island's salt marshes, work Sam had been part of during his previous assignment before he moved in with Charlie. He was counting the wildlife that was returning, establishing the success of the restoration. Hot, tedious work that left him too much time to think and only one day off per week.

Without Elizabeth, Greg and Sam, Charlie was at sixes and sevens with herself. Her interest in cleaning out the refrigerator, rearranging the linen closet, and replanting the terra cotta pots on the front porch ran out after one week. The fall semester had been incredibly busy, the spring quieter, and the summer seriously boring. Though Sam's phone calls helped, she needed something to do, so when Tessa called about making a trip to San Francisco to see Jimmy, Charlie was more than happy to keep her friend company.

"Harold's office is moving into their new building in Eureka. He can't get away." Tessa's voice sounded as though she'd been crying.

"Is he okay? Jimmy, not Harold."

"I—think—so."

Charlie waited.

"He's living in a group home, sort of a halfway house for people who've been in rehab. He didn't want to get in touch with us until he was settled. Now he needs more of his clothes and a few other things. He has a job with Goodwill."

The trip gave Charlie something else to think about. She and Tessa shared the driving, stopped for lunch at a freeway off-ramp and, in the late afternoon, checked into Executive Suites. The next morning, while Jimmy showed his mother where he was living and working, then introduced her to his boss, Charlie visited the Museum of Modern Art and, that afternoon, revisited the Columbia Avenue coffee shop where she and Sam had spent time when they were in the city, falling in love. It was early evening in Florida when she called him. "I'm in our coffee shop. The Beacon. Remember?" For the first time in days, she felt close to him.

"I do remember. Terrific espresso." His voice was wistful.

"We should come back to San Francisco for a day or two when you get back."

"We should."

"I miss you."

"I miss you too." She wondered whether she should have said *love* instead of *miss*. But she'd already pushed the red dot to disconnect the call.

On the drive back to Arcata, Tessa was wound up, needing to talk about Jimmy. "He's quieter and seems to be thinking about the future. Though it's not the kind of future I imagined for him."

"What's he thinking?"

"In the short term, trying for a promotion. Right now, he's sorting whatever discards come into the main warehouse. He'd like to make more money."

"Any interest in going back to college?"

"He didn't mention it. Harold will be upset. He figures Jimmy should instantly bounce back. Revert to being the same boy he was during his Freshman year at San Jose State. All I care about is that he's stayed clean since he left rehab. All Harold seems to care about is that Jimmy hasn't fulfilled the expectations he had for him before everything fell apart."

"I suppose most kids manage to disappoint their parents about something. I sure did."

"I don't know whether I did or not, other than only having one child. My folks had their sights set on having a lot of grandchildren. My brother only provided two."

Charlie sighed, "I was never sure how my mother felt about my not wanting to raise her granddaughter but, to her credit, she was the one who arranged for Missy to take Elizabeth. My dad was definitely against the adoption. And said so—often. Having her with Missy allowed them to see her occasionally when she was a toddler. After my mom died, my dad moved to L.A."

"Is that why your father told Elizabeth the truth?"

"I don't think so. He honestly assumed I'd told her—and felt bad about upsetting her."

"Are you and Elizabeth doing better since the great revelation?"

"A little, only because I'm at the edge of what she's doing with Andre and now she's at camp. She's probably never going to forgive me but, since I'm her guardian, she has to deal with me for another year."

"What does Sam think about Andre being in the picture?"

"Not happy. He doesn't trust him and maybe doesn't trust me. Mostly we talk around the issue."

"How do you feel about Andre?"

"I'm surprised and grateful that he's taken to Elizabeth so easily. She's rather intrigued with having a couple of brothers and a set of replacement parents, even though one of them is me. He's still very good looking—but no, I'm not attracted to him."

Camp: This is the first night I've had a moment to write anything. It's raining buckets so the nightly campfire was canceled. Julie and I are in our cabin. She's giving herself a pedicure and listening to some awful Rap. Because we're counselors this summer, we've been super busy. Every morning, I have to set up the craft space in the Rec Center. There's a different age group each day. A teacher comes in to give a lesson like drawing trees or animals. Using watercolor or clay. I help the kids during their class and then clean up afterwards. I like the primary kids best. They get so excited.

Julie teaches swimming late in the afternoons because the lake water's warmer then. So we don't spend much time together. I've been doing more horseback riding this summer, following the trails in the hills. I'm in the intermediate group. Thursday we're going on an overnight trip. Riding all day, then camping out. The horse I've been riding is a three-year-old quarter horse named Penelope. I'm looking forward to the challenge. After that, there's just a week more of camp.

Grandma's house fell out of escrow—whatever that means—but there were other offers so it probably won't be long until it sells.

Since Julie's stopped being mad at me, she's lobbying for me to board at the academy during my senior year. I'm not sure. What if she gets mad at me again? And I don't think I want to live in a dorm. I don't like any of my choices. Grandma will be in Florida and won't have room for me in her new place. And living in an old people's place would be horrid. Rowena isn't offering her house and anyway I wouldn't like living with her. Charlie of course has to take me in. I'm sort of guessing things aren't quite right between her and Sam. And then there's Greg. I don't know whether he's going to be at Charlie's again.

When Charlie began teaching, she was delighted that publishers sent advance copies of textbooks and new editions of the literary masters. No such thing as too many books. Now, however, the shelves in her office were full and running over, especially since she'd moved most of her personal library from the house to the university to make room for Greg. It was time to draw the line between books that were or might be necessary and those simply taking up space. For an English professor, books were tough to get rid of. Old friends.

With nothing else on her agenda, she put on an old pair of walking shorts and a faded t-shirt, fixed a thermos of coffee and a sandwich, and drove to campus. Cleaning and sorting would take her mind off the unsettled parts of her life.

She started with the Freshman and Sophomore-level writing texts; books with a copyright over two years old went into the give away pile because the publishers were probably already revising them. A marketing trick that forced teachers to change texts way too often. And since many students were now downloading textbooks onto their tablets or laptops, whatever she chose for a class had to have an e-text edition. Pretty soon the bookstore would be unnecessary.

The literature texts were harder to get rid of. She usually taught classes covering Sixteenth and Seventeenth Century literature. Especially

Shakespeare. She kept the editions with scholarly criticism, regardless of the copyright date and all the poetry texts.

While she ate her lunch, she immersed herself in a new collection of Twenty-first Century poets she hadn't looked at yet.

"Dr. Ames?" Charlie jumped. Angela was standing in the doorway.

'Hi, you startled me. Need any old textbooks?"

"No thanks. Do you have your cell phone with you?"

Charlie reached into the side pocket of her purse. "No. I must have left it in the car."

"A Dr. Winslow is trying to reach you. He says it's an emergency. Something about Elizabeth. He wants you to call him on his cell."

Without thanking Angela, Charlie ran toward the faculty parking lot, her heart racing.

The phone was on the passenger seat. She fumbled through the contact list. When Andre answered, she was hardly breathing.

"What's wrong? Where are you?"

"South of Boston."

"Tell me."

"When the camp couldn't get you, they called me. Elizabeth put both our phone numbers on her information sheet. Her horse threw her. She's in the hospital in Bangor. The Eastern Maine Medical Center. I don't have any details. I tossed a few things in the car and took off. When you weren't answering, I decided to try the university."

"I accidentally left my cell in the car. I'll be there as soon as I can get a flight."

"Go into Boston. It has more flights than Portland. And bring the insurance information." He stopped. "Oh hell, I'm getting into major traffic. Keep me posted about your arrival."

Charlie hurried to her office, locked up, and drove home, cold with fear.

She pulled up the United Air website and stared at it vacantly, her brain refusing to help her find a flight. *I can't do this.* After a few minutes, she called Tessa, grateful that her friend was home, and poured out the story.

"I can't seem to figure out how to—I'm—can you come over?"

"I'll be right there. This is a medical emergency. Flights will be expensive."

"Just come."

Instead of staring at the computer, Charlie began packing the roll-on bag that fit in the overhead space. Slacks, tops, nightgown, tennis shoes. In the midst of packing, she went to look for the insurance papers she kept in the pantry safe.

When Tessa let herself in, Charlie was zipping the suitcase. Tessa put her arms around her. "I called my friend Maria, who works at Travel Time in Eureka. She'll find something faster than I will."

"Thank you," a whisper. "I'm so scared."

"Where's your phone. I'm going to call the hospital. I want to leave my line available for Maria's call. Do you want me to pretend I'm you?"

Charlie nodded.

Tessa googled the Medical Center phone number, then tapped it in. Getting medical information on the phone was never easy. Whoever was on the other end was trying to put her off, but Tessa was tenacious. Ten minutes later she ended the call. "The best part of the answer is she's critical but stable. I couldn't get anything else."

"That helps."

A few minutes later, Tessa's cell rang. She listened, making notes on a pad of paper she found on the table. To Charlie, "I need your credit card."

Tessa's intervention had taken just under an hour. "We need to get you to McKinleyville. There's a seat on the 3 p.m. United Air into San Francisco and a US Air flight to Boston at 8 p.m. You'll land just before dawn. Maria reserved a rental car for you with Avis."

"All I can think of is what if she dies, what if I don't get there in time?"

"Charlie, don't do that to yourself. She's going to be okay. We need to get you on that plane. The sooner you're en route, the better you'll feel."

Charlie doubted that.

During her layover in San Francisco, she bought dinner and ordered wine, hoping it would relax her. Then she called Andre. "Are you on your way?" He sounded tired. He'd already been driving several hours.

"I have an eight o'clock red eye into Boston. I land some time around 5 a.m. I'll pick up a car when I land. How long will it take me to drive to Bangor?"

"Three to four hours. Most of it's Interstate. Make sure there's a GPS in the car." Static, then silence.

Days later, Charlie couldn't recall much about the flight to Boston. Perhaps she had slept after all. She drove out of Boston just as traffic picked up. The clerk at Avis had showed her how to set the car's GPS for Bangor and the Medical Center. Since it was Saturday, the commute was lighter.

The hollow voice of the GPS and memories of Elizabeth kept Charlie company as she drove north.

A kaleidoscope of pictures. Their first meeting in Donovan's office, the second meeting at the luggage carousel in McKinleyville. A girl who was hers and not hers. Quiet, keeping her pain to herself, making friends with Martha, singing a solo in the choir. Her fury on learning Charlie was her biological mother.

Outside Portland, she stopped at an Interstate McDonald's. Besides food and coffee, she wanted to brush her teeth and wash her face, but the water couldn't erase the dark patches beneath her worried eyes. While she was eating a breakfast burrito, she tried Andre's phone but the call went to voicemail. Next, she tried Sam's number and also got his voicemail.

At least, Andre would be at the hospital when she arrived.

CHAPTER 21

Sam had spent a stifling morning in a beach hut covered with palm fronds, counting migrating wildlife. To maintain silence, his cell was turned off so he didn't find Charlie's message until he came in from the marshes at lunchtime.

Elizabeth's been injured; she's in the hospital. I'm on my way. Andre's probably already there. Short and to the point.

He immediately returned the call but ended up in her voicemail. Where was the hospital? And why was Andre going to Elizabeth's rescue? Sam's concern for Elizabeth was interrupted by his knee jerk response to her biological father helping in a moment of crisis. Sam was, admittedly, being paranoid. He should not care that Charlie had talked to Andre before calling him.

Getting no response from Charlie, he called Tessa and heard her *critical but stable* report, wrote down the name and location of the hospital, and listened to Tessa's guess about when Charlie would get to Elizabeth's side. He felt slightly better about Elizabeth's condition. Not about Andre's involvement. Before the call ended, Tessa added, "Charlie's terrified. Maybe she's calmed down a bit by now, but she probably shouldn't be there alone. I don't suppose you could go to Maine to be with her?"

He couldn't. Elizabeth wasn't his daughter and Charlie wasn't his wife. Emergency leave was given only for immediate family members. Besides, he was not ready to share space with Andre.

Elizabeth's trail ride and camp out had been perfect. A warm day without rain. A roaring bonfire after dinner and a quiet night in her cozy tent. But the next morning, an hour before they returned to the main camp, the usually sure-footed Penelope stumbled on a rocky part of the trail and sent Elizabeth flying to the ground, only aware of swirling rocks racing toward her face—then a shattering pain in her head and left side. Then oblivion.

When Charlie reached the Medical Center, she was exhausted and irritable so, when the receptionist at the first floor counter told her to wait while she checked on Elizabeth's location and who her doctor was, Charlie did not take it well.

"I've flown all night and driven four hours from Boston. I—need—to—see—her." She laid her driver's license on the desk. "I should be listed as next of kin."

"Nevertheless," the nurse read the name on the license, "Ms. Ames, you will have to wait while I check. Please sit down."

Charlie continued standing. If she were in a comfortable chair, she might fall asleep.

After two phone calls, "Go to the third floor nurses' station." She returned Charlie's license.

There was, however, no one at the third floor nurses' station so, in lieu of waiting for someone else to tell her to wait, Charlie walked along the hall, checking the patient names posted on the doors.

A voice asked, "Who are you looking for?" Another nurse was directly behind her, a clipboard in her hand and a frown on her face.

"Elizabeth Enright. She was brought here yesterday." Charlie had assumed someone from the camp would have stayed with Elizabeth to run interference. But that did not seem to be the case. After all, the accident had happened on their watch.

And, yes, she was cranky.

The nurse consulted the clipboard. "Please have a seat in the waiting room."

Charlie took a deep breath, "I need to see her—now."

"I'll page her doctor. Her father is already waiting in there." She pointed to an uninviting room, empty except for an uncharacteristically disheveled Andre reading a newspaper. Charlie joined him. "Have they let you see her?"

He looked up, "Oh good, you're here. No. When I arrived in the middle of the night, they were still running tests, so I checked into the Quality Inn down the street and left the nurse my cell number. Didn't sleep much but I did get a shower and some breakfast."

"At least she isn't in ICU. I'll be right back. Which way to the rest room?"

"Alongside the elevators."

By the time she returned, a young man in blue scrubs was talking to Andre. "Charlotte, this is Elizabeth's doctor. Dr. Babcock, this is Charlotte Ames, her mother. Tell her what you told me."

"Ms. Ames, your daughter is still not fully conscious. Drifting in and out. We've run several scans and other tests. She has a slight concussion and a gash on her forehead. She also has four cracked ribs on her left side and her left forearm is broken. She was very lucky that the horse didn't step on her."

"May I"—Charlie stopped, remembering to include Andre— "may we sit with her?"

Babcock hesitated, "Just one at a time. Please be very quiet. I want her to wake up on her own. She's in Room 311." He consulted the clipboard, "Ames, Enright and Winslow—why are all the names different?"

Still having trouble with the word *mother*, "I'm her legal guardian."

"But I was given to understand you're her parents."

From Andre, "It's complicated." He turned to Charlie, "Why don't you go in first. I'll check in a little later."

Charlie nodded and followed the hall numbers to the half open door of Room 311. Pale beneath the bruises on her face, Elizabeth lay on her back in the hospital bed, wires and drips attached to various parts of her body, sending messages reflected in the beeping of the monitors.

Her forehead was bandaged, her left forearm in a cast from her elbow to her hand, with only the tips of her fingers showing. Her ribs were probably taped. Someone had braided her hair into two pigtails, making her look like she was about ten. As Charlie stood in the doorway, the tears she'd been ignoring all day came without warning. Trying to wipe them away, she settled herself in the upholstered chair at the side of the bed, afraid of waking Elizabeth but hoping she'd wake up for a moment.

Charlie didn't understand her tears. Maybe relief that Elizabeth was alive and, in time, would recover. Or was there something else? Fear that Elizabeth would tell her to go away. Fear that she wouldn't know how to take care of her. Caregiving had never been required of her. She'd always believed she didn't know how to express sympathy and empathy. The tears might be some type of delayed mother-reaction. Tessa had once said that, when Jimmy was hurting, she physically felt his pain.

When Andre's hand gently shook her shoulder, Charlie had no idea how long she'd been asleep. As she straightened, he held his finger to his lips and nodded toward the hallway.

Closing the door, he took her hand and placed a plastic key card on her palm. "You need to sleep or at least take a shower and eat. This is the key to room 62 at Quality Inn. It's two blocks from here. Turn left as you leave the parking lot. I'm registered for three days. It has an outside entrance. No one will ask questions. I'll sit with Elizabeth until you come back."

Groggily, Charlie pushed her hair back. "Are you sure?"

"I'm sure." He smiled. "Go."

"Call when she wakes up."

Having just finished making up Andre's room, the maid merely nodded as Charlie let herself in. Nothing special about the room, but the hot shower performed miracles, taking the knots out of her neck, relaxing every inch of her body. She washed her hair, wrapped herself in a bath sheet and sat on the foot of the bed to open her roll-on for clean clothes.

This time she woke when her cell refused to shut up. Andre's voice was lighter. "She's awake and the doctor is encouraged by her alertness and request for food. Were you asleep?"

165

"Yes. I can't seem to stay awake for more than ten minutes at a time. I'll be there soon."

Even though she'd been wearing the same pair of denim slacks since she left California, she put them back on and found a clean top with long sleeves. The hospital room was kept cool.

Before she left the room, she checked her phone and found Sam's call.

He answered immediately. "How is she? How are you, where are you?"

"I'm in Andre's room. I needed some sleep. He just called. Elizabeth's awake. I'm going back right now."

"Are you okay?"

"Stretched thin but not as scared as I was. Can I call you tonight and fill you in?"

Before he could say yes, the connection broke, leaving him with *in Andre's room* playing loops in his head.

When Charlie returned to the Medical Center, Andre met her outside Elizabeth's room with "She's asleep again, but Dr. Babcock says her vital signs are good."

"Were you able to talk to her?"

"Only a few words. I told her you'd been here and would be back. Her face and lips are bruised so it's hard for her to talk. Have you eaten?"

"No. But I did register at the motel. I'm in room 210, second level. Thanks for the loan of your room." She handed him his key.

"While you're sitting with her, I'm going down to the small cafeteria in the basement. Do you want a sandwich? Coffee?"

"Yes to both. I'll stay here so someone is with her when she wakes up again."

Elizabeth hurt all over. Not severe pain, just a pervasive aching. She was having trouble focusing on what was happening around her. She remembered opening her eyes, seeing Andre sitting alongside her bed. He looked tired but, when he realized she was staring at him, he smiled. "Hey, are you really awake or just pretending?"

She tried to answer but her lips hurt, so all that came out was a mumble.

"It's okay, don't try to talk. I'm good at monologues. A professor's stock in trade. Charlotte left a few minutes ago. She'll be back. We're taking turns watching you sleep."

He was teasing her. She liked that.

At that point, a nurse hurried in, then a doctor, and Andre was dispatched to the hallway while they checked the monitors, shined a light in her eyes, asked if she was in pain.

As soon as they left, she slipped back into the soft gray webbing surrounding her.

The next time Elizabeth opened her eyes, she didn't feel as woozy as the last time she was awake. She tried a tiny smile. Someone had put a soothing gel on her lips, so she could move them more easily.

Charlie was sitting in the chair, sound asleep, her head tipped to the left, her hair loose, falling across her face. She looked vulnerable, almost childlike. Elizabeth studied her mother, her biological mother. Not her mothering mother. Missy had been with Elizabeth through skinned knees, chicken pox, and arguments with friends. She'd taught her to bake, what colors looked good on her, how to talk to older people, how to make friends.

All Charlie had done was have sex with Andre and eventually push Elizabeth into the world and into Missy's arms. It had been half a year since Charlie's father told Elizabeth she was Charlie's child, and she still hadn't come close to figuring out how to absorb that fact into the person she'd thought she was. If only Missy were here to tell her how to fit into Charlie's life. WWMD. *What Would Missy Do?*

Elizabeth didn't hate Charlie—exactly. Missy had always counseled *Don't hate anyone or anything.* But this situation was way more complicated than any she'd encountered before. She couldn't understand how anyone could give a tiny, helpless baby away. Just turn her back and pretend the baby didn't exist even though it had been in her womb for nine months.

She was pretty sure that she and Charlie were stuck with each other for another year. The guardian thing had been so much easier when Charlie was just a cousin and Elizabeth an orphan.

"Elizabeth?" Charlie was leaning toward the bed.

"Uh huh."

"I'm so glad you're awake." Tears filled Charlie's eyes. "Do you feel awful? Should I get the nurse?"

Elizabeth carefully shook her aching head.

"Okay." Charlie reached over and placed her hand on top of Elizabeth's right hand. The tears didn't go away but they didn't turn into real crying either.

Charlie's touch was comforting. Elizabeth tried to remember whether Charlie had ever touched her before. Charlie was definitely not a hugger like Missy. Andre however usually hugged her when they said goodbye on Sundays. Tessa was a hugger too.

Now, Charlie's hand was curved around Elizabeth's, actually holding it.

When Elizabeth woke again, Charlie's hand was still holding hers, but Charlie had fallen asleep, her head resting on the edge of Elizabeth's bed. Neither one of them could seem to stay awake.

Charlie woke when a nurse brought Elizabeth's dinner tray, slowly raising the bed so Elizabeth could sit up, "Are you dizzy?"

"No, just hungry," though the food on the tray didn't look especially appetizing. She'd rather have a sandwich and potato chips instead of a cup of plain yogurt and a bowl of chicken soup.

"Could I have some bread or crackers?"

"I'll ask." The nurse left.

Charlie looked at the tray, "Not enough to keep a bird alive."

Elizabeth picked up the spoon on the tray.

"I'm starving." Her lips were cooperating better.

"Well look at you, sitting up and eating." Andre was standing in the doorway. "I brought you your purse and iPad. And Julie. She can only come in if Charlotte and I leave."

Elizabeth's eyes brightened.

Julie swept into the room behind him, carrying a comb and hairbrush. "Lizzie, I've been so worried about you. Counselor John and

I gathered up all your stuff, and I made him bring me too. I needed to see that you're going to be okay. You gave the whole camp a terrible scare. Pigtails! Really!" She held up the comb and brush. "You need a makeover."

Back in the waiting room, Andre sat on a straight-backed chair and stretched his left leg across another one. "My knee is killing me."

"When are you having surgery?"

"Originally today—but I called and rescheduled. Maybe in two weeks. Of course, once you get out of the surgery line, you might go to the end of the line."

"I appreciate you coming up here for Elizabeth." And she meant it. She was sincerely grateful for his support, surprised that, from their first meeting, he had seemed to care for Elizabeth. Charlie's sixteen-year picture of him as a selfish bastard was being reworked—slightly.

"I was closer than you were and Grace is in Florida." He grinned, "And I'm afraid of Rowena."

"Everyone is."

With the nurse's permission, Julie was allowed to stay with Elizabeth while Charlie and Andre went in search of dinner. Andre drove. "The receptionist on the first floor suggested an Irish pub called Paddy Murphy's. It's not far. I need a beer."

Beer was different. Charlie remembered him being rather snarky about beer drinkers. They both ordered fish and chips. Charlie skipped the beer. "I'm sleepy enough."

When they returned to the hospital, Julie was gone and Elizabeth, her hair brushed out, was asleep, so they drove back to the Quality Inn, agreeing to meet in the tiny breakfast room at seven o'clock before going to the hospital.

Even though she knew Sam was waiting to hear from her, Charlie didn't call him till almost nine o'clock. She was pretty sure he was on edge about Andre being with her and Elizabeth, so she wanted to think about what she should and should not say.

Sam's first question, "How is she?"

"Doing much better. The concussion symptoms are mild; probably the most painful part is the cracked ribs. Moving and breathing are hard."

"How long will she stay in the hospital?"

Her doctor wants to keep her one more day, to be sure about the concussion."

"Then what?"

"Not sure. I hope she's allowed to fly. Otherwise, it'll take us a couple days to drive back to Grace's. The house will close escrow in three weeks."

"What about Arcata?"

"We haven't talked about it. I don't know what she's thinking; I'm just so glad she'll recover."

"If I can get a day off, fly into D.C. in the early morning and fly back in the afternoon, would that work? I'd like to see both of you."

"Of course."

"Let me know which day I should come."

"I'll ask the doctor how soon she can travel."

Not their usual conversation. No *I miss you, love you, can't wait to see you.*

How had this tiptoeing happened? How could she fix it?

CHAPTER 22

Sam caught an earlier flight into Reagan, rented a car, and programmed Grace's address into the GPS. Before he left the airport, he bought a bouquet of mixed flowers for Elizabeth. He should probably have called to tell them he would arrive early but opted for surprise.

However, Sam was the one who was surprised when a man opened Grace's front door. "Can I help you?" His coloring, age, and good looks said this was Andre. With them. At Grace's. Not the scenario Sam had envisioned.

"Is Charlie here?"

"You must be Sam." Andre reached out to shake Sam's hand. "Charlotte and Elizabeth are expecting you. Come in."

The hallway and living room were bare of furniture, a few empty packing boxes along the wall.

"I'll take you up."

As though he belonged there.

Looking back on those few hours with Elizabeth and Charlie, Sam saw the day as a marker in his relationship with Charlie. It was evident Andre, Elizabeth and Charlie had become a family of sorts, maybe sixteen years too late, but a family that had faced an emergency together. And Sam was on the outside, looking in. Though he'd been annoyed that Charlie hadn't trusted him with the truth about Elizabeth, he also realized he didn't trust Charlie with Elizabeth's father.

Andre led him to what probably had been Elizabeth's bedroom during the spring. "Ladies, here's your guest." To Sam, "Nice to meet you. I have a doctor's appointment." He kissed the top of Elizabeth's head and was gone.

On the double bed, Elizabeth was leaning against a pile of pillows, her knees drawn up to hold her iPad. Her color was fairly good. Charlie, however, looked exhausted. Since there was only one straight-backed chair, Sam handed Elizabeth the bouquet and sat carefully on the edge of the bed.

While Elizabeth was filling Sam in on the accident, Charlie went to answer the doorbell. The pizza Elizabeth had requested for lunch. She was back before Elizabeth finished her story. Using a small table that Grace hadn't wanted in Florida, Charlie set out plates, napkins and the pizza, putting two slices on a plate for Elizabeth and handing her a bottle of water. "Eat where you are so you won't have to move too much."

Sam helped himself to the pizza. "I bet it hurts to breathe."

Around a bite of cheese and pepperoni, "Un huh. Better today though."

While they ate, Elizabeth told Sam about camp, her friends, being a counselor, and Penelope. "She didn't mean to hurt me."

He was tempted to ask whether she was going back to Arcata but didn't want to introduce what might still be an awkward topic. He'd ask Charlie later.

"Who wants the last slice?" Charlie slid a table knife under the remaining piece.

Elizabeth smiled, "Me. I had to eat all that yucky hospital food."

Charlie placed the slice on Elizabeth's plate, "Healing takes energy," and busied herself cleaning off the table, setting her plate and Sam's on the tray. She looked at Sam, "What time do you have to be back at the airport?"

"The flight leaves at 5:10. I need to return the car and check in about three o'clock. I'll be in the airport longer than I'll be on the plane."

Elizabeth finished her pizza, "Thank you for taking the time to come see me."

"I needed to make sure you two were okay. You've had a tough week."

"How's Greg?"

"He's decided he likes Spain, but then he's living in a rather lavish house with a pool. He's playing soccer and undoubtedly being indulged by his rich stepfather."

"Is he coming back to the states?"

"No idea. Texting doesn't lend itself to a lot of information." A situation that was probably going to necessitate a trip to Madrid for a face-to-face with Greg and Diane. And he needed to meet Luis.

"Have you given up on him coming back?"

Elizabeth hadn't lost her ability to read other people.

"Maybe." Until now he hadn't actually admitted it to himself. "I'm surprised Diane let him out of her sight the months he was in Arcata. That's probably not going to happen again." Greg was half a world away, he and Charlie were being careful with each other, and Elizabeth was on the cusp of going out on her own.

A little after two, he kissed Elizabeth's cheek. "Take care of yourself."

She almost laughed, then remembered that laughing hurt. "I have no other choice. Andre, Charlie and Aunt Rowena watch me every minute. How long will you be in Florida?"

"Another couple weeks. I have some vacation time. I'm thinking about going to see Greg so he remembers he has a father." A few minutes later, walking downstairs with Charlie, "Is she coming back to Arcata?"

Charlie shrugged. "I haven't asked directly. Andre goes in for his knee surgery in three days, and she wants to be here for that."

He wondered if Charlie did too, but he didn't go there.

"When does school start?"

"The last Monday in August for both the university and the high school. I didn't know you were planning on going to Spain."

"We haven't had much opportunity to talk since I found out Diane enrolled Greg in school without checking with me. I don't want her to think she can totally control the situation. I need to deal with her in person."

At the front door, he gently pulled her into his arms. He needed to feel her close to him. "Are you okay?"

"Mostly." Her arms hesitantly circled his waist. "You?"

"Mostly. Elizabeth seems fond of Andre."

"They enjoy one another's company. Oddly enough, she's never been mad at him."

"Is she still mad at you?"

"Probably. But she needs help right now, so shutting me out isn't an option."

He moved her away slightly to kiss her, a friendly kiss. Not the kiss he intended. When they separated, he opened the front door. "I'll call when I get to Merritt."

She nodded. "Thanks for coming."

Too late to edit the formality.

He stood on the front porch for a few minutes, painfully aware that he and Charlie weren't on the same emotional page.

Charlie and Elizabeth flew back to Arcata three days after Andre's knee surgery. When they visited him, he was already up and walking, albeit with the help of pain pills and a walker. The next day, Elizabeth's decision to spend her senior year in Arcata was made without discussing how she felt about Charlie or how Charlie felt about—everything. The bottom line was that Arcata High was cheaper than Vienna Academy, and Elizabeth really didn't want to live in the dorm while most of her friends were living with their parents. *Too weird.*

Though Charlie was relieved that Elizabeth was back in Arcata, she wished she had someone to wave a magic wand over her personal life. In lieu of a wand, she definitely needed someone to talk to—about Elizabeth, about Sam, about herself.

Sam flew to Spain the day classes began for Elizabeth and Charlie.

September: Finally, the cast on my arm has been replaced by a lighter, removable one so showering is easier. My ribs are almost good, though I notice them when I walk up the stairs at school.

I'm back in Arcata. I'll never admit this to Charlie, but I probably shouldn't have gone to school in Vienna last semester. I was sort of out of the loop there and I'm out of the loop here too. I'm taking choir again (Mr. Hannigan was glad to see me). And Martha and I are good. I don't have a heavy schedule since I almost have enough units to graduate right now so Martha asked if I wanted a part time job at her family's bakery, helping at the counter. The job was her cousin Annie's, but Annie's husband got a good job over in Red Bluff. I work four hours Saturday morning and two hours after school on Tuesday and Thursday. Minimum wage. I told her yes, but I haven't told Charlie yet. She probably won't care. Since we got back almost three weeks ago, we haven't seen much of each other, except at dinner. And she had to go with me to re-register at school.

No texts from Julie. Not surprising. I felt like an outsider last semester. Guess we aren't best friends anymore. Problem is, this isn't exactly my home either. It's Charlie's. Sort of like being homeless without sleeping on the street.

I don't know what's going on with Charlie and Sam. He's due back at the Humboldt Refuge next week. Since Charlie and I don't talk any more than necessary, I don't know whether they're a couple or not. He hasn't called but maybe they've been texting.

Andre calls every few days. His knee is doing well and he's back at work. I'm going to spend Thanksgiving with him. His father will take a train from Saranac to D.C. and my other half brother, Andre junior, is back from Iraq. I'm looking forward to meeting both of them. I'll probably miss my classes Thanksgiving week.

When Elizabeth finally mentioned she had a job, Charlie was momentarily taken aback. So much happening in Elizabeth's life without Charlie knowing.

"Don't you need a work permit?"

"The principal's office has them. I'll get one tomorrow. Then you have to sign it."

"Does Andre know?"

"Yeah."

It figured.

In his last email from Spain, Sam told her he'd be staying at his Eureka apartment when he returned. "I have a lot of catching up to do since no one has been covering my job."

"When will I see you?"

"Would you mind picking me up in McKinleyville?"

"No problem." But clearly there was a problem. She was tired of him acting as though she'd been cheating on him just because she'd introduced Elizabeth to Andre and, as a result, let Andre into their lives. She hadn't done anything wrong—well not recently anyway. A few dinners, co-parenting Elizabeth after the accident. Telling Sam that she was in Andre's room when she was in Bangor had been stupid, but she hadn't realized just how suspicious Sam was. A trait she'd never seen in him before.

She picked him up late Friday afternoon and, because she was always good at pretending there was no problem, she put her arms around him and kissed him. Admittedly a public kiss. He looked like hell, rumpled clothing, in need of a shave. Understandable since he'd been on planes and in airports for over twenty-four hours. As usual, he was carrying his duffle bag with a colorful variety of airport luggage tags hanging on the handle.

"Are you going to Eureka tonight?"

"Yeah. I need to check in at 6 a.m. tomorrow. Herman left on vacation this morning so I'm the only one available to open up. I thought I'd have a few days to adjust to this time zone, but that isn't happening." Eureka wasn't that far away. If he really wanted to be with her—the thought wouldn't finish itself. His work was an excuse. And it hurt.

She handed him her car keys. His susceptibility to motion sickness did not make him a good passenger. He needed to be at the wheel.

"Let's stop at Carmela's and get something to eat."

She had to laugh at the restaurant choice. "Haven't you had enough Spanish food?"

"Spanish is not Mexican. Trust me. I've been craving Mexican food for days."

He chose a table at the back. The waitress handed them menus. "Can I bring you drinks?"

"Two bottles of Tecate." He leaned back in his chair. "No matter how wonderful foods of other cultures are, nothing is quite like your own food. And around here that means Mexican."

The beer arrived.

"How's Greg?"

Sam turned the bottle in his hands, considering the question. "Best answer—in hog heaven. Diane and Luis want him to want to stay in Spain, so he gets to do pretty much whatever makes him happy. All our work to get him to do chores and accept responsibility while he was living here was clearly a waste of time and energy."

"School?"

"An expensive private school. Fortunately, most of the subjects are taught in English. He's studying Spanish and also picking up street Spanish from the other boys on the soccer team."

When he didn't continue, "Diane?"

He rolled his eyes. "Playing the demure bride. Not a role that suits her, but Luis seems content. She's gotten the promotion she was promised—marrying the boss didn't hurt—and is managing one of the company's major clothing lines. Being uncharacteristically nice to me so I won't take her to court over Greg being out of the country. I decided not to go the legal route, not worth the hassle, let alone the expense of lawyers."

She heard sadness in his voice. "You okay with it?"

He set the bottle on the table, leaned forward on his elbows, looking at her intently. "I'm not okay with much of anything at the moment. Greg might—underline might—come for Christmas, but I wouldn't put money on it. A ski trip to Switzerland is being dangled."

Charlie suspected that their relationship was also on his list of not-okay parts of his life. Afraid of his answer, "And us? Me?"

At that moment their orders arrived, steaming enchiladas for him, fish tacos for her. Refried beans topped with cheese, Spanish rice. Only after he devoured one of the enchiladas, did he answer her question, but kept his eyes fixed on his plate. "I need some time."

Isn't that usually the woman's line?

"Because?"

"I'm not sure where all this is going," he looked up, "I love you."

"But?"

"But seeing you with Andre, knowing you've been spending time with him. I guess I'm—uneasy."

177

"I'm not involved with him. Our connection is Elizabeth. Nothing more. I'm not uneasy about you and Diane."

"It's—" he ran his hand nervously through his hair "me. When you didn't trust me enough to tell me about Elizabeth, I guess I started questioning where our relationship was going."

As Sam reached for her hand, she moved it to pick up her beer.

"So since I didn't trust you, you won't trust me. I never talked to anyone about Elizabeth—never. I never saw it as a trust thing. Is this you getting even?" She knew she was being too hard. Sam wasn't a tit for tat person—usually.

"No, I wouldn't do that but it's made me rethink everything. We were doing so many things independently, our jobs, my visits to Greg. You being in London. Maybe we were kidding ourselves. We were living separate lives in many ways."

Charlie felt her throat tighten. She pushed her plate away, no room for food.

This was her payment for what she'd done all those years ago. A daughter who barely tolerated her and, now, losing Sam.

He was watching her closely. "Charlie—I—"

"Don't." She looked at his plate, "Are you finished?"

He nodded

"Then let's go. Elizabeth is probably at the house by now. She's been looking forward to you coming back."

Sam's back but not back here, in this house. Not in Charlie's bed. He was very sweet with me. Asked about school, how I was feeling. I told him about my job. Then he put some of his stuff into the Rover. His bike too. And drove off.

I think Charlie really loves him.

She spent the rest of the evening in her room. Before I went to bed, I checked that the doors were locked and the lights out.

CHAPTER 23

Charlie coped with Sam's retreat to Eureka by making a list of chores to fill up the empty place in her life. One of her first tasks was to stop by the Summers' Family Bakery to meet Martha's mother, Alicia. Charlie should have made the effort a year ago when Elizabeth and Martha started spending time with each other. That's what real parents did. According to Martha, her parents worked sunup to sundown. Her older sister did the bookkeeping and Martha took care of the house and her younger brother. Alicia baked and decorated the cakes, while her husband and his brother handled the pastries and breads. Assorted nieces, nephews and cousins could be called in when someone was sick or during the holidays.

Charlie went in on a Friday morning when the girls were in class. She didn't want Elizabeth to feel she was prying. She did, however, want Martha's mother to know she was interested in what Elizabeth was doing.

The shop was pleasantly warm with the scent of fresh bread. A wiry woman wearing an oversized white apron splattered with assorted frosting colors was behind the cake display, adding an elaborately decorated birthday cake to the refrigerated case.

"Excuse me, are you Mrs. Summers? I'm Charlie Ames."

The woman straightened and smiled, "Alicia, please. You're Elizabeth's mother."

So Elizabeth had confided in Martha. Day-by-day, Charlie was being forced out of the *mother* closet. Alicia slid the back panel into place. "Elizabeth's catching on very quickly. She remembers customers' names and they like her. Thanks for letting her take the job."

"She's enjoying it."

Truthfully, Elizabeth hadn't talked about the job, except to say *fine* whenever Charlie asked how it was going. For the next few minutes, the women made small talk but, when a customer came in to pick up one of the cakes, Charlie left, giving Alicia a half wave as she closed the shop door.

In her effort to ignore Sam's absence, she was rehabbing her garden. The automatic sprinklers and the summer rain had kept the lawns green, but the flowerpots on the porch needed replanting, and the borders in the back yard were choked with weeds. Mindless, physical tasks that would guarantee her a good night's sleep.

Her classes had settled in rather well, and Elizabeth was busy with school and choir and work. They usually saw one another at breakfast. Elizabeth had an eight o'clock class every day. On Tuesday and Thursday, Charlie's first class was at nine, another at one-thirty and the *Women of Shakespeare* late Wednesday afternoon. Elizabeth worked until five p.m. on Tuesdays and Thursdays. Whoever got home first started fixing dinner. Both of them agreed they missed Sam's cooking. Charlie missed everything about him.

In the past, when Sam was staying in Eureka, he called Charlie at least once a day. Since his return a week ago, he'd only called twice. Afraid of leaving too much silence between them, Charlie phoned every other evening, slightly uneasy about appearing to be chasing after him. This Sam was not the Sam she'd fallen in love with, the one who sought her out, loved talking over coffee on rainy Sunday afternoons. The Sam who'd had her back was avoiding her, talking about everything but them.

The same day Tessa remembered to email Charlie the name and phone number of the therapist she'd gone to when Jimmy was having problems—*I like her because she's 75% common sense and 25% psychology*—was the day Elizabeth began crying during choir practice and ended up in the high school Counseling Center.

As Charlie was dismissing her class, Angela entered the classroom, the counselor's name and phone number on a post-it. "Jeremiah Solomon called fifteen minutes ago. He said I should wait until your class ended to give you this. It seems the choir director brought Elizabeth to the Counseling Center because she couldn't stop crying."

Charlie felt her stomach clench; at least this time Elizabeth wasn't in the hospital on the other side of the country. Stuffing her books and papers into her briefcase, she began searching for the eraser to clean the white board. "Tell him I'm on my way."

"Don't worry about the board; I'll deal with it."

The Counseling Center was directly across from the principal's office. Two small offices with a receptionist to keep track of the students and appointments. Charlie was short of breath by the time she walked in. Nerves did that to her. "Mr. Solomon called about Elizabeth Enright."

"Just a moment." The woman picked up the desk phone and pushed the intercom. "Ms. Ames is here for Elizabeth Enright."

As she hung up, the door on the right opened and a stocky, gray-haired man in chinos and an Arcata High sweatshirt came out. "Hi, I'm Jeremiah Solomon." He extended his hand.

"Charlie Ames," she took his hand and relaxed a little when he smiled.

"Let's go into Sheila's office. She's off today."

They sat side-by-side on comfortable upholstered chairs, no desk to intimidate the students. It took Charlie a moment to ask, "Is she okay?"

His voice was reassuring. "A little calmer. Today, the choir began working on a new piece of music, *Danny Boy*. Do you know it?"

She nodded.

"Well, it seems that it was one of her late father's favorites."

Charlie guessed. "And it triggered the tears."

"Exactly. Music taps into our emotions more easily than we expect. I'm betting her emotions have been close to the surface for quite a while."

"Did she talk about anything else?" *Like hating me.*

"In detail, no. But when I asked what she was feeling, she said she didn't know who she was any more, and there wasn't anyone to help her figure it out." He paused, "I wonder if she really meant there wasn't anyone to love her."

Elizabeth's sadness washed over Charlie. Elizabeth had every right to feel that way. Grace had skipped town, neither Rowena nor Andre had offered her a home, so she was at Charlie's. "My fault." *I should be able to love her.*

"Because?"

She looked into his kind eyes and explained about Elizabeth's life this past year. Reluctantly admitting she hadn't yet arrived at loving her daughter. Liking yes, admiring her strength, definitely. But those feelings were different from loving.

He listened patiently. "It's evident she's been trying to cope with her new circumstances on her own but hasn't found a way to get rid of the pain. If she'll agree, I'd like to set up a schedule with her, just let her talk everything out. Provide a neutral ear. She's had a lot to deal with. Getting her to talk will be a beginning."

Charlie took a deep breath. "Anything would help. We, well, we don't have a close relationship."

"How are you doing with this situation? It can't be what you expected either."

"Not great. I don't know how to help her." *Because I can't help myself.* He waited.

"Ironically, just this morning a friend gave me the name of a therapist in Eureka. I probably should do some talking too."

"Agreed." He stood up. "Elizabeth's embarrassed about having to leave class like that. She needs some TLC tonight. The less ruminating the better."

"We could go out for pizza." *Not sure that qualifies as TLC.*

"Good idea. She has a free period every morning at ten. I'd like to see her tomorrow. Is that all right with you?"

"Of course. Thank you for helping. I don't seem to be what she needs."

Elizabeth came out of Jeremiah's office slowly, her book bag over her left shoulder, her eyes watery, her mouth a bit wobbly; it wouldn't take much to set off the tears.

In the car, "Pizza?"

Her *okay* was barely audible. But she didn't say *no*.

October: I haven't written anything since I fell apart. No one in choir has mentioned my meltdown, or I'd die of embarrassment. I still have moments when I want to cry and cry. It's like when my parents died. That time though, I knew the crying was from grief. Now it's harder to explain, and so I'm talking to Jeremiah (he told me to call him that). He's really laid back. A good listener. He doesn't tell me I'm being foolish and doesn't tell me what to do. He just asks a question or two and that opens up all sorts of stuff that I've been holding onto. By the time I finish, I'm crying again.

Yesterday, he asked me what my parents and I did on a typical weekend. A nice question. Dad always fixed breakfast on the weekends, and I could smell the coffee brewing as soon as I woke up. Mom and I would do the dishes, then we'd do stuff around the house. Like work in our vegetable garden or Dad would play golf and Mom and I would go shopping, not necessarily for clothes, maybe to the open market or go visit Grandma.

Sunday we usually did special things. A drive to something educational, like one of the museums in D.C. or out to the coast to walk on the beach. Just doing whatever. Weekends were always family time. Writing about it, makes me cry. I want all of that back but it can never ever happen.

Pretty sure she didn't really want to take Tessa's advice, Charlie made a Wednesday morning appointment with the therapist, Dr. Gail Stein. Her Eureka office was in a two-story medical/dental building on a side street. If Elizabeth could let Jeremiah Solomon help her, Charlie should give therapy a try too. Elizabeth seemed calmer and less withdrawn since Jeremiah entered the picture, though there still wasn't much talking around the house.

Gail Stein was probably in her forties, short blonde hair, designer denims and a loose, long-sleeved top. Perhaps an attempt at making herself less intimidating, but Charlie was intimidated anyway. At the first appointment, Stein asked Charlie where she grew up, about her education, job, family. Love life.

Uncomfortable talking about herself, Charlie tried to keep most of the focus on her wanting a better relationship with Elizabeth, but Dr. Stein had a different agenda. Bluntly: "What are you so afraid of?"

It was several minutes before Charlie answered. "I'm afraid that I'm hurting Elizabeth. Well, I've already hurt her, am hurting her still." It seemed the right thing to say, a safe direction.

"Understandable, but there's more to your fear."

For ten minutes, the office was silent. Charlie closed her eyes against the steady gaze of the therapist: seeing Andre's anger when she told him she was pregnant and her parents' distress about the adoption. Revisited Sam's reaction when she told him Elizabeth was hers. Hearing Elizabeth slam the bedroom door the day she found out Charlie was her birth mother.

"I'm afraid—of never getting past everything that happened when I got pregnant. That I'm permanently scarred," she stopped to take a deep breath, "and even though no one says they're judging me, they really are. My daughter, my aunt, Elizabeth's aunt, my father. My boyfriend. The only safe place is my classroom because the students don't know about my private life. My past."

"Do you feel safe with Sam?"

"I did but, once he realized Elizabeth was my daughter, not as much. He believes I didn't trust him enough to tell him. And that has led to his not trusting me when Andre and I have contact because of Elizabeth."

"Let's go deeper. What are you afraid of, in the deepest part of your thought?"

After a while, Charlie whispered, "Not being loved."

CHAPTER 24

For Charlie, the weeks leading up to Thanksgiving were made up of appointments with Gail Stein, trying to *be there* for Elizabeth while staying in the background, and the painful realization that her relationship with Sam might truly be over.

Relationship.

Such a generic, cold word for what Charlie felt for Sam.

Dr. Stein was encouraging Charlie to look at what she believed love was. "I want you to find a definition that works for you. Look at how you show love to others and how you feel about being loved."

When Charlie told her she was puzzled that the therapy was focused on her own issues with love, instead of on Charlie's relationship with Elizabeth, Dr. Stein's answer was rather upsetting: "You need to know how you feel about the people you love, or have loved, before you can understand how to love and be loved by your daughter." Charlie wanted to tell her the odds of Elizabeth loving her were low. Charlie's odds of learning to love Elizabeth were only slightly better.

While Charlie did agree that she needed to understand what love was, she wasn't sure she needed to talk to Dr. Stein about that. The issue was Elizabeth. However, Elizabeth's sessions with Jeremiah seemed to be providing the kind of support she needed. She was smiling more and talking to Charlie more comfortably. Not about personal issues, but about what to fix for dinner, asking Charlie to make her plane reservations for Thanksgiving week. Suggesting she needed to shop for new winter clothes before she went to Virginia. They were back where they'd been a year ago—tentative but not at war.

And then there was the problem of Sam staying away. Just phone calls. The few miles between Arcata and Eureka had become impassable. Maybe Dr. Stein had a point. It wasn't just her relationship with Elizabeth that needed therapy.

Elizabeth was due to leave for D.C. the Sunday before Thanksgiving. Late Saturday afternoon, she suggested that they go for pizza. Charlie was surprised and pleased. They hadn't gone out to dinner since the day Elizabeth had cried during choir.

The weather had been threatening all day, and the rain began as they pulled into the parking lot. Instead of fumbling with umbrellas, they made a run for the front door. And waiting near the hostess station was Sam, wearing a plaid flannel shirt, Levi's and his work boots. Roughly handsome and smiling. Oh, God, she'd missed him. Charlie was tempted to throw herself into his arms. Settling instead for a kiss on her cheek, the same kind of kiss he gave Elizabeth.

As they followed the hostess to a booth by the windows, Elizabeth took his arm, "You beat us here."

"I was already in Eureka when I got your text."

So Elizabeth had arranged this accidental encounter. They sat across from Sam. The hostess left menus and promised a waitress would be right over.

"When do you leave?" he asked.

"Tomorrow." Obviously they'd been communicating. Charlie was definitely out of the loop but that was okay because Sam was sitting across the table. "My aunt will pick me up at Reagan. She hates having to drive to Dulles."

"After that?"

Elizabeth looked up from the menu she was studying. "Monday afternoon, Andre and I are going to the new African-American History Museum. He doesn't have a class on Mondays. On Tuesday, Julie and I are going shopping if she can use her mother's car. Then late Wednesday, Andre and I will pick up his father—my other new grandfather—at Union Station. Since Andre doesn't have a guest room in his condo, his father and Andre's younger son are staying in a B & B in Georgetown. His son's stationed at Quantico."

"And you haven't met either of them?"

"No. Only his other son, Nick, who's in North Carolina, clerking for a judge and too busy to come. Andre thinks a new girlfriend is the real reason he's not coming."

"Are you cooking the turkey?"

Elizabeth laughed. "No way. We're going out for dinner. Andre made reservations. It'll be fun being in Virginia for the holiday. There's always something going on in D.C."

When the salads arrived, conversation moved to what was happening at the refuge but, when the waitress set the extra large pizza in the center of the table, most of the conversation halted while they concentrated on eating. So far, Charlie had kept herself on the conversational sidelines, grateful Sam had come, uncomfortable about what Elizabeth had in mind but glad she seemed happy.

As Elizabeth polished off her third slice of pizza, her phone chimed the arrival of a text. "That's probably Martha." Glancing at the screen, "She's just pulling into the parking lot." Elizabeth stood up and reached for her purse. "Gotta go. I still need to pack. Thanks for coming, Sam." And she hurried outside.

Not what Charlie had expected. The surprise on Sam's face probably mirrored the surprise on hers. Finally he grinned: "I think we've been set up. Clever kid."

"And devious." Something deep in Charlie softened and expanded.

By the time Charlie got home, Elizabeth was conveniently asleep or at least giving a good imitation. Just as well. Charlie didn't want to talk about the arranged reunion. Not yet. It felt too fragile, too precious to risk conversation. With one pizza, Elizabeth had successfully by-passed the emotional walls Sam and Charlie had erected over the last months.

After Elizabeth left the restaurant, they laughed about being managed by a seventeen year old. Spent time reminiscing about the first months Elizabeth was in Arcata, Charlie explaining about Jeremiah and about her sessions with Dr. Stein.

"Do you mind telling me what you talk about in those sessions?"

"About me. Why I have trouble loving and feeling loved." She was fiddling with her napkin, folding and refolding it.

Sam reached across the table and gently took the napkin. Softly, "Charlie, I love you. I've never stopped loving you."

She nodded very slowly, afraid to trust her voice. He took her left hand, lifting it to his lips. Then releasing it. "I've been an ass. About Andre."

Another nod from Charlie.

"Elizabeth wrote me an email last week. She said she hoped I would move back, that you were depressed and she was pretty sure it was my fault. No punches pulled with that girl. And even though she hadn't forgiven you, maybe I should until she could."

When Charlie didn't respond. "Pretty grown up idea. She's looking out for you."

She hadn't thought of it that way. "I suspect Jeremiah may be behind the forgiveness thing. She doesn't tell me what they talk about, and I don't ask. She may never reach the point of trusting me with much of anything beyond getting her plane reservations because that's what a guardian does. And I'm okay with that. She doesn't have to love me." She stopped. "I'll settle for her looking out for me."

The talk switched to Greg. "He's not coming at Christmas. Swiss skiing beats a father in Arcata. It feels like he's moving farther away from me, and I don't mean geographically."

Sam sounded so sad that this time Charlie reached for his hand and took a chance. "Shall we cook a turkey on Thursday?"

He searched her face and saw a soft smile. "We? If I recall you have no idea how to cook a turkey."

"True. I can be your *sous* chef."

The day before Thanksgiving, a storm front dropped down from Oregon, swamping roads, ripping branches from the trees, inflicting misery on those who were traveling to share their holiday dinner with family and friends. Charlie was grateful she'd shopped on Tuesday—not because she'd known about the storm but because the Wednesday before Thanksgiving was never a time to fight the grocery store wars.

Sam called a little after nine Thanksgiving morning to tell her he was leaving Eureka and, since two of the supermarkets were staying open until noon, did she want him to pick up anything.

"Depends on how much wine you want. I have two bottles of white, no red."

"How about beer?"

"No."

"I'll stop for some. See you soon."

He sounded more like the Sam B.A. *Before Andre*. Still she wasn't going to hope for too much, better to err on the side of caution. She had just finished peeling the potatoes and placing them in a pot of water until it was time to cook them when Sam came in the back door. He'd left his slicker in the utility room, his face and hair still dripping. Charlie handed him a t-towel and took the six-pack of beer.

"Is the highway flooded?"

"Not yet, but it could be later. Nasty day all round. Good day to stay at home."

All Charlie heard was *home*.

Sam poured himself a cup of coffee and began buttering the inside of the turkey. While he was getting it ready for the oven, she chopped celery, onions, and apples for the dressing. Sam decided to cook the dressing in the turkey even though it would take an hour longer. "It just tastes better."

The kitchen's warmth and the aroma of the roasting turkey were comforting contrasts to the wind and rain. Charlie had bought packaged soup and crusty rolls—they needed a bit of lunch to tide them over. Today felt like their first Thanksgiving—before Elizabeth arrived.

Everything was ready a little after four. During dinner, "Tell me about Elizabeth."

Charlie poured more gravy on her mashed potatoes. "She's okay— mostly. Having Jeremiah to listen—and maybe counsel her—is, I don't know, letting her relax more, but we only talk about superficial things. No confidences."

"What about the job?"

"She doesn't talk about the bakery much but, according to Martha's mother, Elizabeth is very good with the customers. She's been going in early on Saturdays to learn how to make bread. The bakery gives her another place to be. She still loves the choir and I suspect there may be a boy she likes. Just a guess. Have you heard anything more about Greg and Christmas?"

"No," Sam pushed his chair back a little, "I'm afraid I've been bested by all the advantages his new stepfather can offer. Greg's more like Diane than I care to admit. Having "stuff" matters. He's getting new Rossignol skis. They'll be in Davos during Christmas."

"I really thought you two had made progress while he was here."

"Me too." He shrugged. "Maybe he'll come in the summer, but I'm not counting on it."

Charlie couldn't think of anything to help his sadness. "Do you want more wine or coffee?"

"Coffee. First, let's get the kitchen mess cleaned up."

They stored the leftover food, loaded the dishwasher, wiped the counters. Familiar territory.

While Sam made a fresh pot of coffee, Charlie took the tray from the top of the refrigerator. Two cups, saucers, milk for hers. Sam carried the tray—Charlie always managed to spill coffee into the saucers. She closed the shutters against the darkness and the rain, then sat beside him on the couch.

"Thanks for coming today."

"We couldn't disappoint Elizabeth after she went to all the trouble of re-arranging us."

Charlie smiled. She loved how he could bring lightness into her world, loved being with him in the kitchen today, loved that he didn't need to watch holiday football games or be in a noisy crowd of people. They'd always been good at being alone together.

Setting her cup down, she looked at him so intently that he asked, "What?"

Before she lost her courage: "Are you staying tonight? I mean, it's really raining hard—" and her confidence slid away.

He took his time answering. "Are you asking because it's raining?"

"No. I'm asking because I want you to be here—with me."

"My toothbrush and razor are in the truck."

"Oh." She felt a bit light headed.

He moved closer, placing his hand at the side of her neck, remembering the subtle excitement that always arced between them, her hair soft against his fingers.

The kiss lasted a long time, not a kiss of newness. A kiss of knowing and belonging.

Sometime after midnight, they wandered into the kitchen, wrapped in the sweet softness of lovemaking, fixed themselves turkey sandwiches and finished the wine.

Thanksgiving night: Last Thanksgiving, of course, was different, the first one without my parents. So was this one.

Andre's father, Milton, is way different from Andre. Kind of gruff, but nice. What mom would call rough around the edges. Andre junior just returned from Iraq. He's cuter than Nick and was really glad to see his grandfather. They both seem a little uncertain about being confronted with a foundling (which of course I am) being left on their doorstep. I'm on the outside. I don't have any history with these people. It'll take time. Maybe I'll always be on the outside.

Dinner was okay but not like having it at home. Mom's dressing was way better.

Tomorrow, I'm having breakfast with Andre's family—not sure I should call it my family. Then we're taking Milton to the train station. He lives in a small town and doesn't like the bigness of D.C. I can tell he's proud of his son and grandsons but none of them seem very close.

Julie and I shopped all day Tuesday. I only bought a sweater, pale yellow. Saturday, Rowena will deliver me to Reagan and, in my new ping-pong life, I'll be back in Arcata in the afternoon.

I wonder what happened with Charlie and Sam after I left the restaurant. Won't know till I get back. Charlie didn't say a word about it when she took me to the airport the next morning. I tricked them because Jeremiah made a good point. Until I reentered Charlie's life, she and Sam were okay, not that their problems are my fault. Nothing about any of this is my fault. I didn't ask to need a guardian, didn't ask to know who my birth parents are. Sam being stupid about Andre is NOT MY FAULT. Jeremiah thinks things might be easier for me if Charlie is happier. And I suppose that means getting Sam back into her life.

He also said I don't have to love Charlie, and she doesn't have to love me. Not required—though lots of people think family has to love family. Like your blood type is some sort of magic love potion. I need to be who I am, not who my parents are or were. Just me. Never quite got that before.

Then Jeremiah asked me about college next year. I told him that Andre really wants me to apply to the important East Coast colleges. Charlie has never said anything specific, but the way she's worrying about the money in my trust fund suggests she expects me to go to a big college somewhere. If my parents were alive, I'd probably go someplace in Virginia or Maryland, close enough to come home weekends. But I'm not so sure that I want to go to a big school right now. It's been a tough year. I feel like I need a gap year or a year doing something I really love. Not slogging through a bunch of GE courses and dealing with all the stuff about dorms and sororities. Ugh.

Jeremiah asked what I want to do with my life. I'm still thinking.

CHAPTER 25

Wednesday afternoon, Charlie was in Greg's room, grading lit midterms. Since it didn't look like he was coming back anytime soon, she and Elizabeth had managed to move her desk from the garage into his room so she didn't have to work in the dining room. She heard Elizabeth come home, drop her book bag on the floor in her room, then go to the kitchen. Since the exam Charlie had just read gave little evidence of the student having studied any of the material, she mumbled, *This is upper division, not high school*, and wrote a D on the front of the booklet.

"That's a very large D." Elizabeth was in the doorway, half a sandwich in one hand and the last of the day's coffee in a mug.

Charlie turned, "True. It's my way of yelling at the student without actually yelling."

Elizabeth sat on the bed, facing Charlie. "Do you have time to talk?"

"Absolutely," Charlie laid her pen down.

"I mean—well—*talk*."

Ominous.

Charlie nodded. "Okay."

"When Andre and I were having lunch, after we took Milton to the train station, he asked me what our meeting was like that day in Mr. Donovan's office."

Not the topic Charlie expected. Or wanted.

"What did you tell him?"

"That you were already in the office when Aunt Rowena and I came in and then, all of a sudden, they left us alone."

Charlie felt the stress of that day crawl out of her memory.

"I told him I was terrified. Aunt Rowena hadn't told me anything about you, not how old you were or what your work was. Only that you lived in Northern California and that legally I had to live with you until I'm eighteen."

"I didn't know anything about you either, except your age and that you probably had Andre's coloring. Your eyes were red, almost sunken, and I knew you'd been crying a lot. Then you said," Charlie wasn't prepared for her throat closing around the memory, "that for the second time you were on the open market because your birth mother hadn't wanted you either."

Elizabeth finished the sandwich and took a sip of coffee, remembering that she had said all of that. "But then you cried too. Why? I mean you hadn't seen me or my parents all those years. Why did you cry?"

Charlie had invented dozens of dialogues in case she and Elizabeth ever had this conversation, but she'd never thought she'd have to explain the crying.

Begin at the beginning.

"When I realized I was pregnant, I was so excited that I didn't mind spending most of every day throwing up. I couldn't wait to tell Andre." She took a deep breath. "I was 23. And seriously naïve. I thought he'd be as happy as I was, that he'd divorce the wife he was supposedly separated from. But as soon as I told him about you, he told me he'd pay for an abortion and stormed out of the coffee house where we'd been sitting, leaving me there, feeling as though I was the biggest fool ever."

Elizabeth didn't move.

"In a few days, he sent the money and the name of a clinic." And there was the information Charlie hadn't wanted to tell Elizabeth.

"Did you see him again?"

"No. The semester was ending and he returned to Chicago. And his wife."

With the hint of a smile, "Did you get a good grade?"

She nodded. "He probably didn't want to risk my going to the administration because professors aren't supposed to sleep with their students, and especially not get them pregnant."

"What would have happened to us if you hadn't given me to my parents, if you'd kept me?"

Sam always said Elizabeth was good at going to the heart of issues. "I would perhaps have taught high school English, but I'd have had to find child care until you were old enough to go to school, and then there would be after school care. I doubt I'd have been as good a mother as Missy was."

Elizabeth processed Charlie's explanation. "He hurt you."

"I was an emotional mess. You needed love and, at that point, I couldn't love anyone, not even you, and I didn't feel able to love anyone for years."

"Until Sam?"

"Yeah. Until Sam."

"So why did you cry?" The question wasn't going away.

"Fear maybe—at having you unexpectedly returned to me. I guess I felt sorry for you losing your parents like that."

"And sorry for yourself too? Because now you had to take care of me."

"Maybe." No maybe about it.

Elizabeth got up and walked to the door. "Thanks. I'm going to start on my homework. The choir has new Christmas music."

Without any warning, the long awaited talk about the elephant in their relationship had happened. Charlie was pretty sure there would be more talk. She stared at the pile of exams, knowing her brain could not cope with them right now, and went for a long walk.

Halfway between Thanksgiving and Christmas, Sam and Charlie decided to get married. No down-on-one-knee with a ring in Sam's hand, more a gentle tiptoeing into knowing they'd wasted too much time already. A consensual proposal of sorts. He still had the ring he'd bought while she was in London, though he hadn't told her about it when they purchased their wedding rings, hoping the diamond he'd been keeping would look good with the matching bands they'd chosen.

After Christmas morning's pancake breakfast, as the three of them were opening gifts, Charlie unwrapped Sam's gift, a box within a box, within a box—down to a small velvet box holding an engagement ring.

She stared at the ring, a modest emerald cut diamond set in white gold. "Oh my, it's beautiful." When she didn't touch it, Sam gently took the box from her, removed the ring, and slid it on her finger.

"Merry Christmas." He kissed the ring in place and then kissed her—a soft promise—aware Elizabeth was sitting across from them, watching.

As the kiss ended, Elizabeth reached for Charlie's left hand. "It's just right." She turned to Sam, "You're supposed to ask first—on one knee. The whole proposal thing."

"Sort of did that already—well not the one knee." He grinned at her. "We thought you might enjoy a surprise, so we waited until today to tell you."

Elizabeth let go of Charlie's hand, "When's the wedding?"

"The Friday after New Year's. Tessa offered her living room—it's bigger than ours—and I'd like you to be my maid of honor."

Elizabeth was caught off guard. "Really? Sure. What do I wear?"

"We'll go shopping. It's going to be a simple ceremony. Sam's brother is coming from Seattle to be the best man, and Nora and my dad will fly up from L.A. If you'd like to invite Martha so you have someone your age in the mix, she's more than welcome. Her mom is doing the cake, and Tessa knows someone who caters appetizers. As I said, simple. Then Sam and I will spend the weekend in San Francisco. He already used up his vacation time going to Spain."

"All these plans. Even Alicia knows! I'm going to have to give her a hard time about keeping secrets. What about Greg?"

Sam frowned a little. "He knows, but he'll be in school. He wasn't terribly enthusiastic about coming all that way. In his words, *Just for a wedding.* Getting two stepparents in less than a year is probably daunting. Now, open our presents to you."

Charlie's gift to Elizabeth was a Visa credit card in her own name, which Charlie would underwrite. Sam's was a message inside a Christmas card. He would teach her to drive Charlie's car—no more

Julie debacles—and he'd included a duplicate key to Charlie's Subaru. Since she was now almost eighteen and her learner's permit had expired, she could prepare to take the test like any other adult. Elizabeth leaped up and hugged him. "Thank you for both of these. I've got to call Martha," and hurried out of the room.

Charlie couldn't take her eyes off her ring. "I thought we agreed not to exchange presents this year. Our weekend in San Francisco would be our present to each other."

"I've had the ring since you were in London. That predates our agreement."

"But you never—"

"I know. My bad. First Elizabeth came, then Greg, then they left and then I began behaving like an idiot. I just wanted the time to be right, for both of us, and for Elizabeth too."

"What made you stop behaving like an idiot?"

"I reminded myself that I loved you, knew you wouldn't do what I was afraid of—though Andre might try what I was afraid of—and gave myself a good talking to. Also, Elizabeth can be a nag. And here I am."

Charlie leaned against him, feeling his arms tighten around her, feeling safe and cared for. They were kissing when Elizabeth returned. "Hey, impressionable teenager entering."

March: On my eighteenth birthday, I finally took my driving test at the DMV in Eureka. The woman at the counter laughed when she saw that it was my actual birthday. "In a hurry, are you?" I can now legally drive by myself though I can't go beyond Arcata and Eureka for a while. Not so much because I don't drive well, I do, but because I don't know the territory all that well. And I have to have my cell phone with me at all times. Charlie is getting a bit protective.

I got a fairly substantial check from Andre and one from Aunt Rowena. Not sure how I want to use them so they're in my checking account right now. Grandma sent a quilt she'd made and Julie missed my birthday completely. So much for BFFs. Charlie and Sam updated my phone to an iPhone7. Alicia baked me a gorgeous applesauce cake. It was a good day. I almost forgot to be sad about my parents.

Charlie and Sam's wedding was really sweet, and we actually had sunshine. They did the old-fashioned vows instead of writing their own. She wore a long, filmy turquoise dress—a good color for her, and I wore a rose sleeveless dress that'll work for other events. Martha put my hair up with Baby Breath tucked in. Very stylish. Sam and his brother Clark wore dark suits. His brother is a football coach at a Seattle high school. They look alike. A good day and, while Nora and John were here "babysitting" me for the honeymoon weekend, we drove up to Redwood National Park. I'd heard about the Coast Redwoods but to see how tall they are and the way the fog hangs over them along the coast is really cool.

Andre has called several times about what colleges I'm looking at. It's too late to apply for the really big colleges, and he's annoyed that I haven't sent in applications to any four-year school. I guess he also gave Charlie an earful for letting my chance to go to a high-powered college fall through the cracks. She informed him it was my decision not his or hers. I suspect she enjoyed telling him to back off. The topic is probably not finished.

The thing is, I don't have any idea what I want to do or where to go. It seems like all I've done for a year and a half is redo my life. First here, then there, now here. If I go to a big college, I'll be leaving again, living in a dorm or a sorority house, coping with another new life.

It sounds exhausting right now.

Besides, I sort of have a boyfriend. Henrique Solis. Everyone at school calls him Ricky. He's a junior. He came from Argentina three years ago, and it's taken him a while to learn English, so he's not in the right grade for his age. He also speaks German and Spanish. He's good looking, blond, not what I'd expect from South America, but one of his grandfathers was German and he looks like him. He sings baritone in the choir and writes music and plays the guitar. We're not dating dating. Just coffee, eating at McDonald's, and attending school events. Sam saw us leaving McDonald's one day, and so Henrique isn't a secret anymore. Charlie made me invite him to dinner so she could meet him. Another parental thing she's done. It turned out okay. Sam and Henrique talked about boats because Henrique likes to sail. He doesn't have a car so, if we go someplace beyond walking distance, I drive. Martha laughs at that but it doesn't bother us.

Martha plans to enroll at the Eureka campus of College of the Redwoods.

It's a community college south of Eureka. They have lower division music classes, and I can take them without enrolling in a specific degree program until I know whether I want to major in music. Mr. Hannigan knows some of the music teachers there. I could take theory and start learning the piano.

I haven't told anyone but him and Martha what I'm thinking of doing. Andre will have an absolute cow. He thinks community colleges are educational slums.

I just want to settle in for a while. When I first came, I thought I was just marking time till I graduated and then I'd be out of here. Go somewhere to begin my real life. Now I don't think I'm ready to leave. It's not about needing to stay close to Charlie or Sam or even Henrique. It's more about me wanting to have new roots. If I pull up what tiny roots I have now, then I might not have others for a long time.

CHAPTER 26

Elizabeth's senior year came with so many extra activities that Charlie bought a separate engagement calendar to keep track of them. Senior pictures, class rings, senior prom, annuals, a cap and gown, as well as choir performances. Rehearsals for the choir, rehearsals for graduation itself, plus Elizabeth's school and work schedules.

Along with maintaining their own work schedules and juggling Elizabeth's activities, Charlie and Sam invited the bits and pieces of Elizabeth's family to attend her graduation. Other graduates would have family and friends in the audience. Elizabeth deserved to have an entourage too. But putting all those disparate people in Arcata at the same time could prove—difficult. So far, Rowena and Grace had accepted. Grace would stay in Greg's room. Rowena was more than willing to rent a motel room. Charlie's father and Nora would also attend. Charlie was nervous about Andre coming, but at least he was coming, though he was not at all happy about Elizabeth's decision to stay in Arcata next year. The decision had surprised Charlie too, but she saw the wisdom of it. Another occasion when Elizabeth was wiser than the adults in her life.

Graduation began at 4 p.m. Thursday.

Late Wednesday morning, Rowena landed in San Francisco an hour before Grace arrived from Florida. Then they flew into McKinleyville together and rented a car. John and Nora spent a few days with her family in Marin, then drove from San Francisco, arriving around dinnertime Wednesday. Andre arrived late Thursday morning. Because everyone else was busy, Rowena volunteered to pick him up at the airport. Elizabeth was at school until noon, Sam had to work, and Charlie was getting the house ready for a small celebration after the ceremony. Since there was no time to cook a large meal, Elizabeth requested Chinese takeout.

Charlie was pretty sure Andre would have chosen almost anyone else but the sharp-edged Rowena to be waiting for him at the airport. Fun to contemplate the uncomfortable silence in the car on the drive to Arcata.

No matter how much the graduates and their families look forward to graduation ceremonies, they are, face it, boring. A speech by a member of the school board, another from Principal Severin, and one from Arcata's mayor. Student awards and scholarships, speeches by the Salutatorian and Valedictorian. And finally the alphabetical calling of each student's name.

The graduates were seated on a raised platform in the middle of the football field so they could be seen by the audience, which was sitting on seriously uncomfortable folding metal chairs. Seated at the end of the second row, Elizabeth had plenty of time to study the seven people who were sitting together in the fourth row. Her totally non-traditional family.

Grace was in the aisle seat so, if she needed to go to the bathroom during the ceremony, she wouldn't have to climb over anyone. Elizabeth thought her grandmother looked happy—she had a tan from playing golf, and she'd put on some of the weight she'd lost after Kevin's death. Florida must agree with her.

Rowena was seated next to Grace, wearing dark slacks and a white silk tunic, by Rowena's Virginia standards, casual dress. As usual, Rowena had been helpful—even picking up Andre. Elizabeth guessed she was already looking forward to the flight home. A small California town was not her style. Andre was between Rowena and Nora. A safe arrangement, though probably accidental. Nora had tried to smooth the edges of the moment when John was introduced to Andre, but the temperature in the room dropped a degree or two. Sam, who had been coolly polite to Andre, was between John and Charlie, Sam's arm lying along the back of Charlie's seat. Since their wedding, they were more relaxed about showing affection in public, holding hands whenever possible, stealing kisses when they thought no one was watching. Charlie looked pretty, much happier than the first time Elizabeth had seen her.

If only Missy and Rick were sitting with the others.

The principal was already calling student names. The row Elizabeth was in stood up together and began moving closer to the podium.

"Elizabeth Ann Enright." The voice sounded very far away. She forced herself to concentrate on walking smoothly, ignoring the wiggling tassel she could see from the corner of her eye.

Principal Severin extended his hand, "Congratulations Elizabeth," and deftly handed her a diploma folder—which would remain empty until she collected the actual diploma from his office tomorrow. As Elizabeth moved past him, all seven people in the fourth row shouted her name and someone whistled, probably Sam. She turned toward them and smiled—really smiled. She'd almost forgotten that she could smile so happily.

And then the next graduate was at the podium and his family was yelling his name.

Watching Elizabeth, Charlie had tears in her eyes. That lovely girl on the stage was her daughter—yes, daughter. Sam noticed the tears and tightened his hand on her shoulder.

Once the students moved the tassels to the left side of their caps, all the important parts of the ceremony were over, but it took a long time for the 127 students to march off the platform and into the waiting arms of proud families. On the way to the ceremony, John had purchased a dozen long-stemmed roses and presented them to Elizabeth as he kissed her cheek. One by one, her family hugged and kissed her, careful not to damage the roses she was clutching.

Charlie was last. Before she had time to overanalyze the moment, she put her arms around Elizabeth, unaware she was crushing the roses. "I'm so proud of you." Then kissed her cheek.

It's almost midnight. By the time everyone got back to the house, it was 7:30. Sam stopped on the way home to pick up the Chinese food, and Charlie left early to get the house ready for everyone's arrival. After I turned in my gown, I rode home with John and Nora; Andre rode with Grace and Rowena, staying at the house only long enough to toast me with a glass of wine, then asking Rowena to take him to his motel. He has an early flight. It was lovely of him to make the trip—especially since he's not especially popular with the rest of the family. I'm surprised he didn't mention the college issue. I sense I've disappointed him, but I'm not going to let that influence me.

Rowena and Grace will stay over until Saturday, same with John and Nora. I have to go to school for a little while tomorrow to get the actual diploma and say goodbye. It's a bit sad. Public school hasn't been all that bad. Afterward, Henrique and I are having lunch with John, Nora, Rowena and Grace. I hope he won't be bothered by everyone checking him out. John will behave but Grandma can ask rather awkward questions.

Most surprising moment today, Charlie hugged me and then kissed me. Not a forced hug. A sincere one. And told me she was proud of me. My mother would have said the same thing, but Charlie wouldn't have any way of knowing that.

Her hug felt like she cares. I've never been sure she cared. But then I haven't shown her affection either. I need to think about that, but I'm too tired right now.

Maybe tomorrow I can find a reason to hug Charlie.

Printed in the United States
By Bookmasters